Stories
by the
Fire

Stories
by the
Fire

Connie Miller Pease

A Note From the Author

I started a blog at the behest of my publisher. I decided to just do what I always do, which is to write.

This book is a compilation of short stories I've posted on my blog, *www.myfiresidechat.com*, over the years. There are certainly better stories out there, but, dear reader, I wonder if there are authors more grateful for the gift of writing and the blessing of readers than I.

Soli Deo Gloria

Preface

As the sun sinks lower in the sky and the cooling day begs for something to warm it, some light to once again clarify its beauty, and some sound to break the quietness of approaching night, we light a fire. The crackle of the fire excites the silence, and its light reaches into shadows, and it gives us warmth and reassurance.

Stories do that. They reveal ideas to a thoughtful reader, provide warm company, and fill our imaginations with the sounds of another place and time. So we tell stories to communicate more than fiction and to cross that bridge that otherwise keeps us apart.

Pull up a chair by the fire. It's time for a story and a fireside chat!

Treasure

I t was the shoes I noticed first. They were brown and clompy and worn, with traces of mud and dead grass stuck to the sides. She was drinking a cup of black coffee, some of which now spilled on the newspaper she held in front of her but did not read. Instead, she held it up to hide the fact that she stared into space; her thoughts breaking long enough for her to look around the small café and then drift back to whatever it was that drew her imagination to another place and time.

With nothing better to do and too little in my own life to merit attention, I resolved to catch her eye. I did, but not of my own effort. I had just searched my bag to see whether a piece of blueberry pie was in my future. It was not, and as I glanced around for a waitress to order my tea, I felt the stranger's eyes on me. I looked her way, nodded, and then surprised myself by walking over and asking if I could join her. The stranger looked at me hard, nodded that I could indeed join her, got up, and walked out. Stunned at her rudeness, I stood motionless for a full minute until I turned and saw her at the door, motioning impatiently for me to follow.

Startled as I was, my grasp loosened for a split second, spilling some of the contents of my bag. I knelt to scoop it up, but her wave was so insistent and hurried that I took what was in my hand and left the rest to fate; a faint peach lipstick that I loved and two quarters.

As I started toward the door, she turned and jaywalked at a brisk clip across the street, a little to the left, down an alley, and back onto another street. I trotted to catch her, nearly close enough to ask her name a couple of times; but I was so out of breath, I could only wheeze. As we neared the edge of town, she slowed and looked northwest of where we now stood.

I looked intently in the same direction, but couldn't see a thing despite my eye-strained efforts. My stomach growled and the woman, tired of what I supposed she saw as my ineptitude, turned her head slowly to me, then started off again. Ambling now through the long grass of the field we reached, she headed toward the wooded coolness at the far end. We'd entered the woods only slightly when she bent down and wisked a handful of blueberries from a bush.

Holding them out to me, she said, I couldn't tell apropos of what, "It's early yet, but maybe . . ."

It was the first time I had heard her utter a word. Her voice was surprisingly lovely; soft and – I will acknowledge this much – lilting. It made me think of a song or, perhaps, a story I had heard a long time ago, but couldn't quite remember.

I was just about to reply, when a piercing shriek caught my voice in my throat. My leader paled slightly, and searched the distance from where the horrible sound had come. She involuntarily, barely perceptibly shook her head and hesitated for a moment.

"You look as though you could use a rest," she said, looking as though she wanted me to negate her observation.

It was not in me to let this advantage pass, though, and I eagerly assented that I did, indeed, need not only rest, but some more blueberries as well. Without waiting for further suggestions, I plopped down where I was. I quickly stood, having poked myself with a sharp stick or stone, and moved to sit on a fallen tree instead. I reached for some more blueberries and ate uninterrupted for at least five minutes straight until I felt sufficiently full. The whole time the woman in front of me looked toward her destination, then down at the decaying leaves at her feet, then off again in the same direction.

Destinations can change on the simple turn of a phrase.
"What is it?" I finally asked.

"What?"

"What is it that you keep looking for or toward or whatever it is you're doing?"

I swatted a mosquito and began to itch with zeal what promised to be a generous patch of poison ivy on my ankle.

I spoke quietly to myself now. "What in the world am *I* doing?"

"You asked if you could join me," she replied.

"At the *table*. I meant to ask if I could join you at *your table*," I answered her, frustrated with my stranger's assertion and amazed at the misunderstandings this world holds and how destinations change on the simple turn of a phrase.

"You followed me. No. You wanted to join me. In fact, when your little Honda pulled into the café, you looked," she paused, searching for a word which she couldn't quite find, 'lost'."

I stared at her, baffled that she'd not only noticed me come to the café in the first place, but also that she'd studied me. It was she who I had thought distracted, but her narration challenged my blazingly astute observation.

"Let's see. You've, on impulse, decided to pull up roots, that is if you've ever had them which is doubtful; a result of something in your past, perhaps."

A lump began to form in my throat, but I stared sullenly past her; a habit I'd found useful in life.

"You've used your last dollar for a week's worth of cheap motel and a full tank of gas; and after a few days of little sleep and not much food you're wondering if you're still sane."

She was about to continue, but, to my strange relief, another shriek split the air. At this she jumped to her feet and flew from the woods, running in the same direction in which we had first started.

The day was by now growing toward twilight, and having been afraid of the dark since my childhood, I sprinted after her. After all, it's one thing to follow a stranger in the daytime, but quite another when the dark closes in. As the moon rose, she was – being the only human in sight – in an instant, my friend.

She was fast and seemed to know the terrain well. I was neither, and fell farther and farther behind. It was luck alone, although I think she would have disagreed, that brought me up short when I tripped over her as she squatted near the ground. She was peering in the dark for some small landmark, some indication she was near whatever it was that she sought. She motioned silence, and I acquiesced, too out of breath for words anyway. She straightened and we had taken only a few steps when I felt the very earth give way below me and I fell smack onto a pebbly, hardened space a good twelve feet beneath the surface. I rolled to a sitting position, moaned, and saw that she was climbing down some mismatched boards nailed into the side of what appeared to be a cave wall.

I began to groan. It was not involuntary, I'll acknowledge, but I thought by this time I deserved to whine. However, the instant a sound escaped my throat, she held up her hand to silence me and walked into a short tunnel. I found her scraping away some dirt from the wall with a little tool. It was apparent that she knew this place. The earth was packed solid, and she seemed to know exactly what she was doing though it was very dark despite the flashlight she had flicked on upon our descent. I tried to while away the minutes by chatting with her, but getting no response, I went back through the tunnel. I'd had enough. She could have the silence she seemed to crave for company. I climbed the "ladder" to the ground overhead, peeped out, recoiled at the black night, looked down again at the darkness beneath me, then, gathering my courage, swung my leg up and pulled myself out. I started off unsteadily, uncertain of my direction. The moon shone only dimly, and there was no trampled path, no recognizable landmark, no inner sense of direction.

I had walked for a few minutes when I heard a rustling. Scared out of my wits, I searched in vain for the hole I now wished I had never left and then ran into a bush under which I promptly sat as far as I could manage. There appeared, not too far distant, a large bird with black feathers and no markings.

"Black feathers," I silently scolded myself, "Of course its feathers are black! The whole world is black in this darkness!"

It stood waiting; looking around excitedly like some kid at the first football game of the season. It didn't wait long. Four birds of similar size joined it. They immediately raised such a scream as I've never heard since. The sound inhabits my dreams still on nights when the dark seems to close in so near that I can touch it.

I heard a scrambling and saw the stranger throw a wooden box the size of a small trunk out first, then hoist herself outside.

Looking at the birds that crowded around the box, she said, "So now you come! Now when I've done all the work!"

One of the birds pecked at her shoe.

"I've nothing more left. Thank you for your help in finding it, but it's all gone now." She shooed them with her hands. "Go on. All gone."

They squawked loudly, and she raised her voice over theirs, "The lady that came with me. She might have something for you."

I suppose there are worse things than being found when you wish to hide, but I can't think of many.

I shivered for a moment, enough to give myself away. They all looked my direction. I suppose there are worse things than being discovered when you wish to hide, but I can't think of many. I crawled out from my place under the bush and took a few steps.

"The box," I said, rather crossly. "What's in it that you come so far from town, at night, with these, these . . ." I interrupted myself long enough to scratch my ankle furiously.

"Birds," she finished calmly. "It's a treasure I've been hunting for – oh, so many years I've lost count now. My husband buried it after a fight we had – years ago. He died not long after, but had left a note in his will telling me of some little birds he'd trained to show me where the treasure was. He always did love gamesmanship."

"You've been hunting a treasure."

She nodded.

"The birds led you to the treasure?"

"They led me to this little spot. I had to figure out for myself where exactly it was."

She paused. "It took awhile," she concluded.

I pointed to the chest. "I don't suppose there's anything there for me."

"Not in this lifetime," she said without malice, to my dismay.

"What do you think *I* can give those shrieking things?"

"I always gave them little pieces of meat. And berries. They seem to like berries."

"Berries!"

What kind of mundane, insane conversation was I having with a stranger in the middle of the night? I began to walk. Then I ran. I must get to some place normal; a place that carried familiar scenes and scents; a place where people and birds said and did what they were supposed to say and do. I left town that same night.

I returned to the little town later and stayed in the same "cheap motel" as it had been so kindly described by what I was now referring to in my thoughts as "my stranger". I had taken odd jobs here and there, long enough to save money enough to pull up roots and wander again. I had felt unsettled, admitting now that I had felt that way since I was a teenager, and, as inexplicable as it seemed, this was the one place I had lost that unsettled feeling one evening turned to night about one year ago. I picked up the paper in the tiny lobby as I sat down to eat my continental breakfast. As I turned a page, a small obituary stopped my hand, leaving my next bite untaken. It was she, no doubt: the dry, black hair; the harsh, definitive profile; the eyes the color of a turbulent sea.

I felt a hand on my shoulder, and looked up. An overweight man in a black silk suit asked my name and sat across from me.

"Ah. I see you've been reading the death announcement. She became very ill a few months ago, called my office and asked that I find you and give you this."

It was a copy of her will.

"She wrote it in my presence. It's all legal."

I scanned the type.

"Everything?" I asked, stupefied, unsure what I would do with worn, clompy brown shoes.

"She had no one. Not after her husband died. Here are the keys to the house. It's the stone one on the hill. I'm sure you noticed it as you entered town."

"I only recall a . . . what looked like a large . . . house." I gave up trying to describe what I had seen.

He nodded. "Moved in as a young couple. Crazy in love, those two. He was away on business when he was hit by a little Honda. She wished she'd died with him. Never got over it."

Upon those words, I was immediately transported back to the day when, as a careless teenager, driving much faster than the limit, I had killed a man. I felt the blood drain from my face.

He shook his head and then roused himself. "A very large estate indeed. That's the one."

He fished out another set of keys.

"Here," he said handing them to me. "The keys to her cars. The Mercedes is parked in front," he nodded out the window. "You might call the salvage yard to pick up that piece of junk," he chuckled as he pointed to my Honda, the only car I had ever owned.

As he rose to leave, I called, "Wait! I . . . I don't know what to do."

"Why don't you go home?" he laughed as he walked out the door.

I found it the moment I entered the house. A note lay on a table in the large entryway of the mansion. It said simply, "Do you wish to play a game?" Then I heard a familiar shriek.

It's been four years since. I've met some people from town, but mostly prefer the solitude of this place. The vastness of the grounds does something to you; something forgiving, maybe. The quietness feeds you.

I found it finally; pulled it out of a very twisting, very dark, very wet cave underneath a small waterfall. I dragged it home, the birds and their progeny following me hoping for some fresh berries in the rookery I had built up for them.

I turned on every light in my vast house, made a celebratory cup of tea, scratched my ankle vigorously, and opened the trunk at last.

I've been reading its contents for days now; love letters written over many years from a man to his wife; flirtatious notes, long letters of yearning, crisp pieces of ordinary detail, always signed the same way: "Undying love". Treasure indeed.

The Yes Man

His heels clicked on the polished floor as he walked quickly to suite 300. The low buzz of his watch alarm sounded only once as he raised his wrist to press it off. This was exactly the time he usually sat down at his desk, placed his coffee cup neatly its coaster, and began the day's work. People joked they could set their watches by his movements, and he felt proud. Not every man could join precision and structure so seamlessly. It was, to his mind, what made a man dependable.

He briskly knocked twice on the door and entered at the invitation of the voice within.

A smile tugged at his mouth, though looking at him, one would not have known. Madeleine wore a red skirt and red and white pinstriped blouse with matching shoes. Her short, red hair just touched the back of her collar. Looking at the combination made him wince. A gold bracelet hung heavy on her small wrist. He noted one earring lying on her desk by the phone. It was her habit to remove it to talk on the instrument, and she invariably forgot to replace it. He had once overheard her in the lunchroom saying that she had lost three earrings because of her habit, but it was obvious to him now the losses had not deterred her.

Madeleine was sitting at her desk typing and spoke above the tick-tack of the keys. "I buzzed her when you knocked, Mr. Nordrum. She's expecting you. Go on in."

"Thank you, Ms. Hallowitz."

He nodded once and stepped toward the double doors. He knocked twice and turned the shiny knob. Its click was music to his ears. The doorknob was such a simple device, beautiful in its simplicity and precision. He wished he could have met its inventor.

He clicked the door shut behind him and stood, his hands clasped behind his back.

"Mr. Nordrum. On the dot as I knew you would be," she said with clipped articulation, motioning to a chair in front of her desk.

"Ms. Marley."

He sat soundlessly in front of her. Her black suit matched her hair which was pulled back into a neat chignon. Her nails were polished with a color that matched her skin. He looked at her now; her face was carefully made up so that no blotches or variations of color were evident – only a clean layer of peach tone. Her eyes were as gray and direct as her speech.

"Mr. Nordrum, it has come to my attention that there is a poster – unapproved, of course – hanging in the hallway by the lunchroom."

"I'll take care of it, Ms. Marley."

Ms. Marley leaned forward, touched her thumbs, and tapped her fingers together above them forming a triangle.

"I've been giving this some thought, Mr. Nordrum. We've had trouble with this for three weeks in a row."

"Yes, Ms. Marley."

"It makes me wonder what our staff believes about this office. In fact, Mr. Nordrum, it makes me wonder what the citizens of this state believe about this office."

"Yes, Ms. Marley."

"I was elected Governor not once, but twice."

"Yes, Ms. Marley."

"I have served our citizenry well, Mr. Nordrum."

"Yes, Ms. Marley."

"It is time for a change, Mr. Nordrum, and," Ms. Marley nodded her head slightly as though she was about to bestow a great honor on her employee, "I have determined you are the man best suited for the job."

The import of such a nod from his superior was not lost to Mr. Nordrum.

He replied in his most confident voice, "Yes, Ms. Marley."

"I have thought this over for some time. I can assure you, Mr. Nordrum, this has been long in coming in a state that begs for decency and order. There is far too much," here she searched for a word and, finding it, spit it out like an air drill, "difference," she pursed her lips as though she was tasting something sour, "difference," repeated, "in our diversity."

"Diversity is something you have given much time in promoting," he answered.

Ms. Marley stood from her chair and threw back her shoulders.

"It has been a very effective effort," she agreed with just the right amount of modesty and pride.

"However," she continued, "not everyone cares as deeply about it as they should."

"Excuse me, Ms. Marley," Mr. Nordrum interrupted, "but you made the word 'should' a misdemeanor offense last month."

His boss's face reddened slightly.

"How careless of me, but," and here she directed a steel-like gaze on her employee, "I think you know what I meant."

"Yes, Ms. Marley."

"I would like you, Mr. Nordrum, to make a list of all of the variations at work against our contemporary society; deviations from what we consider acceptable and appropriate in this state."

The tall woman turned to face the window. Her eyes darted over the traffic beyond it to the commons spreading like a wide sea in front of the grand building.

Abruptly she spun around and commanded, "Have it on my desk day after tomorrow."

Mr. Nordrum nodded.

"Yes, Ms. Marley."

He rose from his chair and walked to the door.

"Mr. Nordrum."

He turned slightly.

"Yes, Ms. Marley?"

"9:01 a.m."

"Yes, Ms. Marley."

He silently shut the door behind him.

As he walked through the reception area a muffled, "Goodbye, Mr. Nordrum," came from beneath the desk.

The top half of Madeleine Hallowitz was enveloped underneath, undoubtedly looking for a lost earring, leaving the bottom half still in the chair to unwittingly entertain those awaiting their appointments.

Plato street

The Inheritance

A lone street lamp shone its dim yellow light over the pocked and crumbling pavement beneath it. The lamp, green from years of neglect, stood sturdy and dignified nevertheless; its scrollwork base and lantern top the result of the insistence of a tenacious city council member long since forgotten. Its light spread over the area like a thin blanket, not quite reaching the ends of the old street.

A socialite famous for a gluttony of grand parties, an unquenchable thirst for written works of philosophy, and a limited understanding of himself had once owned all of the land through which the street now traveled and some of the adjoining property, as well. He was the son of a railroad baron, had observed his father's business from bottom to top, had never been invited to take over the business and had never asked to. In all of his life, the son, Courtney Clive Tice (Clive after his grandfather on his mother's side), had never known want. He had never had to care for himself in all of the ways mankind finds it necessary to survive, he had never had to sweat, nor to make his own money. It was all there for him from the time he was born until his last breath.

It was this last breath, this last uttered thought, that had made his land even more marketable to those who had the means to buy some of it. So it was sold in large parcels, then later resold in smaller pieces, then divided into lots that were smaller still. The passage of time, the decline of societal standards, and general neglect had finally led to the street's current condition. Most passersby made a wide detour around it, but those who had the nerve to pass by that now decaying part of the city still recalled its first owner's words: "What was good could have been better." Those were not his only words, but since they were the last sentence of his final musings, they were what the people recalled.

A sarcastic city planner had later named the street 'Plato Street', thinking to himself that its owner, his head full of useless philosophy, had thought in vain the property could be improved. Indeed, its current conditions proved the planner right. Ramshackle houses dotted the small, crude lawns, and those who now lived on Plato Street wished Courtney Clive Tice had told the truth. But it was obvious to all who passed by and especially to those who lived there that he had not.

One house, by now nearly bare of paint, though the chips that remained told of an original Hershey's chocolate brown, stood on the exact spot where Courtney Clive Tice had once slept – and where he had died. The plat reached to where the edge of his smoking room had been. A hard-packed dirt path led from the boulevard in front of it to the street beyond.

A "For Sale" sign had stood in front of the house some fourteen months, taken down several weeks here and there to fool passers-by that it had been sold and really was worth something. Up it would pop again, though, in a renewed effort to bring something – anything – from property whose owner had since died in a nursing home. Then one day it was taken down for good.

It is this house – and the people in it – that taught me about the man Courtney Clive Tice could have become or maybe *had* become unawares to those who were closest to him.

They moved in without fanfare and I expected they were the kind that lived quietly and unobtrusively, for that is how they lived. At first.

I was pulling some stubborn crab grass from around my own crumbling steps when I was called away by the insistent ringing of the phone (it was my daughter from the next county wondering if I would join them for their annual 4th of July barbecue – I answered with my usual agreeable "No").

By the time I had returned to my task, a boy I judged to be about 10 stood, slowly, but with great delight, peeling strips of bark from a birch clump on the boulevard in front of my house.

"Hey!" I yelled, startling both the young chap and myself. My voice has always been gruff. Even as a youth it stood out like thistles next to new grass. Age had given it as low a note as time had supplied an edge.

"You can't do that! It's agin' the law!" I scolded, and was, for a minute, reminded of my old bloodhound who'd been dead 5 years last month.

The boy looked at me with fear in his eyes, but his posture remained unchanged and his brows scrunched together in a wide "V".

Soon he replied, "Why?"

"Cuz it's, it's . . . agin' the law, that's why!" I spat back, irritated with his, by now, expression of disbelief.

He took hold of the bark again.

"No intelligent person would make a law about a tree," he said quietly. It appeared he had decided I was belligerent and crazy, both.

I proved him wrong at once by running over and bodily shoving him into the street. He fell, and I could see one hand was skinned; tiny pricks of blood began at once to trickle to his wrist. I turned back to my house, and by the time I'd reached my steps he was gone.

"Stupid crab grass," I muttered.

Not many days later I was sitting on my porch, reading the paper. I had read the obituaries – first, as always – and was now engrossed in the comics. It was evening, but the sun tenaciously held its place these waxing days of summer. I swatted in the air at a fly, which promptly landed on my nose. I have a respectable nose. No small speed bump this, but rather long and straight and glad-to-be-noticed. Impatiently, I let the paper fall to my lap and swatted with one grand smack. Unfortunately, I caught sight of a woman standing at the bottom of my steps just as the fly, now as flat as flypaper and sticking to its chosen landing spot, met its demise. I've always been a good aim. This was one of the rare times I regretted it.

I quickly brushed it from my face, hoping it had been a small fly with few guts.

"Hello," she said brightly. A smile cupped her face.

I cleared my throat in a friendly manner.

"I thought you might like some cookies."

She climbed the steps and handed me a plate of oatmeal raisin cookies without the raisins.

"My favorite," I said doubtfully, taking the plate and turning a cookie over to look for at least one raisin. There were none to be found.

She looked around the porch and nervously rubbed one hand with the other.

"Have a chair?" I responded.

She pulled a rusty metal rocker from a few feet away. The scraping sound pleased my old ears, like a snare drum in a rock band. She sat down, facing the street.

"We moved to the Johnston house two months ago," she pointed to the one that had been for sale for so long. "We've been so busy getting settled, we haven't had time to meet everyone."

I lifted my head in acknowledgement.

Then, thinking how I might be neighborly, I said, "This whole area used ta belong ta a rich good-for-nothing."

I took her silence for interest, and continued, "Oh yeah. Near scoundrel he was. Courtney Tice. Never lifted a hand in his life. Had everything handed ta him on a silver platter. Born with a silver spoon in his mouth, as they say."

"Where, exactly *was* his house?" she asked.

Her eyes roamed the street in front of us.

"All over. It was a mansion. I seen it in some hist'ry pictures some fella with glasses and a button-down sweater showed me. Long time ago now."

The woman looked at me curiously.

"I don't know who he were. Just walkin' up and down Plato Street. Talkin' ta people."

She squinted her eyes.

"Oh. You mean . . .?" I gave my chin a good scratching.

I reached my bony hand out and made a broad sweep.

"I'd say, if mem'ry serves, it stretched from that brick apartment over there to the corner past your house. The rest was gardens and grounds."

The woman sat looking at the space for a time. The sun lit her hair in a way that made me wish I was young, but her hands were callused. She wore a pair of jeans and a sleeveless denim shirt. The rubber around her shoes was pulling away.

Suddenly she stuck out her hand.

"My name's Sally. Sally Cortland."

I shook her hand.

"You are . . .?" she asked.

"Right. I'm Bill Bingham."

"You must be retired?" she asked.

It struck me funny and I snorted. It was a good snort as snorts go, but she looked startled. It reminded me of someone.

Suddenly I exclaimed, "You're that boy's mother!"

She cocked her head and I continued, "The boy. The boy 'twas here pulling the bark off my tree. He's about yeah high," I measured with my hand, "and freckly."

"I'm sorry if he upset you, Mr. Bingham."

I started laughing again – so hard I had to get up and spit.

"Honey, if you call anyone 'mister' around here, everyone will think he's a drug dealer."

Somehow I sensed I'd offended her. Then I figured it out.

"Oh. Right. You asked if I was retired. See, it struck me funny, 'cuz I been on some type o' public assistance er 'nother since I were a pup."

She remained silent.

"Bad back," I explained, rubbing it.

"You said the man was a . . .," she paused, as if searching for a phrase, "good-for-nothing scoundrel?"

I nodded knowingly.

"Don't ferget. He was rich," I added. After all, some things bear repeating.

She got up, shook my hand, and left.

The sun was nearing the horizon now. Its brightness colored the street in gold and orange. Sally, now at her own house, bent to deadhead some potted petunias, turned and waved at me, and slipped inside.

I sat on my sagging porch, chewed on a cookie, and let my memory have its way. It began to sprinkle. I went inside and watched out my window as the rain first pelted my newspaper and then spit into the wind; which blew it, page by page, down the street.

The Invitation

Fanny Smith. The name makes me grimace and the woman who wears it makes me groan. She moved in next to me twenty years ago. Her voice makes me feel as though I'm at sea: sick and hearing a foghorn. Its blaring never changes in pitch nor in volume. By the time its over, I'm in need of at least an hour's nap to calm my nerves.

Here she was. Standing on the walk in front of my house, calling to me in that voice. I pretended not to hear her.

"I said, Bill, there's going to be a par-ty," she drew the word out as though it was in a foreign language, "a par-ty next Friday."

I coughed up a good one and looked at her.

"Oh. Didn't see ya standin' there, Sniff," I said.

I'd always called her 'Fanny Sniff'; it just came to me out of the blue, first time I met her. She hated my calling her that almost as much as she hated me. It, of course, brought me great pleasure.

She threw back her shoulders and smoothed the front of her dress. I never could bear a woman who wore a dress with flat shoes. Her shoes looked like she'd bought them at a men's shop, except they didn't look as feminine.

"I told her you shouldn't be invited," she said with that perpetual sound of authority she always had. She would've sounded like that even telling a joke. If she ever told one. Which she never did.

"Who, Sniff? Make it snappy – you're wastin' my time."

That woman always made me impatient. Looking at her made me impatient. It made me want to swear, which I did obligatorily, just to show her.

Fanny began walking away. I chased her down the street. She turned on me so suddenly, I nearly fell over.

"Get away from me, you old coot! I'll tell you, but only because I told her I would. Sally Cortland is having a party next Friday. Seven o'clock. Now get away from me before I lay ya flat."

This last statement was no idle threat. The woman was, after all, a good six feet at least.

I went across the street to the old Johnston place.

After nosing around a bit, I found Sally in the back yard, up on a ladder. The boy was at the bottom, holding it steady.

"Whatcha doin'?" I asked.

"Oh, hi, Mr. Bingham," she called down.

The boy eyed me with a fearful look, but held his ground.

"Don't worry, boy," I said, friendly like, "Your ma's a friend o' mine."

I spit in the grass, and wiped the rest off my chin.

I sat down in the grass a while and watched her work. The day was nearing noon and the sun was piercingly bright. Her shirt was starting to show sweat. Even from where I was, I could see a trickle make its way from her temple to her jaw.

An hour went by. I wondered why she chose this hot day to paint, and I asked her.

Sally gave a short laugh, though she sounded a little out of breath.

"It's hard to predict a cool summer day," she smiled, and winked at her son.

"Especially in the city," she murmured under her breath.

By now she had the top half painted, and no longer needed the ladder. The boy took up another brush, and they worked together to finish the back of the house.

I began to feel restless. She looked so tired and hot.

"Never liked the color yellow," I commented.

"Mr. Bingham," she replied, "would you go inside and grab two pops for us, please?"

I hesitated.

"Grab one for yourself, too," she added.

Never one to waste time, I walked through her back door. It was warmer inside the house than it was outside. I nearly suffocated looking around. I'd been in there just once before, two owners back. Something was different now, though. The whole of the rooms I investigated had been newly painted, the floors had been polished, and the woodwork stained. The rooms were furnished simply, certainly, but still felt very complete. I almost wished I could sit down, but there was still the upstairs to see.

I hurried up and looked in three bedrooms. They showed the same attention to cleanliness and neatness that the downstairs did. One room held a small desk, a wooden chair, a stuffed chair with a braided rug in front of it, and two large bookcases full of books. The other two obviously belonged to the boy and his mother. On a small table by the bed in each room were two pictures of two different men. One was quite handsome and looked as though the outdoors was his friend. I couldn't tell much about the other one.

I went down to the kitchen again and poked my head into the refrigerator. It felt so good that I stood there for awhile to cool down. I pulled out three of those generic brand sodas and took them outside.

The boy came over to me and took two of them. He handed the first to his mother, and then opened one for himself.

I love the sound a soda can makes when it's opened. The snap is so definite, so deliberate, so . . . so . . . confident. That's it. It makes me feel confident when I open a soda can. I took a long swig. The biting coolness made its way straight to my gut.

I lay down in the grass, looked at the sky with barely a cloud crossing its expanse, closed my eyes and fell asleep. I snoozed off and on through the day, monitoring their progress as well as I could.

I woke up to see Sally bent over, cleaning the last of the brushes. She must have sensed my gaze, because she looked up and smiled.

"Have a good nap?"

"I always need a nap after I hear Fanny Sniff's voice," I replied.

"Thanks for keeping us company, Mr. Bingham."

She straightened and looked at the house.

"It's a good week's work," she said.

"You been doin' this for a week?"

"I guess there are so many things going on in this neighborhood, it's easy to miss some of it," Sally commented in an amused voice.

Indeed, the house did look as though it began to be cared for. The creamy yellow was pared with a gray-green trim. Looking back, I admit I didn't appreciate her taste at the time, but even then I could see it was an improvement.

"Stoppin' already?" I asked. I thought she should at least work the day out.

"It's 7:00, Mr. Bingham," Sally answered, "It seems the day got away from you."

I watched as she pulled out her ponytail and let her hair fall as the door closed behind her.

I'd have to make myself a quick supper, if I wanted to get to the comics before daylight faded. Some days are just like that. They are so full, that there isn't time to fit in everything. I blamed it on Fanny Sniff. If she hadn't interrupted my morning, I might have not had to hurry like I was now. That darned woman!

The rest of the week I spent on my porch, watching Sally and the boy. No matter what time I got out there, they had beat me out. The woman had kept her weeds mowed since the day they'd moved in. I had noticed that right away.

I do like putterin' in the yard. It lets me keep an eye on things. And one more thing. I hate crab grass. Now Creeping Charlie I like. It's pretty. It perks up a yard a bit. Clover has a sweet smell. Plus you never know when you'll get lucky with clover. Old sayings always have some truth to them, and you just never know where a four-leaf clover will take you. Dandelions are a fine little flower. I always said 'If dandelions are good enough for a President of the United States, they're good enough for me'. Crab grass is an entirely different matter, though. Some loud-mouthed kid not worth the gum on his shoe once made a comment about my yard fitting its owner and ever since, I've been death on the stuff.

It nearly met its final doom. I was outdoors so much – keeping an eye on things at the old Johnston place – that I swear I nearly dug it all up. I never worked so hard in my life.

The worst, of course, was when they went around to the back of their house. I ended up having to walk around the block and take a shortcut through their back alley to see anything at all. I heard Sally talking quietly to her son before I could see them. They were kneeling there not three feet from the alley. A box lid was crowded with little cups: some of them broken at the lip, some of them old plastic ones someone had thrown out, some of them Styrofoam ones in good shape bearing the logo of the donut shop three blocks down. I wondered if the owner was sweet on her. The cups held seedlings she must have planted a few months back.

She and the boy had measured out a little garden in the back and were planting the seedlings. I was sure she wouldn't get anything from it, starting so late in the year. Still, she nursed those things in her hands as though they were her own babies.

I kicked a rock and scuffed my shoe so Sally would hear me. Someone had to tell her the garden wouldn't do any good.

"Those ain't gonna grow big enough by the time it frosts, ya know."

She didn't stop working at all. She just answered, "I know."

"What?!" I couldn't believe my ears.

That was it for me. I marched from there in such a huff that I had to rest by the time I got home.

She cut up some wilted hostas on the side of the house one day. I never sat so still in my life. The woman reminded me of a Samurai warrior, slashing those things the way she did. For one dreadful moment I thought she looked my way, but to my relief, she picked up her shovel and started planting what she'd just so viciously attacked. Funny thing is, they lived.

The Party

Sally was beginning to cause a bit of a problem for me. One morning I headed down to my basement. I mostly stayed out of it since I couldn't abide the cobwebs. I had a few things stashed down there – mostly bits and pieces the previous owner had left behind. There was a package of mousetraps, of course. Some Shell No Pest strips were down there along with a big hammer, a baseball cap, (I had brought up the bat that had stood next to it to keep under my bed for protection right after Pearl, my bloodhound, died), a few old paint cans, and a growing pile of shredded paper. I considered the latter and decided the mice might as well stay comfortable for awhile, so I left it alone. Besides, I could ask my daughter to clean it out when she came at Thanksgiving. She was always on the lookout for something to ease her guilt for not coming to visit me more often. The paint cans were so old, they'd gotten lightweight. The other thing that was down there was a putty knife. I'd seen Sally had one around, so I picked it up. (Heart glad I was to find I had one!) I climbed back upstairs and settled on my porch.

See, I'd moved from the yard to my porch by now. I thought it best to leave some of the crab grass just in case I ran out of things to do. Like I said, Sally was causing a bit of a problem for me. If I stayed indoors, I wouldn't know what was going on across the street. If I sat out on my porch it might start tongues flapping about comparisons I wasn't willing to have made. I wasn't on any account going to let a woman best me. If Sally was working up a sweat, I'd at least pretend to. I had started by sweeping twenty-five years worth of dirt through the porch cracks. It took a surprisingly little bit of time to do. If I had known that, I might've done it sooner. Then again, why do what would just need to be done again the next year? The wind mostly took care of the upkeep of that porch anyway. I swept over the same two feet for about half an hour, but my arms began to feel stiff, and Sally was so much in and out of her house, it was hard to keep track anyway. Still, I would have hated to miss anything, so I had to get creative. That's why I had hunted for something to bring out with me to the porch. I sat with it in my hands for awhile, but then it occurred to me that I might raise suspicions, just sitting like that. So I figured I'd scrape with it like I'd seen Sally do. No one could fault that. After all, that little woman was beginning to make a name for herself. Every day folks would stop and check on the old Johnston house. She must have met everyone in a two-block radius in record time.

Friday was a very long day. The Johnston place was as quiet as the suburbs. At the moment I was scraping peeling paint with the putty knife. Fanny Sniff had been sitting on her porch most of the week, watching Sally and the boy. If that woman ever lifted a finger in her life it wasn't enough for anyone to detect any movement. It was almost an embarrassment to live next to such an idle woman. However, there was one thing at which she excelled. It would be no exaggeration to put her in an Olympic contest of the greatest busybodies that ever lived. She would win the gold.

I called over to Sniff's house, "Seen anything of Sally Cortland, Sniff?"

"If there was anything to see of her, *you* woulda' by now, ya been keepin' watch nearly a week!" she hollered back.

You would've thought she meant to notify the neighborhood of my own private business and I set her straight right then and there.

"You just can't stand to look in the mirror," she answered; an answer which made no sense.

"I can look in the mirror same as you, you nosy old woman, an' get a better picture back in the process."

Well, she started to yell then, and that teenage boy from the other corner – the one that wears his pants halfway down as though he has his heart set on being a plumber – happened to walk by. His face sprouted a sarcastic smile, and I ran down my steps to the rocks that I keep handy in one corner against the house. He spied me out of the corner of his eye, though, and jogged away. He'd had a couple thrown at him before for one offense or another, so he'd learned his lesson. 'Kids these days,' I thought.

People started filtering over to Sally's place around 6:30, so I started over, too.

I heard a voice from behind yell to me in a whisper, if you could call it that, "Bill Bingham, the party ain't 'til 7:00. What you doin' goin' over an' disturbin' that woman a whole half hour early?"

"Can't you see all the folks already goin' there?" I answered the Sniff.

I kept walking, and in another minute I could feel her monster steps behind me.

"What're you doin', Sniff? 'The party ain't 'til 7:00,'" I mimicked her in a whiny voice and she thumped me over the head with something.

I looked behind me, and she was placing the hat she had whomped me with back on her head.

"What you wearin' a hat fer?" I said in a disgusted tone.

Fanny threw back her shoulders and walked past me as though she was some kind of queen.

I caught up just as she reached the door and rang the bell. It didn't work, so she poked her head through the door and yelled, "Sally, dear?"

Sally weaved her way to meet us through the nearly ten people already there.

Sniff leaned over and whispered to Sally, "Can you believe these people! What can I do to help?"

Sally squeezed her hand and said, "Dear Mrs. Smith. Whatever would we do without you? Would you be so kind as to keep an eye on that tray over there and refill it from the kitchen when it gets low?"

Sniff beamed, looked over at me condescendingly, and started over to 'her' tray which she watched like a hawk the rest of the evening.

I looked around the room. Five of the folks there were from the brick apartment at the end of the street. There was the old couple, Gladys and Manny, that breakfasted at Marv's Café every morning. She started using a walker about a year ago and he was bent, but they still got out every morning for their Number 2 special and coffee. Julie, that flighty woman who worked at Stellard's Grocery, was standing frozen in the corner, her eyes darting around the room, until Sally went up to her, linked arms and brought her over to visit with Gladys and Manny. Bud and Ashley were making out in the corner. I saw an empty envelope (I know it was empty because I checked) with his address on it in the gutter one day. It was addressed to 'Thom Winston'. Ashley's name was underneath his, so I knew it was Bud's name. I've never trusted the name 'Thom'. It seems somehow deceptive to me. If a person wanted to stick in the 'h', he might as well add the last two letters and get a whole name out of it. But this. This I judge to be either pseudo sophistication or stupidity. You can be sure that the last follows the first no matter where and when it shows its silly head. I guess Bud never trusted it either.

All the while I was thinking this, Sally had spotted them. I watched her as she quickly fixed up two plates of snacks and two lemonades and brought it over to them. They had to unlatch then and act interested while she visited with them. Ashley actually looked engrossed in the conversation, but Bud looked peeved.

I went over and helped myself to the food. There was a huge bowl of popcorn, some Chex mix, little circles of bread with what looked like Ranch dressing and cucumbers on top, brownies, and oatmeal raisin cookies without the raisins. As I sized up that last plate, I shook my head in despair and loaded up. I'd have to come back for my lemonade once I got settled.

The Wang family from the house on the other side of Sniff's jostled in just as I reached my chair. I had my place staked out just in time! There are a lot of them, and once they started finding places to sit, there was certain to be no place for anyone else.

Neighbors filed in and out for over two hours. They came mostly to check out Sally and her boy and, of course, because, other than the gatherings of loud music and beer cans, we never had parties on our street. It was a novelty, and no one wanted to be the only one to miss it.

Sweet Beat walked in around 8:45 or so. His name is Kevin, but no one in his right mind would ever dream of calling him that. Some days he seemed almost normal, but other days he seemed wound tight as a champagne cork. It was at his house that the loud music and beer cans had their parties. Maybe he thought he'd see what a party with people was like. I said as much in a jokey sort of way, and he popped a switchblade out at me before you could say 'thou shalt not kill'. Sally hurried over and asked if she could admire it while he helped himself to the snacks. She held that thing in her hands and examined it like it was a lovely antique, but I saw her glance at her watch when she thought no one was looking. Sweet Beat came back over to collect his knife, but Sally kept it in her hand and patted the seat beside her on the couch (the Wangs had left by this time, so there was room for others again).

"Would you like me to hold this for you while you eat?" she asked, as though they were old friends and she was doing him a favor.

He grunted, and started in on his plate.

"I noticed you have a new bike," she continued.

Sweet Beat looked at her sideways.

With his mouth full, he said, "Harley ".

"Right. Harleys are the best, don't you think so, Mr. Bingham?"

I looked at Sally like she was out of her mind because I was beginning to think she was.

"Mr. Bingham," she persisted, "Harleys are by far the best, wouldn't you agree?"

"I'd agree with anything you say, Ms. Cortland," I answered truthfully. For at the moment that, at least, was the truth. I added the 'Ms. Cortland' part to amuse myself, but after I said it, I really began to think she ought to be shown some respect and that Sweet Beat ought to show it. Here she, the newest kid on the block, had invited all of us to her house. We barely fit in there and, even with two fans going, it was one warm party. Then, in addition to the three lemonades being spilled, the uninvited pervert she'd had to ask to leave, her little vase she had rescued just before it walked out the door, and an odd variety of other little incidents, she had Sweet Beat pulling a knife.

I decided I'd had enough then, so I got up to leave.

"Thank you kindly, Ms. Cortland, for the lovely party," I said, looking at Sweet Beat out of the corner of my eye, so he could hear how it should be done.

I heard someone say that on television once, and it stuck with me, I guess.

"Thank you kindly," I repeated.

"I'm glad you came, Mr. Bingham," Sally said brightly. Her smile was tired.

I didn't leave, though. I thought I'd check out the kitchen. Sure enough, Sniff was in there.

"Eating the leftovers?" I asked.

There was a brownie crumb on the corner of her mouth, which was full. She glared at me.

I stuck some Chex mix into my pockets and peeked into the living room.

Sally was still talking to Sweet Beat – something about the lunar cycle and meteor showers.

I leaned against the archway until he left. I was the last one out.

There are times in the years that count a man's life that he regards as markers on his journey: incidents of great proportion that all around him notice and which, by virtue of their enormity, stand like a totem pole of meaning. There are other times, however, that are quite inconspicuous to all, and nearly unnoticeable to the man, himself: yet by the insight they spark, inscribe upon his life that indefinable mark of understanding that his Creator gives as pavers along the path of wisdom.

Standing there in the archway, waiting for everyone to leave Sally's party was such a time for me. Sally could take care of herself. That was obvious to anyone who met her. It seemed to me, though, as I watched her visit with the leader of a neighborhood gang that life hands us duties to each other: obligations like protection and, if we are unequal to that, duty to "keep company". At the time, I couldn't have put into words the feelings that began to force such thoughts into my hard head and harder heart. All I knew was that I needed to be the last man out. I remain amazed to this day that I was.

Changes

By Labor Day weekend Sally had planted a vegetable garden of a respectable size in front of the apartment building. Gladys and Manny tended it like it was their sacred charge. Manny would pick up his hoe the minute they got back from Marv's, and Gladys would sit in a lawn chair and tell him what to do. Then he would do it while she talked to the bean plants.

The Wangs had pulled out the overgrown jungle in their backyard and a few other neighbors up and down the block started mowing more often. It was the "keeping up with the Jones's" thing and it disgusted me. If a man can't be who he is, it ain't worth livin'. I said as much to Sally one day when she brought over some sugar cookies without frosting.

"I agree, Mr. Bingham, a man should be who he is, but. . ."

I coughed and spit then. I hate 'buts', large and small. The only ones I ever liked were in an ashtray, and even they get stale after a time.

Sally stopped.

"I'll be heading home now. Nice to visit with you."

She started toward the porch steps.

"You didn't finish your sentence, missy," I remarked.

That threw her, I could tell, for she just stood and looked at me for a minute.

"It bothers you, Mr. Bingham? An unfinished sentence?" she asked.

I squinted at her.

"Maybe an unfinished sentence bothers you like an unfinished man bothers me."

She smiled, waved, and left.

Now I ain't dumb. I resented that woman, Sally. She tweaked
me on purpose, and it wasn't the first time.

The rest of the neighbors took to her pretty well, though.
Sniff copied her like a scribe – not one jot or tittle was omitted.
She had a red potted geranium balanced on her porch railing.
She got it at K-mart. I know cuz I saw them on sale there for
99 cents. Sniff pretended it was from Bachmans, though; like
she was some sort of landscape expert herself.

I started a game of throwing pebbles at it. She caught me at
my game, though, and you would have thought Armageddon
itself was located on Plato Street and the good Lord sent His
angels for the last war. That explosion lasted at least a week. The
problem, of course, was that the corner column of the porch was
in the way. Otherwise I would've taken that stupid geranium
out for sure.

I started making a habit of walking down Plato Street every
day. Someone needed to keep track of things and, as usual, I
could see it would fall to me. No one else was up to it.

Sniff sat out on her porch drinking Coke all day long. There
were too many Wangs for them to keep track of themselves,
much less of anyone else. Gladys and Manny had their garden
to tend. Julie was too scared to leave her apartment for anything
but work. Luckily for her she worked at a grocery, so she didn't
have to make special trips for anything. I rarely saw Bud, although
Ashley came out to visit with Gladys when Bud was on his shift.
She wore dark glasses sometimes or long sleeves in the sunshine.

No one said anything, but everyone knew what was going on. But I'm getting sidetracked.

Anyway, as I said, it fell to me to be the neighborhood monitor. When I was in grade school, the teacher would appoint a hall monitor while we put on our coats. One time she appointed me, and I had them kids in line, no question. A classmate, Martha was her name, started to cry when I yelled at her. To this day, it bothers me. At any rate, I've always liked that word. Monitor. It sounds business-like.

It fell to me to monitor Plato Street, and I noticed before long that it began to look, well, for lack of a better word – clean.

The sidewalks, though still jutting up in places for all the world like a California fault line, were clear of weeds and gum. Even the gutters were swept at some houses. That was going too far to my mind. Didn't people have anything better to do than sweep a gutter? I said so under my breath. It happened, though, that I mumbled this just as Sweet Beat walked past me.

"What'd you say, ol' man?" he yelled, jostling me with his shoulder.

I looked at him and spit. I was tired of that fool of a kid. Well, he pushed me against a tree and caught my throat in his hand and pulled back the other for a good punch when we both heard a whistle pierce the air.

Sally was running full tilt our way, and when she got within a couple of yards she slowed, bending over double to catch her breath.

She walked up to us, spit on the ground, and said, casual like, "I was wondering (pant) if (pant) you two would be (pant) interested in a book club this fall?"

"Why'd you spit, lady?" Sweet Beat frowned.

"Kevin. Have you forgotten my name? I'm Sally. Sally Cortland. And, although I'm grateful you think me a lady, I prefer you address me less formally. At any rate," she continued as Sweet Beat squinted, trying to figure out if he'd been cut down or not, "I'm going to host a book club in my home during the cold winter months. A lady (as you so ably noticed, Kevin) must plan ahead, and I need to know if you'd be interested."

"Of course," she continued as we both began to decline, "I'm only asking those who I think could keep up. You see, not everyone is *man* enough to take on something like this."

Well, I wasn't going to let anyone beat me out. I spoke right up.

"You can count on me, Sally."

She nodded and raised her eyebrows at Sweet Beat. He shrugged.

She continued to stare at him until he grunted, "I'm more a man than he is," and walked off.

"We'll start the first Thursday in November, then!" she called after him. "7:00 sharp, 6:30 if you want snacks."

She turned to me, then, and said, "I suppose if spit remained in one's mouth, one might retain more of one's teeth. I see today you are that lucky one."

I had to give her that joke and laughed out loud. I supposed I could forgive her some things after all.

The sticky hum of summer began to be visited by cool nights that extended their arms into evening and morning respectively, until the air was again palatable. Neighborhood tempers followed suit. The neighbors somehow seemed to stroll more; the kind of taking a walk that led to nowhere and was just for pleasure.

I noticed kids walking down Plato Street on their route from school to wherever the heck they lived. I piled up more rocks in my rock pile near the corner of the house. I've always believed in planning for the future. A man who doesn't take care to plan for the future, well, he might as well wear a skirt to a penitentiary, that's what. I'm no fool. Who knew when I might need to hurl one of those things? And where were those kids coming from, anyway? I got so mad thinkin' about it, I selected a small projectile from the pile and threw it at Sniff's geranium pot. I was standing where the porch column didn't obstruct my aim. That thing went as straight and true as ever any guided missile did. It whistled through the clear, fall air and knocked that planter smack against the siding faster than you can bite your lip. Which is what I did when Sniff came barreling out of her house like a moose on a rampage. Not one to be discourteous, I got out of her way. She chased me around to the back of my house and down the street until she tripped on a jut in the sidewalk. I didn't turn to look at her. I just heard the sound of her large thighs slapping the cement. Well, I thought. Well maybe she'd learn her lesson about letting her temper fly like that.

Later, though, I got to thinkin'. It weren't her fault the sidewalk was stickin' up like that. I slipped into my house for a Coke and came out with two.

"Want one?" I asked just as she was limping by.

She stood in front of my house for a full minute, then kept walking. She could suit herself, I thought, leaving the Coke on my porch railing. I went in to get my paper. When I came out, there she sat in one of my metal rockers on the porch drinking the Coke, so I graciously handed her the business section. I figured she could use it for her parakeet, Fred, if she wasn't inclined to read it. I know *I* wasn't. I read the obits until the sun set. She got up in the fading light and slowly walked to her porch where she sat until the stars came out. I went inside. After all, something was bound to be on the TV and I don't much like sitting in the dark.

The Book Club

"Halloween is over, thank goodness. Having to sit in a dark house half the night just to keep greedy little kids away is not my idea of a holiday."

"I appreciate your frustration, Mr. Bingham, but I believe I asked what you thought about Captain Bill's wild stories and songs."

I settled back then to consider it. You see, this was the second meeting of the book club and, while I was glad for a night out, I couldn't make heads nor tails of Bill nor Dr. Livesey nor why in the world anyone would give a motel the name of a person. I mean, for Pete's sake, call it by a number. There's nothing wrong with numbers. Or directions, like Eastside something or other. Or even the name of a street or a town. But a person?

Sally cleared her throat.

"What, for instance, do you think of the song that goes 'Fifteen men on a dead man's chest'?"

Well now, we were finally getting somewhere.

"That's my favorite so far. I 'specially like the part about the rum," I answered knowledgeably.

"You fool, that's the only song so far," spouted Sweet Beat.

"Ah! Kevin. How astute of you to note that it is the only song to which the author gives words. Yet, Mr. Bingham, you're right as well. There are more songs noted in the first chapter. We just aren't made privy to their lyrics."

I caught Sally somewhere between a smile and a frown. I think now, years later, what I would say was that a look of apprehension crossed her face, but only for a millisecond; like the ember of a lakeside bonfire landing on the water and quenched the minute it hits. Then, however, I was too busy with what I regarded as my triumph.

I looked condescendingly toward Sweet Beat, he smirked my way, Sniff licked her finger to turn the pages of her book as though she was searching for something, and Julie and Ashley alternately crossed and uncrossed their legs and looked around the room. There wasn't much to look at: just the sixteen of us scrunched up next to each other in this one little living room and the leftovers on the snack table along the wall. That was really why most of us came, I figured. There's nothing like free food.

That first meeting, in fact, had been all about food: who was willing to bring something and when. We considered this carefully as we munched on blonde brownies and drank RC cola. After that Sally told us we'd be discussing *Treasure Island*, passed out books she must've gotten from Salvation Armies all over the city, and told us more than any of us wanted to know about the guy who wrote it. After a few snide comments and one or two polite questions from the group, Sally said she'd read aloud the evening's chapters to anyone who came for snacks in order to refresh our memories. Yeah, right. I, for one, know that Sweet Beat couldn't read a stop sign much less a book. I guess *he* lucked out.

"I don't like he stayed without payin'."

I started, since the comment came like a shot out of nowhere. It was only Ashley.

"Tell us why, Ashley," Sally encouraged her.

"I, I just don't. He like as promised he'd pay, but he didn't."

"He didn't no such thing," Bud said quietly but with an intensity that made me scared.

Ashley eyed him for a minute, then slumped back in her chair.

"Maybe he didn't say no such thing, but he made 'em think he would," she muttered under her breath.

Sally ran her thumb back and forth across her fingernail for a few minutes.

"I suppose," she said, "what we're examining here is whether Captain Bill is a man of truth. The question then becomes not whether he paid, but whether implying something is the same as saying something outright. Can one be accused of lying, of not meeting his obligations when he hasn't said something, but has rather behaved in a way that said it?"

That was really too much for me. I got up for some more weenies in barbecue sauce. I could feel Sniff raise her eyebrows at me clear across the room.

By the time Christmas came, we were knee deep in mutiny and I moved the bat from under my bed to right next to me where I slept. I started to think Dr. Livesey wasn't so bad after all, and I grieved anew for Pearl.

Just as the crocuses started poking their heads through the melting snow, Ashley moved in with Julie and, shortly after that, Bud left town for someplace in Arkansas. That was fine with me. One less person meant more food for the rest of us.

"But *why* do you think it was so important for Jim to strike the Jolly Roger?" Sally repeated with some exasperation. She was talking to Sweet Beat.

"It's their colors," he said at last.

"Right, Kevin. Their colors, as you say, tell who's in charge. They tell where their loyalty lies. But beyond that . . ."

"Beyond that it tells their future!" interrupted Sniff exultantly.

If astonishment could be described, that moment was an apt description. Sniff had had an original thought. We all looked at her in wonder. Sniff, herself, was so overcome with surprise she started crying. Then Sally started chuckling until the whole room was laughing right along with her, even Sweet Beat.

After we'd wiped our eyes, though, he said, "I just think Hawkins was crazy to give the wheel to Hands."

"What else could he have done?" Sally asked.

It wasn't a question, though; like maybe she'd given Hawkins' decision a lot more thought than she let on. She got up from her chair and started clearing the snack table.

* * *

By the time the church choir down the street was practicing the *Hallelujah Chorus*, Ben Gunn had led them to the treasure, that traitor, Long John Silver, had cut out with some of the stash, and Jim Hawkins had said all he had to say.

We all stayed later than usual that last night. It didn't seem quite right to stop meeting every Thursday, and someone said as much. Sally just nodded. We all waited for her to say something; to say we would start another book, for instance. She didn't. She just started clearing the snack table alongside her boy, calling 'good night' to us over her shoulder.

We all just stood there looking at her as if that would change things. No one moved. No one said anything.

"The book club, as you will recall, was for the cold, winter months."

No one answered.

"It's officially spring now," she persisted.

The house creaked.

"Bulbs are sprouting, soon the grass will be green instead of brown."

She looked at all of us for a minute. Then, with a slight smile, she shook her head.

That shake of her head, that short laugh tinged with a sigh said either that she didn't understand us or that we didn't understand her. I guess I'll never know for certain.

There was nothing else to do then. We started leaving by ones and twos and threes. Before I left I kissed her on the cheek.

"Thank you kindly," I said. I meant every word.

Then, as had become my habit, I was the last man out.

Overheard

It was one of those late Spring days when life wraps its fresh sweetness around every tree branch and bud; its tendrils wind through the grass, full of earthy, musky fragrance. The air nearly sings out loud with the intensity of the lushness of hope. No one in his right mind can stay indoors on those days because doing so would be like whacking himself with a wet fish; slimy, crazy, and slightly painful.

After I'd finished my breakfast burrito with hot sauce and two cups of coffee, I sauntered out to the front lawn. I had to cut down since my stomach started giving me trouble. Coffee used to be my mainstay for breakfast: four cups and a piece of toast with orange marmalade. I suppose, though, after awhile an old leather bag gets so soft it gets loose at the seams. That was my stomach. Loose at the seams. So I had to cut down, you see, from four cups to two.

I turned and looked at my house as I had done every day for the past week. Although I'd grown kind of fond of the weathered look my house gave the property, I had been feeling more than a little pressure to fix it up. The drip that burst the pipe came over a month ago in the form of chocolate. Sally had brought me some frosted brownies without the frosting and some cardboard squares of sample paint colors. Since she had them with her, I looked through 'em. It's kind of like buying a lottery ticket, only not as exciting. I chose gray with dark gray trim so it would hide the dirt. Sally said she'd get some neighbors together if I would supply lunch. That was asking a lot, I tell you, but being the generous person I am, I consented. About a week ago now a bunch had come and painted my old house. Sniff had played the lottery, too, but she chose white with green trim. I secretly hoped for a little dust storm.

I started down the street at a slow pace. Being the unofficial monitor of the neighborhood did not require speed. Gladys and Manny and were back from Marv's Café, already poking in the garden they had planted. Julie was already at work and Ashley was heading out the door. Over the winter she'd gotten a job at the flower shop five blocks away. I cleared my throat in that friendly way I have, and she waved back. We all started choking on fumes as Sweet Beat rode past on his Harley. I made a mental note in my monitor's mental notebook. The boy was up before noon. I looked at Manny and he raised his eyebrow (he had just the one that went straight across the top of his eye sockets.). I scratched my chin in response.

I was still puzzling over that when a child's voice made me stop in my tracks. I was, by now, in the alley behind Sally's house and could hear a conversation as clear as weak tea with no sugar.

"Do you think they'll ever know, mom?"

"Probably not."

He laughed then, and mused, "To think all this could have been mine."

Sally chuckled, too.

"Yes, Court, in another time and another world it would have been yours. Still, your great great grandpa, my great grandpa on my mother's side, may not have been the type to care one way or another about the fortunes of his descendants."

"He did leave the stock. You've got to give him credit for that."

"Yes, Court, for that I would thank him if I could."

"Why don't we use it?"

I nearly fell over.

"We like our independence."

The boy persisted, "How much are we worth again?"

Sally answered without a moment's hesitation. "We're priceless."

There was a long silence and I nearly passed out from keeping my breathing shallow enough to escape detection. The screen door slammed, then slammed again.

"Ah," Sally breathed with a noise that sounded like a very long stretch. "The first lemonade of the season; home-made and sweeter than the law allows."

She said it with a laugh in her voice.

"What do you think Dad would have thought of what we're doing?"

"Oh, your Dad would have thought it a great adventure, I'm sure. Though he probably wouldn't have wanted us here, he would've given us credit when he saw we got through safely enough."

"I miss him."

"Me, too."

More silence than I could stand.

"I wish we could go back, Mom."

"Mmm. Well, we never did get around to selling the place, did we? How 'bout it? Let's go back, Court. I'm missing our little mountain cottage more than anything. Of course, there will be a lot of work, you know. . ."

"I know, I know. . ."

"Grass grown shoulder-high, tree branches helter skelter, leaves all over everything."

I guessed there was nothing more to say because they didn't say it.

I went back down the alley the way I came, and crossed over to my side of the street. Sniff saw me coming. I felt her hawk's eye on me.

"Do you know that boy's name? Sally's boy?"

"C.T. That's what he told me to call him," she answered. Then she scrunched her eyes at me.

"Why?"

"Just curious," I replied.

The next week there was a realtor's sign in Sally's yard. The place sold within a week.

At her going away party, I cornered her.

"Why?" I asked.

"Why what?"

"Why'd you move here?"

She thought for a minute, then looked me in the eye. "About three years ago my son and I decided to explore our roots. You know, mill through old cemeteries, read faded obituaries, tour places our ancestors lived. We thought we could learn from them.

"The bad and the useless, you know, can't be undone. A person can't redo yesterday. However, we thought that maybe we could continue something of the good they started."

She stopped abruptly and looked at me.

"But then, as neighborhood monitor you knew that."

I smiled until my face hurt.

The End of the Sentence

When I first moved onto this street – Plato Street – so very many years ago now, I had no illusions of it being anything other than what it appeared to be: a rundown street in a rundown part of town whose inhabitants chose because they could afford nothing better. Nothing better. That was what we all believed as we sat in our own raggedy rundown houses sitting on our own weedy, wilting, waste-filled yards perched on the crumbling street that historical rumor and historical rumor alone had said was once something worthwhile. We had taken our assignment, some full of rebellion, others with acquiescence, and lived it because, whether we admitted it or not, we believed it was ours to accept. We lived our days full of an image of our neighborhood and ourselves that said we could not do better. We could not *be* better. We branded that image into our brains with a thousand little acts and a million little thoughts. No one did it for us. We did it ourselves.

Then Sally moved in. She didn't accept that image. She didn't even seem acquainted with it, and when any of us would attempt – even remotely – to show it to her, she seemed puzzled. Maybe it was an act. Maybe she saw it, the picture of our neighborhood, as clearly as everyone else did and simply ignored it. We'll never know because we never really got to know Sally. The little that we did learn of her, though, was like a blast of Arctic air on a sweltering day. She treated us like the people we could be, not like the people we had become. She jolted us from our hazy lethargy and sent shivers down our collective spine.

Plato Street: simply the pitiful result of a vain thought that the property could never be improved. We thought that image was as immovable as the street, itself. That image hung over us as faithfully as the sun rose every morning; a permanent presence we'd grown to accept as completely as corn stalks in the summer or dead leaves in the fall. How strange, how funny, how amazing it is that we lived with that image believing it to be as real as the stars in the sky. It wasn't.

Necessary Chocolate

It was going to be one of those days, she thought; a day when chocolate would be more than a treat. Chocolate would be a necessity. First of all, she had slept through her alarm clock which wasn't alarming in the least. It clicked on the radio that told her the news and the weather and offered a song or two. Today those voices had seeped into her dreams, and she had dreamed of a train crashing into a burglar and a state legislator who were having a heated argument while it rained sporadically. Then she had burned her ear with her curling iron, spilled coffee on the cat, and stepped in a puddle walking from her car to Allmart, a store her great-grandfather had started.

He had opened it under the family name, but for reasons still unclear to her, her father had decided to change the store's name to something more generic and all-encompassing. It was an average store, but it was under her management, and Julia felt a sense of pride over the variety it offered and customer service it provided. Sure, there were larger stores of its kind and smaller ones, too. But this was the one where Julia had learned about business. This was the one for which she was responsible. This was the one she owned. She was satisfied.

Caesar O'Swiffy peeked his head into her office as he knocked lightly on the door.

Seeing him, Julia stood quickly, bumping her knee on a not quite closed desk drawer.

"Mr. O'Swiffy! I didn't realize you were coming today," she said, surreptitiously glancing at her desk calendar.

Caesar O'Swiffy softly laughed in his low, reassuring voice.

"Please. Have a seat," she said as he shook her hand and sat in the chair across from her desk.

He reached into his briefcase and pulled out a Dove caramel milk chocolate, tossing it on her desk. He had remembered she liked chocolate.

"Actually, our meeting was scheduled for next week, but I happened to be in the area and thought I'd see if we might go over the books today."

He said it in a way that sounded like the most reasonable request in the world.

Julia made a quick phone call to her assistant and assured the accountant hired by the newly formed business cooperative she had joined that they could, indeed, move the meeting.

She cleared off a table in the conference room while she made fresh coffee and as the lovely caramel chocolate melted in her mouth.

The meeting had gone smoothly and was over in less time than Julia had anticipated. It would be nice to have a second set of eyes look things over, especially at tax time. Mr. O'Swiffy had quickly gone over the store's profits and losses and commended her on her management skills.

"One thing, Julia," he said after they had returned to her office and settled into their respective chairs. "I noticed there isn't much for the staff."

"Much . . .?" Julia attempted to follow Mr. O'Swiffy's train of thought.

"Oh, you know, something to keep them happy in the break room. For instance, do you think a few packages of chocolates every week would perk people up a bit?" He laughed and gestured out the window. "Especially on a day like today!"

Julia followed his gaze. The rain was coming down steadily now. It made her long for the warmth of her living room. She wished her cat was there to jump into her lap like a purring blanket. Chocolate would be wonderful. She had thought so, herself, this very morning.

"I agree it would be a nice addition, Mr. O'Swiffy, but I need to count costs here as you saw from the books. I do bring in cookies every once in a while, and the employees seem to like that," she offered.

"Oh, Julia. There's no need to worry about it yourself. I'll just enter it as a regular delivery from the coop."

"You can do that?"

Julia's heart lifted in a way it hadn't all morning.

"I can do anything and I will. For you, Julia. We want to keep everyone happy," Mr. O'Swiffy reassured her as he stood.

He started for the door, then turned.

"I nearly forgot. You will need to sign here," he pointed to a line on a paper he quickly pulled from his briefcase, "to authorize it."

"Of course," Julia replied, signing on the line indicated.

As the door closed quietly behind the accountant, Julia sat back in her chair and smiled. Oh yes. Necessary chocolate. Just what the doctor ordered. And the rain began to subside while the sky temporarily cleared, just as the weather forecaster had predicted.

The clerk behind the counter at Allmart waved cheerfully to Julia as she stepped over the threshold of the store. She nodded an acknowledgement and headed straight to her office. She nodded, because that was what was allowed. If she had waved, it could have been interpreted as something other than a greeting according to the manual adopted by the coop three months ago. Heaven forbid she stop to chat. Julia stopped the thoughts strolling through her mind. No, she told herself, she would not be negative about a regulation intended for her own protection.

It had been exactly six months since her first meeting with Caesar O'Swiffy. The first delivery of chocolate had been wonderful, and it really perked up the entire staff. Julia was glad she had joined the business coop. Mr. O'Swiffy, their accountant, seemed like a dream come true.

The fourth week after that first chocolate delivery had been icy, and three employees were in fender benders; one, a rear end bump at a stop sign, and the other two, minor crashes on side streets. Julia, herself, had had a near miss. So when their accountant had suggested providing transportation to workers who faced some difficulty getting to work, everyone in the coop had agreed. It was worth it to keep their employees safe and, besides, it would minimize hours missed due to taking care of car repairs.

That icy week had made everyone hesitant to make the short run to the McDonald's down the street over their lunch breaks and those who hadn't packed a lunch had gone without. Well, that wasn't entirely true. There was chocolate in the break room, and some of them had a few pieces. The next coop meeting had resulted in a lunch provision to employees. Breakfast soon followed.

With the provisions had come more paperwork, though. Julia had found every increasing demands on her time to follow coop regulations and to record any deviations from them.

Julia looked up at the sound of a knock on her door.

"The mail came early," Julia's assistant, Lexie, said as she walked into the office. "Umm, let's see, not much here except a few flyers and something from the business coop. The electric and water bills are usually here by now. Would you like me to make some calls and see what's holding them up?"

"No, Mr. O'Swiffy said we would get a lower rate if the businesses in the coop were billed all together, so the coop is taking care of it now. You have to admit it's more streamlined."

Julia slit open the coop's envelope with her letter opener. She held the contents up for Lexie.

"See? Here are those bills. We just pay the coop instead of the electric and water companies now."

Lexie bent over and peered at the multiple lines in small print.

"What's this?" she asked, pointing.

"It's the charge for the coop to pay the bills."

"And this?" persisted Lexie pointing to another line.

"That's the charge to help any business in the coop should they they fall short a month."

"Doesn't that negate your savings?" Lexie asked under her breath.

Julia laughed.

"You'd better not let Mr. O'Swiffy hear you. He'd be offended. This is his baby, you know."

"Hear what?" asked Mr. O'Swiffy as he entered Julia's office and tossed a Dove sea salt caramel dark chocolate on her desk.

Picking it up and unwrapping it, Julia thought that she could find it in her heart to love this man.

Lexie quickly left as Julia answered, "I was just explaining about the utility charges arrangement."

Caesar O'Swiffy massaged his back and carefully sat in the chair in front of Julia's desk.

Julia jumped up.

"How's your back, Mr. O'Swiffy? I heard you had a run in with a stack of boxes. Here, take my chair. It's padded."

The accountant moved to Julia's chair as Julia sat in the one she reserved for office visitors.

"Thank you, Julia. Yes, it was at Norton's Grocery during inventory."

"Why were you there during . . ." Julia began, but Caesar O'Swiffy cut her off.

"I think it's important, Julia, that the staff is made aware of expectations. That," Caesar O'Swiffy waved in the direction of the door through which Lexie had recently left, "assistant needs to be reprimanded for her lack of support for our efforts."

"Oh Lexie's fine. She's always been a great employee and is an excellent assistant," Julia replied.

"Hmmm, we shall see," Mr. O'Swiffy countered. "Our efforts here are only because we want to make things easier on everyone. Don't you want to make things easier?"

"Of course!" Julia assured him. No one had ever accused her of a lack of compassion and no one ever would.

"Everyone needs to be supportive. A house divided against itself, well you know the rest. It's employees like that who bring everyone else down."

"Lexie has never broken a rule, Mr. O'Swiffy," Julia defended her assistant.

"Rules can be broken in thought as well as deed," Caesar O'Swiffy cautioned her.

He placed a stack of papers on Julia's desk and stood.

"I'll be back next week to check on staff compliance," he said, tapping his finger on the papers he'd brought.

Julia stood as he left, then sat back down, then realized she was sitting on the wrong side of her desk.

"I'm just saying that if everyone does what Norton's is doing," Julia swallowed, "there won't be anyone left to pay the utilities."

It had been nine months since she had first joined the coop, and Julia was sitting in their quarterly coop meeting. Since the coop had started, they had gained three new businesses. They were bound to run into difficulties here and there, she knew; but when she'd received her last utility bill, she'd nearly fainted. Three businesses had followed Norton's lead and declared that they could not meet their utility payments, leading to larger bills for everyone else.

Caesar O'Swiffy cleared his throat.

"We all know that Norton's had unexpected legal expenses,"

"From the lawsuit you filed on account of running into a stack of boxes," thought Julia.

"And the other three had lower profit margins than expected," he declared. "I suggest you just calm down, Julia. You seem, hmm, rather unregulated in your comments today. It's bordering on hateful. What do you have against these four businesses anyway?"

Everyone turned toward Julia, and she sank down in her chair.

"Nothing. I have nothing against them. I just don't want to use my profits to pay for their electric. . ."Julie's voice faded under Caesar O'Swiffy's gaze.

"I didn't realize the depth of your selfishness, Julia," Mr. O'Swiffy countered.

Members of the coop began mumbling to each other, but Julia didn't stay to find out what they were saying. She wanted some chocolate, wanted it now, and the candy dishes set out at the beginning of the meeting were empty.

* * *

Julia stared at the wall wondering how everything could have gone so wrong. After the meeting three months before, the one from which she had walked out, things had gone from bad to awful.

A series of events including unexpected expenses with the meal programs had led to her finding it necessary to lay off some of her employees. Julia, herself, had taken a cut in pay and could barely meet her mortgage while she juggled bills from the coop. As it was, she was eating breakfast and lunch at work to save on personal grocery expenses, and her cat refused to eat the generic cat food she was now buying and most days had taken to hiding under the couch.

Her alarm woke her gently, as always, but each morning she had begun to feel alarmed at the sound of it. Allmart employee morale had sunk to an all time low, and although Mr. O'Swiffy had tried to encourage and support Julia by increasing her

56

allotment of Dove Chocolates, Allmart became a place where dissatisfaction was palpable.

There was a knock at the door, and Lexie stepped in quietly.

"Thank you for hiring me back," she said as she sat some papers down on Julia's desk.

Julia waved away her thanks.

"I shouldn't have fired you in the first place. You were — are — one of my best workers. It's just when Mr. O'Swiffy kept suggesting things about you, I lost my focus."

Lexie nodded imperceptibly.

Julia looked at Lexie who looked steadily back at her. She opened the store account book and threw up her hands.

"Look at this! I don't even know where to start. I feel like I don't know anything about running a business anymore! And, and I'm losing my self-respect," she finished softly.

Julia jumped up, bumping her knee on her drawer.

"This is where the trouble started," Julia mumbled as she caught sight of a Dove caramel milk chocolate just inside the barely opened drawer. "Mr. O'Swiffy offered chocolate provided by the coop . . ."

"I miss your cookies," interrupted Lexie.

Julia sat back down in her chair, the cushioned desk chair, the one where she belonged as owner of Allmart.

"Maybe I need to withdraw membership from the coop."

Lexie looked hopeful.

"It was such a good idea, though. I hate the thought of losing those connections."

"Must they be lost if you aren't in the coop?" Lexie answered, raising her eyebrows.

"Maybe if we hired a different accountant, one who sticks to accounting," Julia pondered softly, reaching for her phone, "though I do love it when Mr. O'Swiffy brings me chocolate."

As she picked it up, something new dawned on Julia; or maybe she had known it all along. She would always love chocolate with a love bordering on desperation. There would be days when chocolate would be just the thing to carry her through until she got home to the soft cuddles of her cat (although at this point it would take at least a month of coaxing to get it back to its former self). But as wonderful, alluring, and oh so amazing as chocolate was, there was something it wasn't. Necessary. And on those days when Julia could almost believe it was, it was not necessary for someone else to give it to her. She would find a way or make one to get it herself.

A Hiking Lesson

They'd been hiking for hours. Sweat trickled down his face from the top of his hairline to his neck, a tiny drop detouring to touch the corner of his eye, momentarily blurring his vision. The intensity of the day's heat had grown from warm and inviting to suffocating.

"How much longer, Dad?" asked his seven year old son.

He looked three paces back to Corbin. The boy was pushing a wisp of his strawberry blond hair out of his eyes. His freckles seemed to multiply under the hot sun.

He took a breath to answer, then paused. He didn't really know how much longer. He didn't know because he had insisted they wander from the trail. He had wanted to teach this little guy, the one who was too comfortable with quiet pursuits, that the world was big and he needed to match its wildness with strength of his own. It had been his idea to take this hike into the woods filled with blackened trees and matted leaves and heard but unseen animals so that his boy would learn about manhood even at this young age. A boy had to learn.

How much longer? As a father and as a man he had never been comfortable with acknowledging ignorance, even to himself.

When faced with a question, he always had an answer, even if he really didn't. Never in his adult life had he uttered the words "I don't know".

Upon first discovering their situation, they had hiked on and found the opposite edge of the woods. Progress, he had thought. They would certainly pick up a trail without the obstruction of branches to keep them from seeing far. They hadn't.

"Dad?"

Corbin's voice was small in the grand expanse.

He stopped, then turned aside to sit on a large rock near the path.

"Let's sit down for awhile. Pretty out here, isn't it?"

As their breathing slowed from the huff of hiking to the soft in and out of rest, a sound, nearly imperceptible, quenched the silence.

Corbin's eyes followed the sound of a muffled whine, and he slowly got up and tiptoed to where he could better observe its source. It was a puppy, old enough to wander, young enough to need its mother. The mother trotted up from behind some bushes that grew crookedly out of the rocky soil. She sat, nudging the puppy, and licked it with her hot tongue.

"She's kissing him," Corbin whispered to his father.

The dog picked the puppy up by the scruff of its neck and followed the distant call of her master.

Father and son watched as the dog trotted off. He hesitated, then reached down and hugged his son, kissing the top of his head.

"Let's follow them," he said.

Road Trip

"We're gonna die!" we yelled in unison.

The car was barreling down the mountain road at sixty-five. A spring breeze blew through the rolled-down windows, the radio was turned up with decibels enough to break the sound barrier, and our eyes squinted in the sun's flashing pre-sunset glare.

It was great, this feeling of freedom; like flying or shouting at the top of a mountain. We laughed as we yelled and every so often the road twisted sharply enough so that we almost believed the top-of-our-lungs mantra we'd adopted on our road trip.

Bottomless drops became tangled montages of green brush that turned into rolling hills. When we reached a mid-point of the road, we slowed and turned into a barely visible driveway hidden to all but those who knew it was there. Brush on every side walled in the long path, barely worn tire tracks led us onward, the spring breeze that had blown our hair and stung our eyes in our race down the mountain now kissed our cheeks.

Ahead and slightly to our left it rested in the arms of the half acre of cleared land. We stopped, cut the engine, and heard something most of us had rarely heard before in our young lives. Complete silence, a deafening presence.

The faint squeak of an old rocking chair caught our collective attention and only then did we see her. Her wrinkled skin reminded me of ruts in a neglected road, but it was soft and the color of honey and glowed like there was a light underneath that we didn't see. Her not quite five foot stature was slightly stooped, but her step was sure as she rose and lightly stepped off the porch to greet us.

"Grandma," said our driver, Sam.

"Sam, you rascal," she replied, hugging him tightly. "And these are your friends."

"Nigel, Trent, and T-ball."

She hugged us each, and when she got to me she said, "I don't know any woman who likes sports quite that much. What's your given name?"

"Frederick Kellen the third," I said quietly, my face growing hot.

The others chuckled as they did every time I answered that question which, fortunately for me, wasn't often anymore.

"A fine name, Fred. I'll show you all around, but first let's get refreshed."

She seemed happier than any eighty-nine year old I'd ever met, not that I'd met many of them.

Just as we were settling around the sparsely furnished cabin to digest the pork sandwiches, home-made sweet potato chips, and sweet tea she'd fed us, Sam's grandma untied her apron and clapped her hands. We looked up. In the space of time it had taken for us to wander to our chairs and put our feet up; in the short time that we had taken to crack a few jokes and examine the rudely-made furniture; in the time we'd used to watch her fill the kitchen sink from a pump right next to it, she'd cleared the table, washed the dishes, and put everything else away.

"Lesson one: you're lazy," she laughed at the verbal dig.

We didn't know whether to laugh or leave, but Sam didn't seem disturbed by it, and he was our driver. We were stuck here whether we liked it or not until he decided to go. The road trip had been a group idea, one we'd dreamed up around the table at the school cafeteria, one that had grown from midnight texts and Facebook messages and senior year convictions about how we would live our lives without the restrictions of fathers' advice or mothers' apron strings or any other stupid restraints. Sam had always been the one who took our ideas and made them happen, though, and he had taken the lead in finding a route and planning things boys our age should get a taste of; things we needed to know about the world like strip clubs and beer and who knew what else. We were going to be men's men. Nobody would mess with us by the time we went off to college or wherever it was we ended up. We were ready for it all. Well, maybe not all. We had no idea what to think of Sam's grandma.

Before we knew what was happening, she had us outside chopping wood. Using an ax was new to all of us except Sam. We had blisters in no time, and started regretting Sam's turn into the barely visible driveway hidden to all but those who knew it was there. I heard Nigel gasp, and spun around to see Sam's grandma swinging his ax like a seasoned lumberjack. Who knew the old lady could even pick up one of those things? We turned, zombie-like, to look at the wood pile, and at that moment it dawned on us how it had gotten there. Woa. Sam's grandma handed the ax back to Nigel and told him it might help if he pulled up his pants.

"Lesson two. Keep private things private so you can get to what needs to be done," she muttered as she started walking into the cabin.

"It's chilly," she called, "Hot cocoa for whoever wants it when you're done."

Well we all dropped our axes right then and there and started for the house. She was waiting for us at the screen door.

"When you're done," she repeated, pointing to the uncut logs and tools on the ground.

We turned around and spent the rest of the evening chopping. We actually got the hang of it and by the time we were done, we were not just ready for cocoa. We were ready for bed. It was 9:00.

What we had initially thought would be a quick stop for Sam to say hi to his grandma turned into a week. She always came up with a reason we needed to stay one more day. Instead of drinking beer and seeing things our mothers never intended for our young eyes to see, we ended up doing odd jobs around Sam's grandma's property; things like turning over dirt for a garden and planting seeds so small we lost half of them who knows where, and learning how to make lemonade with actual lemons, and how to shoot a gun and field dress a deer. Sam's grandma had us take turns reading Shakespeare and Frost and Thoreau and Lewis to her after dinner while the rest of us listened as we stared into the fire. What school had never done for me, Sam's grandma did, for it was then that I think I really began to love reading and thinking, both. We fell into bed every night by 9:00

and she woke us up with the prickly side of a broom at dawn. She especially liked whapping Nigel. After a couple of days he began to think it was as funny as she did.

That last night there we sat in the dancing light of logs chopped long before, maybe years before we had arrived. Sam walked over to her and told her spring break would be over in two days and we had to get back home. She reached up on her tiptoes and placed her cheek gently next to his.

"I know. Your mother called and told me."

We did a double take.

"Grandma, when did you ever have a phone?" Sam asked, looking around.

His grandma motioned to me and led me over to a closet.

"Fred, would you be so kind as to open this door for me?"

I pulled the surprisingly heavy door open, and inside there was a little room, complete with a desk on which sat a cell phone and computer.

After a couple of silent minutes, Trent stuttered, "Wha . . .?"

Our thoughts exactly.

"Lesson ten: change is a fact of life," she said quietly.

We were quiet the morning we were to leave. I couldn't smile even when Sam's grandma laid into Nigel with the broom. It felt like we were going from heaven to purgatory. The week had been filled with lessons like *listening to nature clears your thoughts;* and one that closely followed it, *how are you ever gonna hear God if you're listening to loud music;* and one especially for Nigel, *sleeping in makes you stupid;* and *animals trust people with kind hearts.*

Sam's grandma packed a lunch for us to take back with us and gave each of us a bear hug that nearly took our breath away.

Last was Sam, and she hugged him for a long time while they swayed together in the clearing. Then she swatted his backside and he got in the car.

Leaning out the window he said, "Lesson eleven: Listen to your grandma."

What a road trip: sixty miles and a world away. She smiled and waved as we pulled out of the barely visible driveway hidden to all but those who knew it was there.

Reel

How it caught his eye, he didn't know. He bent down and picked it up. It was a misshapen stone about 2 inches in diameter. It was the dark gray of river rock, but on one side silver, red, and blue stripes ran up and down along its surface. He turned it over; but no, it was just the one side where the stripes covered the otherwise dark gray. He put it in his pocket and looked at the sky.

The sun would be setting within the hour, he guessed. The air was already becoming that tempered color of dusk, a subtle dimming of light and warmth. The day's brightness had gradually left and with it the cheeriness that sunshine brings. He'd been on the river for two hours doing more strolling and thinking than fishing. It was good out here, away from the pressures of committees and expectations and people needing him. Out here it was the way everything should be; slightly rugged and sparkling and colorful. Out here it was real.

The mayflies would be swarming soon. Trout would race toward them, flashing their colorful God-given Joseph coat and splashing in their leap to catch the flies. Then fishing could begin in earnest.

He cast out. It was a good one. He would have a trout or two or more to take home and show off and fry up. There it was! The familiar tug; the fight for life at one end and for food and satisfaction at the other. He pulled and played with the fish until it was close enough to net. With a practiced hand he unhooked his fish. Just as the splash of the trout sprayed him, he heard it.

The leaves of a bush rustle in a variety of ways. A spring breeze only slightly moves leaves in a playful whisper. The wind that stirs before a storm is faster. It's urgent, a warning. This was neither. It was the sound of someone approaching. But, no. Not someone. The sound was too brash, too heavy.

He spotted it then, the dark brown coat, the swaying posture. The bear looked at him across the river that was suddenly more narrow than a minute before. Snout to the air, it sniffed. There was no way to remove the fish scent that touched his waders and permeated his hands. If he threw the fish to the bear it would be a short time before the bear came closer for more. Slowly he let the fish slip from his hand back to its home in the river.

Fishing was over for the night. He would give the other fisher extra room by his absence. He moved quietly and as quickly as he dared, making his way back to his truck, back to the people who needed him. That was real, too, after all.

The Unimportant Painting

Hundreds crowded the steps and spilled onto the sidewalk, waiting. It was opening day at what was touted as the finest art museum in the Midwest. The Museum of Artwork and Vision, MAV, had been six years in the making; from the first meeting of ideas, to argumentative meetings regarding design, to the ground breaking, to more meetings filled with debate, to the final MAV committee private tour. As opening day visitors paused in front of everything from hand thrown pots to busts to paintings, two children wandered from one room to the next. Their steps led them in an arbitrary tour of things that held little of their interest until they stopped in unison in front of a painting. Small and hung in an obscure spot, it had garnered little attention from most in the crowd. It, however, held the twins with an unaccountable pull, as though they could not move from their spot had they wished. The two understood, in that fuzzy place between mind and heart, that the story behind the painting was one that could change a life. The story had at the very least changed the lives of the ones who lived it, the ones who were in the small painting hung in an unimportant spot in one of the finest museums around.

The painting in front of which the two children stood was awash in colors of black and rust, with splashes of red, and was a montage of well-drawn images. In the center stood a man, his foot on a copy of the Constitution of the United States of America. He was dressed in a shirt embroidered with many words, among them, "women's rights". He was smiling and waving to five happy men with turbans on their heads as they flew away to freedom. His back was to a woman being lashed one hundred times by a man resembling the ones flying to freedom. A noose hung slightly ahead of the woman. Her small child and newborn baby, held back by others, watched the scene. Over two hundred school girls sitting silently and guarded by soldiers with guns also watched.

In the upper left side was a scene of an embassy, lying in charred ruins. Four skeletons lay at its base. Slightly below that scene were guns, many guns with legs, running fast and furious toward a Mexican sombrero. One dead man in uniform lay between the guns and the sombrero.

Giant forms and tax records had been molded into iron gates to restrict some citizens from moving freely. A pregnant woman with hair the color of snow, each strand banded with jewelry that spelled 'fear' was giving birth to cameras and listening devices so numerous that they spilled out of the birthing room, down the hallway, and out the doors of the hospital where she lay. A picture of the hospital she had wanted to use instead hung from her limp hand. A giant eye in the corner of the frame seemed to follow onlookers, in this case, the two children, regardless of the angle from which they observed the painting.

A school building was marred by graffiti, with CC in bulging, garish letters. Tests were stacked neatly on each desk, while textbooks lay scattered on the school rooms' floors. The school's entryway held a picture of a gun with a line through it. Two dots on the top and a half-circle on the bottom made it into a happy face.

Reporters in a busy newsroom stood against a wall while a few important looking people looked through their phone records and emails, patiently crossing out whatever did not suit them.

Throughout the painting in small, nearly imperceptible drawings, was something else. Sprinkled all throughout the scenes was something like golden dust. Tiny images though they were, they drew the children's eyes to them. A soldier stood stick straight, talking to the few who would listen. A woman bent down to help some fearful children and gave them sweet pieces of fruit with wrappers labeled 'truth'. Some people were on their knees, their hands lifted in prayer. There were many, many images of many small, good things. It seemed, almost, that the painting pulsated with the golden dust; the tiny pictures growing more numerous and larger at times, then fading again to their infinitesimal size.

And the two children watched while the museum visitors around them toasted the great building's success.

It Was a Dark and Stormy . . . Well, You Know

"What? Louder! I can't hear you! There's something – crackling or something – on the line. What?" The static ceased as did every other sound. I hung up and dialed. No tone. No anything. Maybe the landline would be better. I walked into the kitchen, muttering to myself and picked it up. It was silent. Maybe it was the storm. Beyond the window glass I could see the trees bending in the greenish sky, branches lashing one way and another all at once. The rain had determinedly increased since the storm had begun nearly an hour ago, and the angry sky was gradually changing daylight to dark.

I jumped at a cannon-fire rumble as lightning flashed just in front of the window. The lights in the living room and kitchen went out at once. I knew flicking the switches would accomplish nothing. I flicked the switch.

It was my way, I admitted maybe for the first time in my life, flicking a light switch back and forth. If something wasn't the way I thought it should be, I always tried to fix it even when

I knew the likelihood of my changing things had somewhere near the same probability of the Kardashians going into hiding.

The truth was I'd always lived my life on the basis of possibility rather than probability. That was the reason I'd been on the gymnastics team in middle school. It was the reason I had graduated from high school even though I could tell my science teacher thought dark thoughts every time I entered his classroom. And it was why I was here in the first place. A relationship, one I valued beyond reason, had soured and, after more than a few unsuccessful, unreasonable attempts on my part to force it back to what I believed it should be, I had run away. At twenty-eight I had actually run away.

I'd known about this old run-down place for many years. It had been my uncle's old house, one he'd lived in and died in. That he'd actually been dead a week before anyone knew it was something we didn't talk about. No one in the family wanted the house and no one in the world wanted it either, so it had sat alone and ignored for the eleven years since he'd been gone. It was four miles beyond the edge of a dying town: one of those towns that has a gas station; a church with twenty pews, one for each parishioner and a few to spare; a bar with the same customers every night; and no police force.

I'd been here exactly one week, arranged for the utilities to be turned on, a surprisingly easy thing to do, and had unpacked all my earthly belongings. And swept. I had swept the building from bottom to top to bottom again. There was a lot of dirt. I'd been in the process of changing my mailing address when the phone had gone dead.

I hadn't gotten a job yet, the nearest job being the factory ten miles south, but I wasn't in a hurry. I had some money stashed away. It was in a manilla envelope under the silverware in a drawer in the kitchen.

As I stood peering out the window, I heard a creak; but it was different from the storm-related creaks and groans the old structure had been emitting for the last half-hour. I turned my head slightly and squinted into the dark.

I was just beginning to think I could make out the form of a person standing in the entry of the kitchen. It was slightly taller than I and lacked the rigidity of the doorframe. It seemed like a person, but that would be crazy, right? It wasn't really all that clear, after all; just a nearly transparent image – more of an outline, one that I could easily be, for who knew what reason, imagining. The dark made it impossible to actually see anything anyway.

There it was again. Another creak. The form, or whatever it was, hadn't moved. It was as still as the wall, itself. Maybe it was just my imagination after all. I glanced out the window again. Lightning danced across the sky momentarily revealing some downed branches and an overturned lawn chair. I loved that chair! I'd rescued it from the dumpster of my apartment building the summer before and replaced the ripped nylon webbing with heavy muslin in a chili pepper print. I hoped it wouldn't be carried too far before the wind died.

I turned to check the kitchen doorway again, and my heart, which had begun beating more rapidly since the last loud thunder, seemed to be of two minds because now it stopped completely. There was no form any longer; only the faint outline of everything that had slowly been growing familiar over the past week of my living there. So *had* I seen something?

The lights flickered on again, though the storm raged on outside. My eyes surveyed my surroundings. Nothing had changed. All was well. Tea. Tea would be good company for such a night. I started over to fill the teapot. I would have at least two cups, and who cared if it was caffeinated on the edge of evening? The floor creaked just as I stepped on the threshold of the kitchen.

I backed up and stepped on the threshold again. It creaked. I took little baby steps along the width of the entry. The old hardwood yielded slightly underneath my weight and creaked slightly every so often along the boards.

I walked back to where I had stood at the window and looked at the threshold. Was there something amiss with the lines of the house? Maybe what I had imagined was actually a bulge here and there. It was an old house, an old *neglected* house. I willed the spot I had peered at earlier to bulge. It didn't.

I let out a deep breath. I wasn't the kind to be spooked. I was probably just tired. It had been a long, empty week for so many reasons. The relationship that had prompted my escape from what was familiar as an adult to what had been slightly familiar as a child was without a doubt behind it. I had done everything I could, hadn't I? Tried to change myself, him, and past arguments to no avail. Tried to make him see things my way, myself to see things his way. Tried. Tried. Then tried to just forget it all and found instead mice nests and cobwebs and dust enough to make another galaxy in making this house inhabitable again.

I always said I believed in possibility more than probability, but maybe that wasn't exactly true. Maybe what I believed was that if I managed something enough – problems, relationships, dreams – I could move them from one column to the other. Anyone who didn't believe Henley when he said, *I* am the master of my fate, *I* am the captain of my soul, was a fool. I filled the teapot, then jumped and nearly dropped it as I placed it on the stove. Whoever designed the jangle of the old phone here should be arrested! Who in the world would be calling since no one in the world knew I was here?

"Hello?"

"Oh yes! I had been trying to change it when the power went out."

"Um, what?"

"Proof of . . . oh. I will come in person then. Thank you."

I replaced the receiver with slightly more force than necessary. Really? Proof of my existence? Maybe their so-called policy should be put in a time capsule along with the old black phone. I stared at the old phone, my mouth going suddenly dry. My eyes darted to the cell next to it, the one I had placed there when I'd lost contact. I slowly picked up the receiver and listened. There was no dial tone. I clicked the little knobs up and down. How in the world . . .? I picked up my cell and tried turning it on, but it remained black. It probably needed recharging. I plugged it into the outlet and laid it on the kitchen counter.

The house still held my dead uncle's furnishings, a good thing since my few possessions fit into the back of my pick-up truck. I eased into his soft, dusty armchair, sipped my tea and stared out the window. I found myself wondering where they had found him — my uncle who'd been dead a week before anyone knew it.

I must've dozed, for when I opened my eyes, my cold tea pooled on the floor and the slightly cracked cup lay beside it. The storm had died and left behind a damp stillness. I felt a slight, cold breeze filter from the direction of the kitchen and shivered. The day's light had truly been stolen by the storm and by this time the trees blended into the starless night.

I grabbed an old quilt and wrapped it around my shoulders while I went to start the water boiling for a cup of tea I hoped this time to finish. As I waited, I scanned the bookshelf replete with my uncle's old books, selected one, and took it with me and my now hot tea to the armchair. The story was benign, really. It was of a silly girl whose efforts in controlling everything and everyone around her irritated me. I was beginning to tire of it, when the pace picked up slightly. She finally encountered a situation that resisted her efforts and wandered away into the night. Two weeks later the few who cared enough to search were on the brink of finding her. I turned the page. The next chapter would finally give some satisfaction! She would get her comeuppance or learn the error of her ways, though I doubted the latter. The page was blank. What? I examined the book. Nothing appeared to be torn out. I turned the next page and the next, suddenly frantic to know what happened. There was nothing. What cruel trick was this?

I turned toward the sound of a sudden creak and felt a slight, cold breeze on my cheek. Then the lights went out.

The Key

Lilies bloomed with glad abandon along the gravel road. The high sun shone bright and hot, bronzing his neck and arms as he trudged along. Dust, kicked up by his worn boots with every step, hung in the air long enough to cover his jeans with its brief touch. The circular saw buzz of cicadas grew louder, then quieter, then louder again.

He hadn't decided where he was going. He just knew he needed to leave. He needed new air to breathe, fresh scenery. What was the purpose of life anyway? Not in his work, at least not the work *he* did. Friendships? Ha. Greetings on the street or at the corner store didn't prove anything beyond good manners. There was that one old woman at Johnson's Foods check-out. He'd always waited to go through her lane. She was nice. He didn't s'pose he had any obligation to anyone. He'd paid his bills. Done his job. Didn't poke his nose where it didn't belong. His eyes roamed over the road ahead. It's undulating path told him nothing of what was ahead.

He kicked an old pop can into the ditch, then stopped. Something was off with the empty sound he had subconsciously expected as the toe of his boot had made contact. Turning back a few steps, he walked into the high grass of the ditch and nudged it with his boot. A lead-like thud answered and a tiny tree-toad hopped to get out of his way. A snake slithered silently through the tall grass. Reaching down, he picked up the can, turned it upside down, and shook it. With a rattle, the noisemaker fell into his hand.

It was a key. Maybe it was to some vehicle. Probably. He slipped it into his pocket and looked around. An old junker roared past, leaving a trail of dust in its wake.

The man made his way out of the ditch and trudged on. Who would put a key in a pop can anyway? Why not just throw it away or sell it for a nickel at one of those sales so popular in the summer where one person sold old stuff and another one bought it? If it was to a car, where was the car – in a junkyard in some other county? Maybe it fit the lock of a house, but he didn't think so. Sweat trickled down his temple and he wiped it away with the palm of his rough hand, then jumped. Yanking up his jeans, he saw it perched on the top of his boot. He scooped up the toad with one hand and covered it with the other. Its tiny presence tickled his hand and he almost smiled.

"You saw that snake too, did ya?"

He was quiet for a moment.

"Hop. How's that for a name?" he asked the toad. "You 'n me, Hop. I got your back. You got . . . you got . . . my hand."

He reached the next rise of the road when he saw it.

It stood there, its tongue lolling out, and looked directly at him. It was a brown and white mutt with friendly eyes. It gave a hesitant wag of its tail and took a step toward him.

"Waddaya think, Hop?"

Hop responded to his whisper by tickling his hand.

The man squatted on the edge of the road and the dog trotted up to him, giving his stubbly face a quick lick with his hot tongue. It nudged his hand with its nose and sniffed. Hop slid through the small gap and hopped on the dog's nose, pausing as the two looked each other in the eye, then up on the dog's head and finally rested on his back.

The man looked the dog over. It had no collar nor tags and its ribs were beginning to show. He petted it for a full minute, then got up and began walking again. The dog trotted sometimes beside him, sometimes nosing into the grasses along the road, then catching up again, Hop clinging deftly to his back.

He watched the dog and its tiny passenger, riding now backward and watching the man as he walked behind them. The ghost of a smile crossed his lips. Nothing had changed. The cicadas still sang their buzz saw song, the sun still beat down its white hot light and the lilies responded with carefree orange faces. Yet he began to feel different; a small excitement somewhere in his gut, a repressed hope he'd denied. He closed his eyes and breathed in the hot air.

"What's yer name? Shep?"

The dog stood still, looking back at him.

"Brownie? No? Look here, I'm no good with names."

He licked his dry lips. He could feel heat radiating from his skin, his body a stove. The dog trotted ahead of him. Dust rose and settled. The sun began its slow descent. One mile. Two. He began to breathe harder. Either he was growing weary or the dog was trotting faster. Every so often the dog would stop and look back, waiting, then trot on again.

One foot in front of the other. Always onward. Why did he do this? Always. His life was a pattern of stay and leave, a wandering mission of disconnection. Five miles farther on, its sound began to wind its way into his subconscious until he heard it: water running over rock.

His life was a pattern of stay and leave, a wandering mission of disconnection.

He quickened his step and came to it, a river half a mile back from the dusty road, hidden by a dry meadow and a sudden drop from the tree line at its edge. The dog rushed its descent as the man followed him, hanging onto a bush here and there for balance. By the time he reached the bottom, the dog was splashing in the cold river, lapping the welcome water, then laying in the shallow edge, panting. He removed his boots and socks, stepped into the shallows, cupped his hand and drank. The cold water sent coolness through his tired bones. Looking down, he saw Hop, tickling the tip of his toe. The man felt hopeful, the first in a long time.

Man and dog lay on a bed of soft pine needles and slept as the moon rose and stars blinked on one by one.

A moist tongue on his face woke him. The sun was just peeking over the horizon, turning the sky from gray to violet to pink and orange and yellow. He waded in the now still water and drank freely, then pulled on his socks and boots. Rising from the piney bed, he stuck his hands in his pockets as he watched the sun's early morning display.

"Hey. Where's the key?" he asked, searching the ground.

The dog trotted up to him.

"Did you see it, boy? Did you see the key?"

The dog barked.

"Key?"

The dog put his front paws on the man.

"Your name's Key?"

The dog jumped around in a circle, then lowered himself in a play bow.

"Waddaya know. Well, boy, it didn't matter anyway, did it? Whatever that key was for might be long gone by now."

The man began following the path upstream, then slowed to a stop.

"Key! C'mon now!"

The dog trotted up to him, looking at him expectantly, then back from where they'd come. He hesitated, looking at the man.

"Ah. Where's Hop? Is that it?"

Key lay in the river, his head on his paws.

Maybe the mutt was more of a key than in name only. How had he gotten to a point when an animal cared more for connection than he did? He suddenly felt — he didn't know — sad, he guessed. Lost. It was a feeling he'd not had since he'd left home at sixteen and never looked back. He'd not been acquainted with it in the twenty years of his wandering since then. He sat down, resting his arms on his knees.

What did it matter? It was just a toad, for pete's sake, hardly as big as his fingernail. But the thought of trudging ahead without Hop — he shook his head. You had to let someone — or something — in to feel the emptiness when they were no longer there. He didn't like it. He started on again, then stopped and looked back. Key waited, cocking one ear. He shook his head at his own weakness. A new knowledge pushed its way through his stubbornness and wouldn't leave. He sighed. Maybe it was time. Perhaps he'd been a loner long enough. And, hard as it was to have the thought, it was possible it wasn't weakness after all. Maybe it was strength. Maybe it was a source of strength he'd missed along the way.

Turning the other direction and starting back, he called, "Okay, Key! We can't leave our pardner!"

Key bounded ahead of him, then began nosing along the water's edge. The man jumped. Yanking up his jeans, he saw it perched on the top of his boot. He scooped up the toad with one hand and covered it with the other. Its tiny presence tickled his hand and he smiled.

It scooted out of his hand onto Key's nose, hopped onto the top of his head, and found his place on his back.

Down the river's path, they walked; one talking, two listening, three together.

On A Golden Afternoon

I could just see the shadow slanting slightly like some willow bending toward the water. It turned toward me then, and I pulled back behind the corner of the building which I told myself hid me. What was I doing? The evening's mystery had begun as an afternoon stroll through the park by my house. Isn't that the way all trouble begins: Innocence pulled gradually by some subtle power until you're standing behind a building a mile from where you should be, trying to breathe noiselessly though you're sorrowfully certain your heartbeat can be heard a block away?

I had begun my walk to see the trees. They were golden this year. Maples splashed red here and there, but the air itself seemed mostly – well, like I said – golden. King Tut's tomb. Pieces-of-eight. The lottery that changed things of value to a thin, printed paper of possibility. I digress, of course, to avoid the obvious.

You see, I was looking up as I walked, the better to take in the fire and shine of the season, when I bumped into something. At least that's what I had immediately thought since it was immoveable, like a lamp-post. My abrupt stop and reverted sight line, however, showed me a person I would guess to be around 6 feet, 3 inches of mostly muscle knit together with intensity. He looked into my eyes for a split second while I stood fixed to the spot wondering how I would explain my disappearance to my dog who I had left at home as punishment for whining into the wee hours of the early morning. Then he was gone and I was shivering in the balmy air of the autumn afternoon.

I'm not being dramatic. He really was gone. I turned to look and there was nothing there. Any sane person would have cut her stroll short and gone home, but I told myself that I wasn't going to allow anyone, even if they were a disappearing man, rob me of my afternoon stroll. So I kept walking until I got to the other end of the park. Then I thought what if I didn't see him because he had hidden? That makes sense, right? Maybe I should go home like the sane person I wasn't and lock my door. But then (I reasoned) if he was, in fact, following me, maybe I shouldn't go straight home. Maybe I should take a divergent path to shake his trail. OR, and this is where the trouble really began, maybe I should try to find him, follow him, and prove to us both I wasn't anyone to be trifled with.

At that point, I turned and started back the way I'd come, eyes darting behind every bush and tree. I kept walking beyond the park then because I thought I spotted him, and that's when I noticed the golden light had turned to muted gray. Dark would follow in a matter of half an hour, fall being what it is, and I was a mile of crooked sidewalks from home.

As the solid cement of the building resupplied my courage, he was suddenly in front of me, and the muted gray of dusk turned charcoal.

"Why do you chase me?" he asked.

"I . . . I . . . you . . ."

His intensity took my breath away. I wiped my clammy palms on my jeans. So what if he could hear my heart beat like the tell-tale heart? I was on the offense, not the defense, wasn't I? I would not let him intimidate me. I WOULD NOT.

"What mindlessness draws people like you to chase me? You're the same ones who would be most dismayed to catch up with me."

I gulped and he was gone. The conversation that had taken less than a minute seemed as though it had lasted an eternity.

I ran back home, knowing he would be able to tell where I lived if he followed. At this point I didn't care. I just wanted to be somewhere familiar, somewhere safe. I slammed the door behind me, locked the deadbolt with trembling hands, and watched as my dog took one whiff of me and hid under the couch.

Later, when my breathing had returned to normal and the sirens of the evening blended with street sounds of my city block, I sat with my cup of tea and thought about what he had said. Chasing him? Well, sure, but only because I wanted to prove I – what was it I had thought at the time? Trifled with? Yes, couldn't be trifled with.

Maybe I did prove it. I'd caught up with him, after all. But to be perfectly honest, it didn't feel like I'd proven anything. I turned to one of my favorite shows on the television, but the evening's murder investigation started me thinking things that hadn't before occurred to me. I switched it off. I grabbed a book I had been reading, and slammed it shut after a paragraph. I switched on the T.V. again and listened as a political ad droned on about someone who thought that I deserved to get what I wanted, not what I worked for. I thought for a minute about what I deserved and threw my shoe at the T.V. It went black.

I switched on a lamp. Who was he anyway, this immoveable, intense man who sent shivers straight to my gut; who I'd never seen before, but who seemed slightly familiar? Not familiar like an old acquaintance. Familiar, maybe like an old textbook. Like that.

No. Impossible.

What if it *was* him? Whether I was correct about his identity or not, there was one thing I *did* know. Loathe to admit it though I was, he was right. I had been chasing him without a thought of what that meant other than my immediate desire to prove something. I hadn't thought of the peripheral, the fall out. And *if* he was who I now thought he might be, my mind had already revealed that I had been chasing him long before he confronted me on this golden day. When I inhaled the golden light of fall, I thought of tombs and pirates, not warmth and light. I really was playing that lottery that had flitted through my brain like a sudden breeze.

There are many things I chase in life, some more worthwhile than others. But on a golden afternoon that knocked the breath out of me with fright I wonder. Should Death really be one of them?

The Twig

He unfolded the paper and reread it one last time.

You want to move on, I know. But in case somewhere down the road when your mind wanders to past things and you want to remember, I'm leaving the twig on the base of the statue in the park we used to call ours. I know how you loved it – that small, silly representation of first love I broke off from a fledgling tree during our first walk there. Remember how every walk after, we toasted the growing tree with that twig? You can have the symbol of its springtime buds and summer leaves and vivid autumn color and sparkling snow resting on its bare winter branches. You can have the path we traced so many times, the faint sound of timeless music playing at the band shell on the other side of the lake, and the pungent scent of lakeshore. You can have the sunsets so brilliant they make your heart ache.

I'm leaving in the morning. I'll always hope for your happiness, for good things to come your way, for blessing to meet you on the sidewalk.

He refolded the note, stooped down and slid it under her apartment door. Turning, his form bathed in a sunset of deepest orange and red, he walked away.

Paper Hearts

She shook the snow from her foot. Stepping into a rather large slush pile on the curb wasn't a good omen for this meeting. Why was she even going? One, she didn't even know the guy. Two, a random drawing at the local coffee shop probably wasn't the best way to meet someone. Three, where was her best friend who had talked her into it in the first place? Half-way across the state by now, she guessed – making a trip home to surprise her family on Valentine's Day. Who surprises her family on a day meant for love?! Well, okay. Maybe that wasn't quite what she meant. But any sane person would know what she meant without her having to clearly articulate it.

She pulled the paper heart out of her coat pocket and squinted at the address. It was just the next block. When the barista had given them each a pink paper heart with their lattes and told them to write their name on it, it had seemed harmless. She had noticed he told his male customers to write their name and also the name of a local diner or restaurant, time, and date. Later, another barista had passed around a glass canister for each to drop in the pink paper. As they left, they were given a heart with a name, restaurant address, date, and time. Her friend's poor guy would be stood up. If she was any kind of smart, hers would be, too. Still, underneath it all she believed everyone should agree with her assessment: Valentine's is a day when corny is cool.

She stuffed the heart back into her coat pocket, pulled off a glove to run her fingers through her hair, and stole a glance at herself in the window of a shop she passed. One more building and she would be there. She stopped. What was she thinking? She would just go home. No harm, no foul. As she turned around, she bumped into a man. Mid-twenties, she guessed. Dark hair. Athletic build. Tennis shoes with a small rip on the right side.

An 'excuse me, maybe you should look where you're going' nearly escaped her lips. It didn't. He looked up from what he'd been reading. In his hand was a pink paper heart.

Valentine's is a day when corny is cool.

The Scavenger Hunt

Looking back, I should have known. I should've seen it coming. But that's the way these things happen, isn't it? Not seeing what is clearly in front of you – so close it can feel your very breath?

You see, we had been on a scavenger hunt of sorts: the kind where you go from place to place and take a picture of you and your partners to prove you found whatever was next on the list. It was actually great fun. We'd eaten our pizza and drunk gallons of sparkling water. Okay. I know that sparkling water and pizza don't really go together, but it tells you something about the complexity of my friendship group. Some of us are pretty normal and others of us try not to be. Anyway, we had eaten ourselves into a state of grease and bubbles that defy description and were all feeling ready for this challenge.

At the third place – it was a statue of a lion by the library – a fellow photo bombed our picture. He was nice looking and made a great face and then he struck up a conversation with a couple of us as we walked to the next place and ended up just kind of joining us.

At about the sixth place, we were missing one of the gals. Everyone looked, but she'd just disappeared. Someone suggested she'd gone in a coffee shop and would probably catch up, so we all agreed that was the case and kept going.

By the tenth place of the thirteen original sites we were given, three more of our group were gone. Vanished like ice on a hot day. The facial expressions of the remaining members varied from annoyed to concerned to downright scared spitless.

You know, I should have listened to my scared spitless self then, but I was too embarrassed to acknowledge the thought that popped into my head. I finished the scavenger hunt with one other guy – the guy that had joined us near the beginning. The team members that disappeared? I never saw them again. They were taken away one by one while I maintained a state of denial because things like that don't happen in my world. By the way, we didn't win.

One Stone at a Time

Sweat trickled from his hairline down the side of his determined face and into his beard. The sun was at its peak beating with glaring force on the hard earth, but there was no time to rest. His eyes darted left then right as he pushed another stone in place. He dug into his pocket and read again the ancient newspaper he'd found during his work.

Headline: Aggressors attack. Houses destroyed. City gates burned. City walls demolished. Families separated as young and strong taken for re-education. All is lost.

He shook his head. All is lost: three of the saddest words ever written.

Such words of totality, 'all' and 'lost'. He ran his hand across his brow. What was needed was another word, one of redemption. One man to hope is what was needed: Someone to travel through the night and avoid notice; someone to rally those left behind; someone to assess the damage and the need, to pray to God in heaven for protection against despair from intimidating letters and lies and against the plots of enemies.

He scribbled words underneath the old headline.

We work with weapons by our side, even when we go for water. We sleep a light sleep in our clothes. We live lives of fear. But we work despite our feelings. We work because hard times demand hard work. The Lord does not strengthen confident hands doing what is wrong, but fearful hands doing what is right.

He folded the shred of newspaper and stuffed it between two rocks, pushing and shoving until it was sheltered from weather of every kind. Then he picked up another stone and pushed it into place.

Story prompt: Nehemiah

Predawn Visitor

I could feel it staring at me though my eyes were closed and the room was still dark. I knew only that it was small with a big presence. I could tell it was small, because its breath on my face was slight. I claim it had a large presence because I had lain there under my covers sensing its proximity for a good five minutes, too afraid to open my eyes.

It was of no use – lying still and silent while my unknown enemy stared. I opened my eyes and met his gaze: small, round, black button eyes blinking in the dark.

I started to speak, but my throat, dry from sleep and fear, prevented me at first.

Finally, I whispered, "Who are you? How did you get here?"

I felt his breath. He blinked once more, and was gone.

Every night after that he returned, watching me until I felt his stare and awoke. I lost sleep, knowing what was to come, unable to keep my drooping eyes open long enough to catch his entrance, not knowing how to keep him from his secret mode of appearance and retreat.

Is this the thing of nightmares? Is this a harbinger of a future of unexpected haunt and impossible solutions to problems I would face?

Beware, dear reader, not of things that go bump in the night, but of things that make no sound at all.

One Soldier

He wasn't sure of himself. He never had been. He'd never been a stand out kind of guy. His grades were unremarkable and he was probably forgotten by his classmates before the last strains of Pomp and Circumstance died away. He had few noticeable skills. He was not the one the coach had depended on or praised. He had been placed in an inconspicuous part of the school choir. Throughout his young life he'd had the same insecurities as everyone else who was so focused on their own they failed to see his.

But that was the thing. Somewhere beyond the self-doubt and feelings of inadequacy he wondered if the inconspicuous life was really the majority life, the ordinary life, the normal life. If that life – *his* kind of life – was one that most knew intimately, yet denied publicly, he was as ready as anyone to do the job before him. Maybe life wasn't about standing out as much as it was doing the work in front of you; not running from it nor ignoring it nor disparaging it, but just doing it.

The whir of the plane's engines grew louder. He stepped into not just a plane, but so much more. He handed over his known for the unknown and took his stand as one more unheralded, noble life.

Armistice Day, also known as Veterans Day, is November 11.

Sum Qui Sum

We'd loved each other forever. Grew up two houses down from each other. Went to the same schools and sometimes, if luck was with us, were in the same classes. We looked enough alike that some thought we were sisters. In a way, we were: sisters with different last names. We held each other's secrets close, and kept promises made with the passionate loyalty of youth. When college years approached, we promised each other we'd choose the same college.

That was the first promise we broke. Her parents wanted her to go east to their alma mater and she agreed. I wanted something close to home. We kept in touch with weekend girlfriend chats, though less because of studies and new friends. Then one week we didn't.

She moved back to town ten years later. I'd already settled there with a husband and two kids in a starter house that was fast becoming our forever home. We ran into each other at the local grocery and stopped at the cafe next door for lunch. By the time we'd caught up, her ice cream had melted and my fish sticks had grown soft.

We fell back into the familiar dance of friendship. My kids thought she was a superhero. Without the extra treasure and tension that mark the presence of a family, she had energy, money, and time to do those kinds of things that lives of mundane structure cannot. I promised I would cheer her on in whatever next adventure she undertook. She promised to understand when I did not join in.

I can see now what I didn't then. Our long, repetitive accounts of years together and apart lasted sometimes into the night. Honestly, I was flattered she was so interested in the time I'd mistaken salt for sugar on Valentine's Day or missed my car payment one December. I was grateful for the sweet little presents she bought for my kids. Her excuses for the missed lunch dates were little bits of nothing I ignored. All were tells I could've noticed.

When she suddenly moved and I was left without an inkling why, I dusted off college-honed research skills to find her. Hours of effort resulted in nothing other than a suspicion of identity theft in different cities across the country. Her parents were of no use, only saying it was her way to visit them on an unplanned day and they were resigned to her preference. My husband told me to let it go. Let it go.

It's been ten years since. Shortly after I'd turned up nothing other than suspicion, I was served with a subpoena for the information I hadn't found. From there it was a hop, skip, and a jump to complex accusations I still don't understand.

My life continues its mundane structure, but my schedule is behind bars. My children grew up to call another woman 'mother'. My friends seem to think she is me, as if that were possible. My husband grew distant and divorced, and my friend?

She broke a whole stack of promises when she stole my identity – complete with its extra treasure and tension. And I broke only one: I no longer cheer her on in whatever next adventure is hers.

Memorial Day Parade

Memorial Day: what a great day! Citizens pulled out grills of every shape and size, stores were busy with celebratory sales, and beaches were filled with winter-white visitors. The brief parade highlighted the day, assuring every attendee of their patriotism.

Five well-spaced lines of an exuberant drill team followed the Grand Marshal, a politician of much note and reputation, in whom even the press found little to criticize. The band with its seven trumpets and eight drummers, its four flutes, three clarinets, and a handful of varied other sounds followed the swishing flags down Main Street. Next came a hay wagon of square dancers, the local gymnastics club cartwheeling to their hearts' content, and the yearly float carrying the newly crowned city queen with her court waving in harmony.

The convertible with two Gold Star mothers that came next received a smattering of polite applause on this unseasonably warm May day. They weren't as pretty as the queen and her court nor as exciting as the gymnasts, but they were included every year just the same. People lining the street began to shake out their blankets and stretch their legs, as just ahead of the fire truck, in the echoing cadence of the band, marched the veterans. The flag they carried high hung limp in the heat and stillness of the day.

But one stood still, watching what others left behind in their haste to find the best place at the park. He stood at attention, his chubby hand over his heart as he had been taught. And then? Oh yes. Then a sudden breeze lifted the drooping flag straight. It flew as it should, with honor and dignity. The veterans looked as one at the loyal little boy standing alone at his post on the curb. And the boy smiled.

Believe It.
Or Not.

There were stories, of course: ghoulish, horrible tales passed down for generations. Everyone in town had heard them, and everyone knew they weren't true. He'd heard the stories all his life and ignored them for the tripe they were. He had better things to do than sit and watch birds and bugs in a cemetery. He was a man of the age. But then the dreams had come and wouldn't leave.

Funny thing, dreams. When they come in sleep, we're certain they're passing fancies. When they're part of waking thought, some view them the same as sleep's imaginings and others view them as possible future fact. He pondered that, for a minute. Did it matter when they came, whether waking or sleeping? Bah! Of course it did! Mind tricks is all they were!

So he'd begun to visit this place because of the dreams – the dreams that wouldn't leave – looking for the thing that would set his mind to rest. And because, if he was honest, he was curious. First, he'd paused as he walked past. A week later, he'd taken a few steps in, then walked away. A few days after that, he'd quickly walked through the grounds; the next day, slowly.

Then he'd begun to stop by every day. He'd found the bench and breathed in nature's sweet air. It was peaceful, actually.

He rested his hands on the concrete and pushed himself farther back onto the pocked bench. A whisper of a breeze touched his hair. He scratched his ear and let his gaze wander over the stones that peppered the green grass and weeds. Gnarled trees, older than anyone living, dotted the place. A rocky stream meandered silently along the edge of a steep drop not three yards away, with only a stray burble here or there.

This was the first day since he'd begun coming here, though, that he'd stayed long enough for twilight to descend and cloak the small acreage in the gray that follows periwinkle. The dreams had told him to, hadn't they? He shook his head. Funny the influence that fiction mixed with the subconscious had on a person.

Still, his eyes searched the ground and he saw what he must have missed the other times he'd come here. It lay just as it had in his dreams. Finally. In his dreams he hadn't been able to make out the scrawl. At last he could. At last the silly visions would leave him and he would sleep undisturbed once again.

A stray breeze, strong for the evening's quiet, rustled his shirt sleeve and he shivered. The stream trickled more loudly now. The weather must be changing. He looked up at the leaves, still in the evening air.

He leaned down, picked it up, and unfolded the yellowed page.

He glanced down at the unfolded paper and scoffed. In spiderwebby scrawl it said, "You're next". That was all.

He leaned back on the bench and crossed his knee. The brook's song was noticeable now, and the occasional breeze had slightly increased. Dark edged closer, but dusk's gray remained.

An amused smile crossed his lips. Sure, some people might be frightened here, at the edge of night with a strange message that came from who knew where, a paper that smelled slightly musty, and words written by what appeared to be a decrepit hand. He wasn't some people. Everyone knew the stories weren't true. Anyway, he came because of his annoying dreams. That was different.

He'd stay a little longer just to show it didn't matter. He was comfortable here – truly comfortable now that he thought about it. In fact, if he wanted to, he would find no trouble in spending the night sleeping on the bench.

His eyes grew heavy, his head bobbed, and he slid down, resting himself on the bench. His breathing slowed. The moon rose higher, the stream sang, and a stronger breeze rustled through his hair. His eyes suddenly opened, grew wide, then closed. The paper slipped from his hand and was swallowed in the weeds. And he dreamed no more.

It is said that as the moon peeks through the leaves of a gnarled tree near an old stone bench, its light signals a nearby brook which raises its voice to call the invisible spirits dwelling there. The spirits have no patience for those who believe they are always right, who confuse opinion with fact, and who indoctrinate those who don't know better. Those who believe the unknown and unseen exist steer clear of its call because they understand people, even very smart, sophisticated people, perceive life through a limited lens. Those folks, the ones who rewrite truth to suit themselves, who think the old stories are rubbish . . . discover they were wrong.

Not Wanted,
But Not For Sale

He had first noticed it in the Spring. It was just a little spot in the grass near the door of a house that had been there as long as he could remember. Not that he did. Who would think of, much less remember such a house? He rarely walked this block. It was boring. It offered nothing. He preferred, and therefore frequented, a route two blocks over. Who knew what prompted him to vary his route that Spring day?

The house, itself, was small enough to be called "crackerbox". It's white paint was not peeling, but it was tired as was the faded trim at the few windows. It looked unwanted, but whether it was wanted or not, someone must live there, and for all the years he'd seen it, he didn't recall it ever being for sale. Not wanted, but not for sale. He didn't recall anyone ever sitting on the front step. He didn't remember evidence of life there.

But in the Spring the little spot in the grass near the door had caught his eye, not because it was pretty or even interesting, but because it was different at a house where nothing ever varied. It had appeared suddenly – the little spot of dirt – and then nothing.

A week later, tiny leaves poked up from the spot and and what had once been weeds along one side of the house had been cleared and hoed.

Curiosity changed his route to a job he neither loved nor despised. After all, other than the nine to five schedule of his week and Saturday grocery shopping, his days were pretty much like that lifeless house where nothing ever varied.

One Saturday changed that.

It was silly really. The minute he'd opened his eyes the thought came to him like a character from a forgotten dream: a ridiculous dream, a dream of nothing but unrelated thoughts and images. He ignored it, but it returned as he whipped two eggs for his Saturday morning omelet and hung around as he buttered his toast. By the time he'd washed his last dish, he'd given in; if nothing else than to make the thought go away.

Now here he was, standing in front of the unwanted, unvarying house with a tiny plant he'd purchased for 89 cents at the grocery store. He exhaled, walked past the spot in the yard and the tiny plants at the side, walked up steps, and rapped on the door. A moment of silence was followed by the sound of a scraping chair and barely perceptible footfalls. The door squeaked as it opened.

Her uncombed hair fell over a brown tee shirt. She tucked one hand in the pocket of her jeans as a confused frown flitted over her face.

He pushed the plant toward her.

"Here. I . . ." He scuffed a shoe against the porch floor and cleared his throat.

"I noticed you were trying to fix up your yard."

She looked at the plant.

"I thought maybe you might like this to add . . ." his voice drifted off and he shrugged.

The hint of a smile crossed her face and she took the tiny flower.

"Um. Thanks. You're the guy who walks by every morning at 7:30."

He nodded.

"And walks past every evening at 5:15."

He pressed his lips together, searching for something to say.

"I . . . When I eat breakfast and supper I can see you from the window. There's not much else that happens around here. Nothing changes. Except you. You started walking past here."

"I started walking past because you started working on your yard. Or at least someone did," he defended himself.

She took a step back, then looked at the floor in thought.

"Would you . . . would you like to sit on the steps? I have some sweet tea inside I can bring out for us."

He nodded quickly. They settled on the steps and sipped their tea.

"My dad lived here. He got sick, so I moved back. He died a couple of months ago," she volunteered by way of explanation.

The man shook his head. "I never saw anyone around this house."

She stared ahead.

"No, you wouldn't have. He was very private. I take after him." She flushed. "But, you know, he had some second thoughts those last few months. He told me to plant some flowers in the yard after he passed. He told me it would be a start. Of what, he didn't say."

His gaze was drawn to the yard.

"His house, your house, it looks cared for with flowers. Like it's wanted maybe. Do you think you'll sell and move back to wherever you were?"

She shook her head.

"No. This is my childhood home. Maybe it doesn't – didn't – look wanted, as you say. But I don't sell memories. I'm stayin'".

"To second thoughts," he said as he held up his glass.

"To new beginnings," she added.

The clink of their glasses caught the ear of a passerby and she smiled.

The Choice

These were dangerous times. Her father had warned her, and he was right. Her eyes moved from the glowing numbers that were quickly counting down to zero to four wires. Only four. It wasn't as though there were multiple wires tangled together. It shouldn't be that difficult. Which one to clip? Which one to stop the bomb?

She reached back into her memory. She was pretty sure the middle two, the white and the yellow wires would do nothing. They didn't have enough power one way or the other. A bead of sweat trickled from her hairline and hit her eye. She wiped it away with a shaking hand. What was it she had heard back when something like this wasn't real, when times were safe and life was good? Which wire needed to be cut to prevent the current from setting off an explosion? Was it red, you're dead or blue, you're through? Red, blue, red, blue, hmm. Thirty-eight seconds. She was pretty sure it was the blue one. Yes! That was it! Except there wasn't a red or blue wire. There were only purple and orange wires left.

She hoped it was the purple one. The purple wire looked pretty sketchy, but what wire didn't? It wasn't about pretty, it was about power. Thirty seconds. She bit her lip. A nagging intuition told her the orange wire was the one to clip to stop the bomb. But the orange one hardly even looked like a wire! Shouldn't the wires look at least similar? She peered more closely. Ugh. It had something on it she didn't like. It was sticky and smelled to high heaven. If she cut it, she might get some of the sticky stuff on her hands, and who knew if the stench would fill the air and for how long?

She looked around her and wondered about the power of the explosion. If the bomb went off, the little church on the corner could be blown to bits or maybe compromised by the blast and fall bit by bit through the years. Of course, churches didn't need buildings, so did it matter? Twenty seconds. The newborn cradled on her mother's lap on a nearby bench would be killed. But who knew what the infant's mother was like anyway? Maybe she would be spared a lifetime of sorrow. Maybe it would be okay if she died so young. A couple of army buddies' laughter momentarily punched the air and she shifted her gaze. The singular reporter nearby, the one who refused to march lockstep with the others, would be a goner. Their eyes locked for a brief moment and she looked away. Ten seconds. Her eyes searched the street. Would the people walking and chatting and dining and shopping even know what hit them?

She looked again at the orange wire. No. She couldn't bring herself to touch it. No one would know she had had this chance to stop the bomb anyway. Why did it have fall on her shoulders? Five seconds. If the orange wire would actually stop the bomb, and she couldn't be certain that it would . . . but no. Any consequence was better than clipping orange. She just DID

NOT want anything to do with the orange wire. It was a matter of principle. She squinted up at the sun, then clipped the yellow wire with one second to spare.

And the sky grew dark with dust and debris while a deafening sound filled the air.

A Seat of Power

Her hand, blue-veined and small, pushed open the creaking front door, and she sucked in a fragile breath of the brisk, morning air. Her eyes searched up and down the street.

There he was. The thirty-something man in his black dress coat with the collar turned up passed by every morning. His morning walk was first on his to do list every day. He would say it was first on his list because it cleared his mind. As usual, he walked with quick detachment as he scrolled through something on his phone. He had important work to do. He was an influencer of many and held great power.

Across the street a younger man by a decade or more strolled home from his night job, his ears plugged with his chosen mind-numbing sound. He did not see the cardinal to his right that swooped past nor the golden splendor of the large walnut tree ahead. He'd spent the night making a buck, and had made his usual stop at an all-night diner for breakfast. It was good enough for him, and now he deserved a morning's sleep before doing it all over again.

Farther down the block a young mother pushed a stroller, reading a book, while her blanketed toddler looked wide-eyed at leaves stirring on the sidewalk beneath. They both glanced up at the click of a door as they passed.

The woman closed the door and locked it. She turned slowly until both hands grabbed her walker, and she made her way to her chair. The T.V. loudly announced the latest news of crime and peace talks and weather and sports while she sipped some tea and munched on toast with orange marmalade. What was that? A president or prime minister? She really must get her hearing aids fixed. She leaned forward and turned up the sound. Finally she clicked off the television, dabbed at her lips with a napkin, adjusted the pillow behind her back, and closed her eyes. Not to sleep. No, not that.

Five minutes later the sound went out in the young man's earbuds. He frowned, pulled them out, and examined his phone.

He turned up the sound on his device. Nothing. Plugging the ear buds back in, he switched from Spotify to Pandora to a generic radio station. His pained expression grew as he went outside to see if it was a connection problem. The phone's silence turned to static. He switched it off and closed his eyes as the late autumn sun warmed his face. He opened one eye as a cardinal chirped above his head.

The old woman breathed an amused sigh and, gripping the arms of her chair, rose to pour herself another cup of tea. Peppermint might be nice. She gingerly placed her cup on the seat of her walker and shuffled to the window. She sipped the strong peppermint, then put it back on the walker seat as she watched the young man who was now lying in the grass looking up at a bird in the tree overhead. A soft laugh erupted from her lips as she walked back to her chair, adjusted the pillow behind her back, and closed her eyes. Not to sleep. No, not that.

The little one in the stroller exclaimed at a busy squirrel next to them on the sidewalk. As she checked on her charge, a breeze blew and the pages of the book the young mother was reading fluttered with it. What?! She flipped the pages back and forth. Finding her lost place shouldn't be this hard. Reaching for her water bottle, she dropped her book and, as she bent to retrieve it, locked eyes with her little one. They exchanged smiles, and she picked up her little girl instead as the little one pointed and chattered.

Twenty minutes passed as mother and infant watched two squirrels chase each other up and down a tree while a third rummaged around in the dirt. A cold wind blew, the mother hastily swaddled her baby back in the stroller and hurried down the street. A frown crossed the old woman's face and her eyes flew open. She reached for her walker and shuffled hurriedly to the window.

She had seen him before, the man standing in the middle of the street. Oblivious to his presence, cars drove past without slowing. The young man who had moments before begun thinking about his life more deeply than he had in years, abruptly rose and went into his house. And the woman stared at the man who she had seen before as he glared into her window. In several steps he was at her curb, in a couple more he was at her steps and with a few short bounds he was at her door. He did not ring the bell. He did not knock. He stood defiantly, his hot breath melting the screen.

The old woman grabbed her walker and hurried back to her chair. She tripped, and just as she began to fall, regained her balance. Breathing a prayer of thanks, she reached her chair, adjusted the pillow behind her back, and closed her eyes. Not to sleep. No, not that.

A chill went through the woman in her chair, though her eyes were closed heavily in concentration. The man's heated breath grew cool. His eyes blazed with anger and his breath warmed again. It cooled, then heated with his anger, and back and forth they went; the woman in her chair and the man at her door. Morning turned to noon and noon to afternoon.

The woman's breath grew heavy, then fast, and she faltered. One more blow and the screen dissolved. She was so tired, so very tired. The woman blinked, and looked beyond the windows to the houses on her street. She thought of the distracted man of great influence, of the young mother and her baby, and of the rudderless young man. And she shook her head. *She might be frail, but she refused to be weak.*

Five more minutes and the screen's wires reconnected, and the angry man she alone could see evaporated in a puff of coal black smoke to wait for another day. She let out a long breath. The expression on her lips was full of years of trials and triumphs, of heartache and hope.

She shuffled over to the window and looked out. Sure enough, there he was, the man with his collar up and his head down examining his phone. The old woman tilted her head and looked up at the sky. A twig on the walk cracked under his shoe and the sound diverted the man's attention. Looking up, he noticed the cardinal across the street. A memory lit his face and he crossed the street just as the young man walked out of his door to go once again to the night job that made money and nothing more. Hellos were exchanged, then tentative conversation turned the corner as the two men sat on the young man's steps and imagined a future day.

And the old woman gripped her walker and headed to the kitchen to make herself a victory supper of soup and toast and tea. Peppermint might be nice.

A Form of Godliness

He had always prided himself on his thoughtfulness of others; or maybe when they didn't deserve it, at least his consideration of humanity. There was so much hurt in the world it blinded him. It made his heart ache. There were so many paths people walked and so many starting points, all different, how in the world could one human being judge another? How could one person speak to good and bad, right and wrong for someone else? How? He would not be one of those: one of the stiff-necked people who put all their little beliefs into organized little boxes and made judgments about wrong and right. That was one thing he knew. One thing he felt right to judge. Those people were wrong.

He worked hard to educate himself about all that was going on in the hurting world. He listened to trusted voices, lights in the darkness. He read essays by lauded thinkers and books by highly regarded writers. There was a cacophony of voices, but these voices – these voices were the right voices, the correct thinkers, the trustworthy ones who carried the torch. He acknowledged with humility that he was an intellectual. At least more than some.

Things weren't nearly as cut and dried as some wished them to be. In fact, it was a rarity. Issues of law were just that: issues. What he knew was that law was made by humans – fallible humans. Obedience to a man-made construct seemed questionable at best. It wasn't like law was written in stone. Take stealing, for instance. Sure, it could be seen as wrong; but it could also be seen as needful if the thief (a term used only for discussion here) experienced great need. Actions were relative. Truth, in fact, was relative. Nothing was static. Everything was fluid.

And when He learned of a person who had admittedly harmed someone else, he knew of one response. To consider the pain that person, himself, had experienced at some other time in his life. Surely hardship must be brought into the mix of criminality, blended together with forgiveness until there was no criminality at all; only sadness and loss. Responsibility should not equal guilt, and, even if it did, it should not equal consequence. There was no place in the world for harsh consequence because there was really no evil, only unfortunate circumstances. The Old Testament with its commandments must be seen in terms of mercy. The judgment of God had surely changed with time. God was love – the Bible said so. Whatever else He was didn't matter.

Just today, for instance, someone had been sentenced to death. For what? Did it matter? Sentencing someone to death was taking a life, a life the same as every other, the same as the act of abortion those foolish people criticized. (And what of abortion? They knew nothing of the hardship of the poor woman seeking help to remove the thing that troubled her.) So putting to death a murderer equaled putting to death an infant. It must be so. The lauded voices asserted it was true. He knew they were to be trusted.

Sometimes . . . sometimes he caught himself wondering about it all, turning over equivalencies in his mind. What if one wasn't enough like the other to merit the voices' assertions? What if lack of consequence didn't uphold life's value, but diminished it? What if God was multi-faceted? What if consequence mattered for some reason he hadn't thought of? But, no. The voices were trusted voices.

And the victims of the murderer and the innocents whose lives were taken with clinical precision called from the grave. But no one listened.

The Day He Left

Evening was just barely touching the late May day. A tangy, sweet scent drifted lazily on the breeze like a sleepy teenager floating on an inner tube, dipping his toes in a quiet river. It reminded her of the flowers he had brought to her the day he left. They were an inexpensive bouquet of daisies, chrysanthemums, and baby's breath – sweet, innocent, and tender, like the kiss he gave her before he turned and walked away.

She closed her eyes, playing with the ring on her finger as she let memory have sway: The funny thing that happened the day they met, their first tentative gifts to each other, quick lunches and long dinners, walks down a familiar country road, the surprise of comfortable conversation, and values and thoughts so in sync they could read them in one look of the other's face.

"Mother! We should be going!"

Waiting at the car was her daughter, now grown, who knew her father through others' stories, but not through her own.

How many years would it take to loosen the knot located somewhere underneath her heart? She had thought it would be gone years ago. She realized now that it never would be. She knelt and brushed her fingers over the name engraved in stone, engraved in memory, engraved in time.

She whispered three words: Duty. Honor. Country.

Then she picked herself up and walked away.

Memorial Day is May 29. Remember.

Something Like Friendship

He would rather have been in a small river in an out-of-the-way spot, casting a fly line for trout. It was that sort of evening, he thought vaguely. A warm breeze fingered his black hair; the musky scent of dry leaves infused the night air; the sky, black above the treetops, was beginning to show a few stars, the rest hidden behind heaven's heavy blanket.

He had always preferred the strength and silence of the outdoors to anything else. A small-time outfitter, though, didn't make much money. He knew that, and acknowledged, too, that life held limitless possibilities.

The sound of voices grew greater and the crowd thicker as the soft notes of a piano danced outside to greet those making their way up the wide cement walkway to the hall. It was a simple affair: an alumni dinner of a small college. Through the double doors, Tab could see long tables set with white paper cloths. Squeals of happy recognition punctuated the steady undercurrent of voices. He hated these things, but had promised to come. He stepped inside and scanned the room for someone he recognized.

"We're sitting over here."

The nearby voice was inviting and familial.

Tab looked into the eyes of a tall man who was his double, aside from a twenty-five year difference in age. Max's hair was graying at the tips and the lines in his face revealed that he was not exempt from life's hardships, but everyone they passed hailed him and he hailed them back in a mild, relaxed manner.

Walking together they sat across from a pretty woman with sparkly eyes who was chatting up a storm with the young girl next to her.

"Tab!"

She reached across the table and squeezed his hand.

"Hi, Mom," he said to the woman others thought pretty.

Such a thought had never occurred to him. She was always there, always making friends. There was something in her expression that told she was one who didn't take life too seriously. Her crow's feet were her signature, witness to an easy and ready laugh.

"I want you to meet Jessica. She's interested in languages, too."

This last statement was spoken with an unmistakable emphasis, and Tab caught his parents glancing at each other.

He looked into the round face of a girl close to his age. Her brown hair that hung in a blunt cut below her jaw line exactly matched the deep brown of her large, wide eyes. She wore a pretty, delicately flowered dress. He reached out to shake her hand as she quickly put her hands in her lap.

"Hi, Jess."

He pulled his hand back, and offered her an uncertain smile instead.

Jessica thought to herself that she had never seen eyes sparkle so. They were the color of the sea at its deepest point, and she wondered if that said anything about the man across from her.

Her mouth went suddenly dry – unusual for her. She sipped from her water-glass

"It's nice to meet you, Tab."

The music suddenly sounded too loud. It seemed a mere ten minutes had passed and it was time to go.

It was nearly 11:00 by the time Jessica pulled out of the parking lot. There was little traffic this time of night. She found herself in her room remembering little of the drive back. Quickly readying herself for bed, she pulled up the covers and stared at the ceiling, wide awake.

Who Was Counting?

He'd driven down the road hundreds of times. More, actually, but who was counting? It was funny how driving the same route, the same distance, the same speed day after day was so much a part of his routine he didn't even think about it. He saw but didn't see the sign posts or the dips in the road. His foot automatically tapped the break before the turns he barely noticed. It was a little like life: going through motions once carefully considered and now unconsciously carried out.

One morning, though, he'd caught something out of the corner of his eye that seemed out-of-place. He'd whizzed past it before he could make out what it was. It bothered him a bit. Not that it should. Why should some little change, some barely noticeable something or other catch his attention and hold it?

He slowed down the next morning and peered off to the side of the road, looking for whatever it was that bothered him. There. There it was. A sign. No, more like a marker. Just a small post really. With a number: 636. It wasn't a mile marker. It was on a simple piece of wood – sturdy, but small. And each day he passed it, he noticed it until he began to notice something else. The number changed every day. Every single day the number increased by one.

He mentioned it at work, covering his unsettled feeling by making it into a joke. Everyone dutifully chuckled. Well, not everyone. An intern looked alarmed, but what intern didn't have that look on her face at some point every day? Later, she poked her head into his office and asked if he had a minute. Annoyed, he motioned her to enter. She stood resolutely as though she'd made some important decision which she was about to announce. He looked pointedly at his watch.

"There are stories. Maybe you haven't heard them."

"I've no idea what you're trying to say. I've lived enough years to have heard every story to enter your young head."

She turned to leave, then turned back.

"It's just – something – I don't know why I'm telling you. It's probably nothing."

"And?"

"There's a story that every Halloween someone somewhere in the world sees a sign post that keeps count of – I don't know. No one does I don't think. But it keeps count, and shortly after they're never seen again."

He shook his head and smirked. "Somewhere in the world. How well-traveled you are. What are you? 22?"

The intern's face crumpled and she walked out.

The next day he looked at the sign. 646. He felt slightly queasy. Okay. This was ridiculous. He'd start taking a different route, end of problem. And the next day as he drove the slightly longer route, he spied the post somewhere around mile marker 10. It read 647. He took a different route still the day after that. And after that.

"You're late again today," his secretary remarked.

He swallowed the coffee she held out to him. It was lukewarm. He was tired of lukewarm coffee. He'd go back to his preferred path. What difference, at this point, did it make?

By the time the sign turned to 665, he'd begun to chill as he neared the spot and could feel a trickle of sweat run down his temple. Something had to be done.

The weather was turning. It always did this time of year. Like a clock. Tick, tick, tick. He felt like he was going a little bit crazy. He couldn't stand it.

The next morning looked like twilight and a misty rain spit down on his windshield whisked away by wipers, an ineffectual remedy to persistent rain. He pulled to the side of the road and put his coat collar up against the wind. Walking over the the post, he knelt down and read the number: 666. He kicked the wood. Stupid, stupid marker. He gripped the post with both hands and heaved. It wasn't so sturdy that a few tugs couldn't pull it out. He pulled again. Once more should do it.

And his hot coffee grew warm, then cold.

Even Then

She laughed until she was gasping for air and wiping her eyes. Doubled over, she grabbed the back of the park bench to help her sit before she lost her balance. She looked up, her twinkling eyes still wet, and tried to talk, but couldn't.

"I'm telling you the truth. He actually did that."

The laughter began again.

"Twice!"

"Stop!" she breathed, "I feel like I've done a hundred sit-ups already."

He sat beside her then and pulled her into his arms.

"I love your laugh," he murmured into her hair.

"Oh now you're just making excuses for my nearly wetting my pants."

He chuckled.

"Even *if*," he said, "Even *then* it would be small payment for the sound of your laugh. I could listen to that music every day of my life."

A small smile crossed his lips as he remembered. Then the steady rhythm of the heart monitor pulled him back to the present. She lay there under the white blankets, as still as the dawn on their first day of married life, as soft as her whispers each night before they both drifted to sleep.

"Don't go," he choked, "Don't leave me. I'll tell you a million funny stories every single day if you'll just stay."

The heart monitor quickened, then settled again to its rhythmic pace.

He wandered over to the closet where only her bare essentials were. How did life distill to a few things in a plastic bag? He pulled out her purse and rummaged through it. Lipstick, a comb, her billfold. He opened it. Ten dollars, her license with the picture she hated, two credit cards. There. There was a slip of paper folded and refolded. He pulled it out. Her handwriting danced across a page that held only the faintest scent of her. He held it up to his nose and inhaled deeply. Then he read: *Dearest, This is in case I don't make it. Maybe sometime soon, I'll be rummaging through my things and find this note and we can both have a laugh over my dramatics. But even if. . . even then I want you to know I love the way you make me laugh, so don't cry too much. It'll make your nose red. On the hard days, just listen until you hear something that reminds you of the good times. Of my love. And, if you insist, my laugh. Someone said: "Life is eternal; and love is immortal; and death is only a horizon; and a horizon is nothing save the limit of our sight."*

The rhythm slowed, and he hurried to her bed and grabbed her hand.

"Thank you," he said.

And all sound stopped except the echo of her laughter.

<hr>

Quote: attributed to William Penn, Ralph Waldo Emerson, or R. W. Raymond

A Dusty Few Years

He picked up another piece of bread and stuffed it in his mouth as he looked at some of the ravens perching on the gnarled branches. Life was weird alright, but he'd always been one to accept that. In fact, he didn't understand how most other folks insisted on life being the way they thought it should be. Should be! Really? Life was breath amidst delight and chaos. What did prescriptive insistence have to do with it? He deliberated over those who required people to fit into certain ideas of dignity or say things the way they imagined things should be said; over life's roads taking particular turns at preordained times. Whose ideas of dignity? Whose way of speaking? Preordained by who? People had plenty of thoughts about him, he knew. They didn't want to accept that God's prophets were rough around the edges. But what was more important – their preconceived notions or the truth? A wry smile crossed his face. They had no idea of how improper and uncivilized God could be when He chose. He picked up the last piece of meat and turned it over in his hands, examining it. Holding it up, he toasted the onlooking birds, and finished his meal. Those people who said what others approved were too prideful to yield. He hoped they'd change, but even with a sign from heaven, he knew they wouldn't. Their ideas about what was most worthy of worship were immovable and their hate for him was too strong. The sun blazed down as he slurped from the nearby brook. It was going to be a long, dry, hot, and dusty few years.

Story idea: taken from the life of Elijah – I Kings: 17:1-6

Opening the Door

He scraped the key back and forth in the lock again. Nothing. He rubbed the tip of his nose with the side of his finger and looked at his watch. Humph. Seventeen minutes. The first minute was annoying, the next four – irritating. The ten after that were demoralizing.

It shouldn't be this hard! He had the key. He was in front of the door. Sure, the lock might be a bit old. Used many times? No doubt.

He took the key out of the lock and rubbed it on his pants, then between his fingers. He prayed. Again. Skritch skritch . . . faster, then slower . . . skritch skritch skritch. He pulled the key out, dropping as he did so. His fingers scraped on hard cement as he retrieved it from the step. Sighing, he put it in his pocket and started down the stairs.

This wasn't the first time he'd worked to get through the door, but maybe it should be his last. He was tired. Disconsolate, truth be told. He glanced over his shoulder and stopped.

Once more. Just once more, then he would leave. For good, this time. He trudged back up the stairs, inserted the key, and

. . . click. It turned like new. No. Really? Really. He turned the knob and opened the door.

It is labour indeed that puts the difference on everything.

135

———※———

Quote: John Locke

How Tor
Saved My Garden

Hi. My name is Ginger Teigh. Yes, it sounds like "tea". Yes, my parents thought it was funny when they named me – each of them having safe names like Gary and Ramona. No, I don't mind when people ask. Yes, I do get tired of the jokes.

I was sitting outside on my rather small deck – large enough to hold two sun chairs with pink and green Hawaiian print, a small stump I lugged up the two steps from the yard on which to put my sweet tea, a couple of flowering plants I picked up on sale at Sam's Club, and the dog. It's not as small as you might imagine. My dog is huge. And my dog is the problem.

He likes to dig. Fine. Dig away. I'm not in the market for a layout in Birds and Blooms, anyway, being the type of gardener with a less than admirable success rate. See, I have all sorts of grand plans every spring. I buy dirt. Whoever thought of selling dirt is probably very wealthy and living somewhere where someone takes care of every speck of dirt for him. He probably sits on a pristine beach and drinks something with an umbrella in it. I don't imagine it's sweet tea. Anyway, I drag the bags over to my "gardens", cut them open, and dump. Then I smooth the area with a hoe, and lovingly plant delightful little plants in even rows. And as the spring turns to summer, I watch them die a slow death. It's tradition. But I digress.

So the dog – I might as well tell you his name – Tornado (Tor, for short) – had been digging up a storm under the deck for two days. This morning as I was sipping my morning brew of green tea and Mountain Dew, I noticed he was heaving and panting; even whining a little. That's unusual for Tor. He's not a whiner. He came out from under the deck as black as sin a couple of times, looked at me, and returned to his digging.

His project had by now become my project. I wondered how big a hole he was making and was wondering how many bags of dirt I'd have to buy to refill them. Then I wondered if it was necessary. Who looks under a deck anyway, right?

I was on my second cup when Tor pulled a huge bag of something out where I could see it. I hopped down to the yard to have a closer look. And immediately wished I hadn't.

Well, that's not entirely true. Can something be kind of true? I mean, at the moment I wished I hadn't looked, but after I examined it more closely, I was of two minds. My mother used to use that phrase a lot. My father would always reply that he only needed one. Getting back to the thing Tor dragged out from under the deck – I guess I'd have to say that I was glad for part of what it was and horrified at the other part. That's not kind of true. It's absolutely a true statement. Score one for clarity.

I knelt down and looked at it. Okay, I admit I jumped back a little after my first glimpse. I grabbed a big stick and, scrunching my face, poked at it. Best guess, originally 145 lbs and maybe 5 feet 9 inches, or 8 or 6. It was hard to be sure. It looked like the body had been buried long enough for the clothes to decay which, in the climate I lived in would take longer than, say, the tropics. Then again, I'm no mortician.

What looked like it had been some sort of bag was stuffed in the mouth of – oh – for the sake of my sanity I'd begun calling him Simon. Giving him a name preserved my humanity (and his) to my way of thinking. The bag was nearly decayed, so its contents were visible. I looked around at my neighbor's yards to see if anyone was watching me. Fortunately, no one was out. Who knew what was behind the curtains, but as far as I could see, there didn't seem to be any activity. And really. If I hadn't been up close, I would've thought it was a big pile of dirt. I hurried into the house for a baggie, then out again, and stuffed it full of the decayed bag's contents. Laying the baggie carefully on the deck's railing, I grabbed my gardening gloves and shoved the body back under the deck as well as I could.

I know. I should have called the police. But here was the problem. The bag had a decent amount of money in it; money I wasn't altogether sure I was ready to part with without some consideration. I coaxed Tor into the house and hosed him off in the tub, but not before pouring the gold coins into a mixing bowl and covering them with the white vinegar I'd gotten a week before to clean my washing machine. It's a good thing I procrastinated.

Once Tor was cleaned up and I was, too, I gave him a second breakfast and sat down to think this through. Whoever had buried the body there must have buried it before the deck was built because it would've been nigh unto impossible to do it flattened out underneath a structure. I started thinking about who had owned the house before me. It was known as the K house, I think because whoever built it had a name starting with K. Once upon a time people probably called it by name, but by the time I came along, it had become just K. I tried to recall what I could of the person who owned it before me.

She was actually, a sweet woman, big-boned some would say, and a little bookish. It was by now close to noon. I got up to make myself a sandwich. Don't judge. I'd washed and I was hungry. And as I was spreading mayonnaise, my thoughts drifted back to the first time I had met the previous owner. I'd seen an ad on Craigslist for an end table and had come to take a look at it. She'd invited me in, and we actually had begun something of a friendship of convenience. Every once in a while she'd call me to do something for her – burn a leaf pile or change her furnace filter – and then we'd sit down to tea and cookies and she'd send some home with me. I'm not much of a baker, so it was a nice little perk.

But as I was thinking about it, I remembered that she hadn't always had a deck on the back of the house. I remembered it because the first time she'd had me over to manage the burning leaf pile for her, I'd thought to myself that it was too close to the house. I'd even told her so. It was after that she'd burned them farther back. Huh.

I didn't want to think it, but I had to admit the evidence wasn't exactly looking good. A body had been buried under my deck – a deck that hadn't existed until the previous owner who, by the way, had asked me to help burn a rather large leaf pile in the general location where Tor had dug it up. Of course, it could've been coincidental. Hope and doubt changed places the more I thought about it.

Then there was the issue of a bag of gold coins; money I was loath to part with. However, I was more averse to parting with my good name. Even if no one discovered my secret, I would know it. The Bible verse, "A good name is rather to be chosen than great riches" had been drummed into my skull throughout childhood, and was now pestering me like a very determined mosquito.

I got up, washed my lunch dishes, and grabbed the leash to take Tor out for a walk until I could safely let him in my backyard again. But as I headed for him, leash in hand, he bolted, and knocked over my coffee table. Darn dog! Now I had a 3 legged coffee table – one I wouldn't be able to replace soon at the same great price I'd gotten from Susan, my house's former owner. I snapped his leash on rather more aggressively than usual. It didn't take long for Tor to do his business. That was one good thing about my dog. He's focused. By the time we got back to the house, so was I.

I called the local police and asked if someone could drop by. Good thing I live in a small town with a bored police force. Thinking I'd better make the living room presentable, I picked up the coffee table leg to see if there was any chance Super Glue could come to my rescue. Ha! No need! It appeared I could just screw the thing in. As I congratulated myself on this bonus and turned the table upside down, a slip of paper fell out of the leg. I should've known they were hollow. You don't get much for five bucks. Weird, though.

Squinting, I peered inside the leg. Nope. Nothing else. I unfolded the paper. It said: *Hypocrisy is the audacity to preach integrity from a den of corruption.* – Wes Fesler. Okay. I'm not much of a sports fanatic, but why was a quote from him written down? And stuffed in the leg of my end table?

Sitting back on my knees, I stared into space, then quickly screwed in the leg and unscrewed the other three. I looked into their small openings and shook each one. The first two were as empty as an old sock, but another slip of paper fell out of the third one on my last shake. *I barred my door to bribery, and knocked it to the floor. He'll eat his gold in silence and bother me no more.* Who wrote it? The former owner, Susan? I righted the table as the doorbell rang.

By the time I'd given sweet tea to the officer, told him and showed him everything, including the two slips of paper, I was ready for an old movie. I was also richer. Detective Timmons informed me they'd do a cursory investigation, but most likely I'd be able to keep the money under the 'finders keepers' law. That's not really what it's called, but that's what it amounts to.

As far as Simon – well let's just say after snipping some pieces here and there and filling some plastic bags with them, Timmons confided to me he suspected it was a fellow by the name of – O why should I spread tales? Suffice it to say that he'd caused trouble for town folks for a long time, including corrupting a number of folks who didn't have it in them to turn down a dollar; and the whole town should be grateful someone finally put a stop to it. The coroner (who I suspect had been on the bullying end of the not so dearly departed) didn't seem interested in storing the body after doing her thing and talking to Timmons. I'd made the mistake of calling him Simon, so she asked if I had a preference for his final resting place. Small towns. Ya gotta love 'em.

It's been a couple of months since. Tor is free to roam the back yard again. I planted my garden and, for the first time ever, its blooms are brilliant.

In the Palm
of His Hand

She'd seen it hundreds of times as she passed it on the street. It was a little storefront with a sign saying simply *Chiromancy*. This time, though,her steps slowed as she approached the window. What would be the harm in seeking out a fortune-teller; more to the point, a palm-reader?

There was enough of the unknown in her life that she wished to peer into tomorrow. Perhaps it would relieve some of her stress or give her a new lease on life! Heaven knew she needed *something*; something to steer her in the right direction. But with the way everything was going, *that* would take a miracle. Even at Christmas, the season of miracles, she doubted one would appear to her, of all people. God, if He did exist, had more important things to do.

Clink. A little round piece of something rolled up against her boot. It was funny she even felt it. She bent down and retrieved it. It was a token, something like you would get at a carnival or party. She turn the gold piece over in her hand. One side was gold and the other held the image of a manger scene. A manger scene? She peered more closely, trying to imagine what sort of person or gathering it came from; then looked around to see if someone had dropped it. There wasn't a pedestrian to be seen, but a scraggly dog trotted near her; abandoned from the looks of him.

She called to him with a click of her tongue and he came near enough for her to reach out and pet him. Her palm would be dirty now, and she wondered what the palm-reader would think. The dog nuzzled closer and licked her hand. Then he trotted a few steps down the street, looking back, as if inviting her to follow him. Her gaze alternated between the storefront and the dog. She really wished for direction; direction a fortune-teller might be able to give her! But the dog came back and nudged her knee for a pet. She absently reached down and gave him one. He nudged her again, and she patted him. He rolled onto his back and she gave him a good tummy rub. Her hand slowed as she felt his heartbeat.

And it was that heartbeat that spoke to her. If God had created even the heart of a scraggly dog and kept it beating day in and day out, did he care for small things as well as big, important things? And she was more than a dog, wasn't she? She turned the coin over in her hand and studied the manger scene. How in the world had it rolled to hit her boot? Where did it come from? Did God know *her* heartbeat?

A new thought occurred to her as she followed her new friend down the street. She still wanted to know what her future held. But maybe it wasn't to be found in the palm of *her* hand.

Charmed

"You here for the speaker?" he asked as he offered his hand and she shook it.

She nodded, then glanced down at his hand. "Whaaat? I have one just like that!" She held up her wrist for him to see.

"Nice. Where did you get yours?"

"College. They were handing them out to whoever wanted one. You?"

"Mine was passed down from my dad and he got it from my grandpa."

She nodded. "Wow."

"Yea," his voice quavered. "It holds a lot of meaning for me."

"Oh for sure," she replied.

"Shhh. It's starting."

They both sank down in nearby chairs and listened to the speaker. He wasn't from around there, but there had been flyers and posters and curiosity simmered quietly in the crowd.

An hour passed quickly by, as one by one their charms had fallen from their bracelets.

"Do you buy what he said about stomping on the rights of the people we claim to care about?"

"I think he was just hung up on the phrase 'right to choose'.

"Right. But the 'stage or age' thing he said about abortion being murder?"

"The thing that got me was that phrase he kept using."

"Your silence is your signature on the death certificate," the two new friends chimed together.

He looked down as his PP charm fell to the floor.

"And the thing about loving someone enough to tell them the truth about God's laws."

He shuddered, "Creepy, right? As though people don't have enough to deal with without someone telling them their sex partner's all wrong."

"I agree! But what if he's right?"

"You mean that our silence is . . ."

"Our signature on their ticket to hell? Our signature on their death certificate?"

"Yea," he answered slowly. "But who am I to tell anyone . . ."

"What's right and wrong? I don't like it either."

"It's their choice, right?"

"But hell . . ."

He pressed his lips together. "I know."

She looked at the LGBTQ charm on the floor.

"I thought there was going to be a riot when he started in on immigration."

"Illegal. He kept pressing that point," she added.

He lowered his voice. "What do you think about the trafficking?"

"I know! And the little kids he talked about."

"And the millions of dollars in drugs brought and sold. My best friend's brother died of an overdose last year."

She brushed his arm with her hand.

The two looked down at the floor as some more charms fell.

"I just can't get that phrase out of my head!" He put his hands over his ears.

"Your silence is your signature . . ."

"Stop!" He calmed himself and gave her an apologetic smile. "Do you think killing trafficked kids for organs actually happens?"

She shook her head quickly and shut her eyes. "Whatever happened to just loving everybody? Can't we just love everyone? Let whoever wants come and go?"

"Legally, remember?" he laughed.

"It should be simpler than he's making it," she said, biting her lip.

"But the worst part was his next point. How silence allows unthinkable things you shut your eyes to. Child sacrifice has made its way from the abortion room to secret rooms and rituals."

He shook his head. "I don't believe it," he whispered.

She sighed imperceptibly. She wondered if her hoping something wasn't true would make it so.

The two new friends made their way over to a table stocked with information and charms.

She looked at her new friend. "It couldn't hurt. I don't have anything left, do you?"

He shook his head as he rubbed his empty bracelet between his fingers, and they sorted through the charms, marveling they were free.

Scripture sources: Romans 1:22-26; Leviticus 18:22, 20:13; I Cor. 6:9-11; Jude 1:7; I Cor. 6:9-10; Romans 1:18-22; I Timothy 1:9-10; Acts 17:26; John 3:16

Enjoyed and Unnoticed

She rocked back in her chair as the breeze played softly with a tendril of gray hair that fell loosely on her temple. Voices of the grandkids shrieking and laughing echoed from the yard below and though she watched them, her mind was in another place and another time. It was a time when she was young, living among the elite in Yugoslavia; a time when her father was in the inner circle of Josep Tito – above the masses' deprived, disconsolate lives; a time when she had everything and felt nothing.

For in that place and at that time Communism had smothered all religions but itself. Citizens worked and loved and read and thought – but work was poorly rewarded and thoughts were stilted by muffled truths twisted into something that served the reigning religion. News was only what those in power wanted those watching to hear. And to think. And dreams? Well it's hard to dream of something you have no idea exists.

When she moved to a place called the United States of America, she had marveled at the freedom everyone enjoyed but didn't notice. The air was different in this country. Freedom made breathing easier. She discovered a Savior here – a name that had been all but banned in her former home. She could be a Christian here, and it made her freedom greater still.

Little feet ran up the steps of the wide porch and little Zuhra climbed into the familiar lap as her grandmother held her close and prayed a familiar prayer with first-hand gratefulness: Let freedom ring.

Why Wine

First of all, no, I'm not a mani-pedi sort of girl. If I wanted someone cleaning my nails, I'd just dip 'em in melted butter and sit down by the dog. But I ended up at Salon de Beauté last Saturday because my best friend has a thing for things like that and I had a free afternoon. It wasn't in France, either. It was on Buford Street tucked in between Matt's Realty and Nuts To You. By the time we had pedis with matching manis, we were hungry. So we sauntered over (I know, what a word; but I believe it matched the extravagance of walking over the threshold of a place using French in its name, don't you?) to Sissy's Diner and ordered soup. Again, I know. But we'd just had manicures. What did you expect us to do? Break a nail carving steak? We considered sandwiches, of course; but by the time we would've handled the greasy fries that came with them, again, why take chances? And it wasn't like we ordered chicken broth. We had the clam chowder Sissy's was famous for. Plus handling a spoon gave each of us an excuse to glance at our newly polished fingertips: Pink Delish for my friend and Why Wine for me.

As we chatted on our way out the door of Sissy's, I noticed a car just a few parking spaces down that exactly matched my mani-pedi color. What are the odds? We decided to walk (done with the sauntering now that we'd had clam chowder) over and take a hand selfie by the car. I mean, the color match was so unlikely – in our minds, at least – that it deserved a photo.

Can I just suggest one thing? If that ever happens to you, don't do it.

I bent at the waist, held my hand next to the rear passenger side of the car, and with my other hand held up my phone. As I was just ready to tap the little white thingy that takes a picture, I felt hot breath on my neck and a strong hand squeeze my wrist so hard I dropped my phone.

"Hey!" I spun around and looked straight into the most angry and glorious set of gray eyes I've ever seen.

"Just what do you think you're doing?" the glorious set of gray eyes said.

"I . . . I . . . I was admiring the color of this car – is it yours? And . . ."

My mouth was dry and my heart was beating much too loudly for me to think, so I held up my newly manicured hand, hoping he could figure out the rest of my sentence for me.

He pressed his lips together. I have to say here and now even *that* was beautiful. Stooping to pick up my phone, he turned, grabbed my shoulders, spun me around so that he and I were facing the car, hugged me close, and took a picture of the both of us. Then he punched in some numbers, tapped once or twice, and tapped again. Handing me my phone, he jumped into the car and started a purring engine. A perfect triangle of tiny dings on the passenger side door handle caught my eye as he pulled into the light afternoon traffic.

I shielded my eyes with my beautifully manicured hand and watched as he disappeared from sight while Tracy (my friend) made gurgling noises that ended in a gaffaw.

"No worries." She held a small slip of paper in front of my face. "I got his license number."

"Well that isn't creepy at all."

"What? It won't hurt to see if you can at least find his name."

Later that evening as I was munching on chips with a lovely little loaded cream cheese and salsa accompaniment, and staring at the picture of the two of us on my phone; he, with his chiseled good looks and me with a startled look on my face and no car in sight, I wondered what else he'd done besides take it. I mean he'd tapped a couple of times. Maybe he sent a copy to himself! Wouldn't that be exciting! Why would he do that anyway, unless he thought I was just a little bit glorious, myself? The deafening silence of my little apartment holding no steamy or romantic memories asked me an awkward question: Who was I kidding? Still, I couldn't think of what else he would've done.

I scrolled through my messages and contacts. A new number was nowhere to be seen. He'd either not sent the photo to himself or he must've deleted the number he sent it to.

I knew I shouldn't, really I shouldn't, but Tracy's slip of paper was calling to me from my purse. I rummaged around, pulled it out, and sat down at my computer. A few taps would give me a name, right? Before I pulled up the DMV website, I checked Facebook to see what everyone had for dinner, their vacation pictures, and anything else that was better and more exciting than my little corner of the world.

As I sped past the political posts and inspirational memes, something caught my eye, so I backed up. It was a picture of someone's baby. Not a real baby, mind you, but a car they had fixed, spit and polished 'til kingdom come. The post said it had been reported stolen, but to please repost and keep our collective Facebook eyes open for it. It had been a gift from his father, and, from the long post, the writer was heartbroken.

I squinted at the picture to convince myself it wasn't the same car outside of Sissy's Diner. After all, the posted car was white, not Why Wine. I know, I know. That's not a real car color. They probably named it something like candy apple red, but, like most of the population, for now I'm sticking with what I know, even if I'm wrong.

But I wasn't wrong. Not about the car. Because there, on the passenger side door handle was a perfect triangle of tiny dings.

You know how when you know you should do something but don't want to do it, you find other things to do? Within an hour, my kitchen was sparkling down to the chrome on the water faucet at the sink and refrigerator grate.

I scolded myself, and, sinking down into my most comfortable chair, called the police. Detective John McBrennain was in charge of car trafficking and, I was told, he would be given the message and would contact me.

The next evening a loud knock on my door startled me, and, although the moon hadn't yet risen, I had my pajamas on — a wild floral combination of red, orange, and spring green. I flew into my bedroom, pulled sweatpants and a sweat shirt over my pjs and raced to open the door before I realized I should look through the peek hole first. My first hope was that it was the rough stranger with gray eyes even though he might be a car trafficker. How desperate was I? It wasn't.

Detective McBrennain showed his badge and stepped across the threshold. I invited him to sit at the kitchen table, made coffee (my policy was no decaf, but he looked like someone who preferred the dark of night to the light of day anyway), and told him my story. I told him about the car, the man with glorious gray eyes, and seeing the same car on a Facebook post of a missing car. I told him the car must have been given a paint job, otherwise – and here I held up my beautifully manicured nails – it had been white. I told him I recognized the car by a triangle of tiny dings on the door handle.

Okay, I didn't describe the trafficker's eyes as glorious. I do have some sense. As I waited for John McBrennain to finish his furious scribbling in a little notebook, I looked down and noticed wild red, orange, and spring green sticking out from under my sweats. I tried pulling the bottom of my pant leg down with my foot, then gave up, reached down, and gave it a yank.

When I looked up, Detective McBrennain had placed a picture in front of me on the table. His eyes looked dead as he stared at me. "Are you playing games with me, Ma'am?"

"What? No!"

"We have been trying to track this guy down for years. And now I'm called to a house and given a story by someone who is next to him in a picture dropped at my office just one day ago. It certainly looks current."

He gave me a perfunctory once over, clearly unimpressed.

"May I see your phone?"

I wondered if he could actually ask for it, but I couldn't think of a reason to refuse. He gave it a couple of taps and frowned.

"You'll need to come down to the station with me."

I couldn't believe this was happening. "No! This . . . this . . . guy, the car owner or trafficker or whoever he is took the picture with my phone."

John McBrennain raised his eyebrows and tilted his head.

"Look, I know how this sounds . . ."

"Do you know how it looks, too?"

I paused, my mind racing. Someone who looked that glorious wouldn't be as awful as I was beginning to think he was.

My mouth was dry as I said, "He set me up, Detective."

The Detective rose as if he hadn't heard me, pulled out a pair of handcuffs, and led me to his car.

I tripped on the last step out of the police station. Oh yes. The mighty Detective McBrennain had decided there was nothing to charge me with after all and released me. Bully, that's what he was: accusing me of things I knew nothing of, twisting my words, and stealing my sleep. I felt like I'd lost half my weight and part of my mind in sweat and anxiety. And now, here I was, picking myself off the ground, wondering if anyone would see me on my middle of the night hike back home, and hoping my wild floral combination of red, orange, and spring green wasn't sticking out from under my sweats. I was absolutely too tired to do anything about it.

"Miss?"

I looked up and a policeman motioned me to his car. I had the crazy urge to make a run for it, and I'd like to say common sense prevailed, but who are we kidding? It was fatigue.

"You look tired. Can I give you a ride home?"

Seriously? I began to regret ever going for a mani-pedi and Sunday School cursed everyone involved, including the lovely Lolita, my manicurist. Despite my newly-found mistrust of detectives in general, I got in his car.

"My name is Sergeant John Don. And you are . . .?"

I gave him my name and address, leaned my head back, and, I'm embarrassed to say, immediately fell asleep. I must've been roused by the engine turning off. And there in front of me was my boring apartment building. I'd never seen anything more beautiful.

"Do you mind if I ask you a few questions?"

Good grief. I was so very tired, but not so tired that I didn't care if people saw me sitting in a police car at 3:00 in the morning. I invited him in.

I flipped the switch to heat the coffee I'd made for McBrennain. Sergeant Don would not get a fresh cup.

Two hours later, I'd not only made a fresh pot, but was more awake than I'd been since my mani-pedi. I'd shown the Sergeant the pictures from my phone, I'd told him everything I'd told McBrennain, and more. I'd even told him how glorious the stranger had been. John D. was a very attentive listener, and I couldn't seem to stop talking. The coffee didn't help.

And he had told me something that not only washed away the shame I'd felt as I was questioned by McBrennain, but gave me hope and energy. It turns out, my interview with McBrennain was the final nail in his coffin. Oh yes! Apparently, he'd been so cock-sure of my pitiful vulnerability, he'd revealed more than he realized. According to Sergeant John D., McBrennanin was a bad cop they had been investigating a long while on the suspicion he covered for the car trafficking ring, one of whom was Mr. Glorious. Huh. Well he certainly was in a good position to do so.

Voltaire said, "Fear follows crime and is its punishment". I believe that it does, but not for everyone. As I warmed my hands on my third cup of coffee (don't judge unless you've had a Why Wine incident of your own), I thought to myself that, as glorious as the stranger had seemed, he didn't seem the kind who would ever know regret. Or maybe even fear. And McBrennanin? I couldn't say. Some people love criminality, either outright or cloaked in authority.

I signed something that said I'd testify to everything I told Sergeant John Don, who by now was beginning to develop his own sort of gloriousness. I swallowed my thoughts, gave him a little smile, and closed the door behind him with my beautifully and dreadfully manicured hand.

I left our coffee on the table, grabbed a blanket to cover myself, and fell asleep on the couch. I'd need my beauty sleep if I was going to have another mani-pedi: and I mean the minute Salon de Beauté opened. Why Wine was my new least favorite color. Maybe I'd replace it with Siren Red.

Fight On

Warm air ruffled his hair, whispering a thousand battles into his thoughts. There had been an explosion – sudden and so loud he felt it down to the marrow of his bones. Immediately alert, he'd fired back with everything he had. Then silence. His adrenaline decreased and the beat of his heart quieted enough to look around. He moved slightly toward his buddy for a fist bump. They deserved at least *that* celebration here in the small outpost assigned them. There hadn't been many of them to begin with and now, down to just two, they had bravely carried on. Duty. Honor. Country.

His battle buddy since the beginning of this military journey was immovable. He gave a low whistle between his teeth.

"Jack! Hey, Jack!"

It was then he noticed the brown stain growing on Jack's chest. He crawled over and cried out, but it was no use. Jack's eyes were unblinking and his face expressionless.

The report of machine guns echoed. He was alone. And he would fight on.

Memorial Day. It's not just for picnics.

Before Winter

The first time I saw it was as I walked past the small woods on my way back from the corner Quick Stop. Its entrance slightly covered with leaves, it was hidden in plain sight; a cozy little home of dried grass and the detritus of summer past. I paused, peering from my spot on the street, my hands jammed into my pockets against the increasing cold of late autumn.

The leaves suddenly rustled a little, and from my spot on the cold concrete of the street I saw its tiny nose poke out, followed by the rest of its striped, furry self, sniffing and scuffing around in the leaves. It spied me in a second, sat momentarily still, then scurried up the rough trunk of the tree. I turned back to the Quick Stop, though by now my toes were beginning to burn. I should've worn thicker socks.

That night as I watched the first snowflakes fall – first tentatively, then in increasing numbers until they infused the dark with their icy sparkle – I distractedly peeled an orange into little bits of peel and fruit. Then I sucked on a sunflower shell, split it, and ate the seed.

The next day I returned to the little spot, knelt down, and placed my gift of fruit and seeds at its door. I stepped back and waited. Nothing happened, so I left.

A few days later, I passed the spot again and felt its eyes follow me as I continued on.

I made my final visit that evening. Squatting on the crunchy leaves, I dropped some peanuts and popcorn on the ground. I glanced up in time to see it staring at me from just outside its cozy hole. Our eyes met; I winked, it blinked, and winter began.

Enough

She spread her hands over the festive tablecloth, smoothing it. Now for the china! It had been her grandmother's, passed down to her mother, and now to her. Tiny flowers and vines in varying shades of pink and green graced each plate's surface. She arranged a centerpiece of flowers, pinecones, and pumpkins in the middle of the table; carefully placed a crystal goblet at each place, the silverware – just so, and cloth (cloth!) napkins folded into the shape of a rose. A slight smile crossed her face as she stepped back and admired her work.

The scent of baked turkey and dressing, sweet potatoes, cranberry relish, and a plethora of side dishes wafted through the house. Her faithful dog, Cam, trotted up and stood beside her, and she scratched the top of his head as they stood together taking it all in.

She walked slowly to her bedroom and, after some time, came out dressed in her Thanksgiving best. Cam joined her as she gazed out the front window for a long time. She shook herself, and got busy dishing up the feast and placing it all on the beautiful table.

She glanced at the clock and took her place at the head of the table. Her breath caught in her throat as she looked at each empty chair in turn. Then she bowed her head and prayed. She prayed for each dear soul who should be at the table with her; for their fears and their trials and the way they blessed the world. She thanked the Good Lord for so many good things despite privations of job loss, loss of friends, and confusion. For there was much for which to be grateful – for food and shelter, well-being and contentment, faith and hope.

Then she paused, and thought of the governors who restricted families from gathering; the very ones who were probably gathered with loved ones at groaning tables and in lovely homes or, perhaps, mansions. She did not pray for them, though she thought she should. She just considered them. Considered who they had started out to be and who they had intended to be and who they had become.

She patted Cam's head, and reached for the turkey.

Videbimus

It was one of those unclear days. Not the kind of unclear that the whole world seems to be living in lately. Not that. But — you know — the kind when fog descends so thickly that you might as well put on a helmet along with your jacket before you walk out the door because you're bound to run into something sooner or later; unless, of course, you're an animal with eyeshine. But I had to go to the grocery store. My cat, Videbimus, Wedee for short, hadn't stopped yowling since early morning and wouldn't just eat the can of tuna I'd offered earlier. I should've bought a dog. I hear they eat anything including crayons and socks. But Wedee was the leftover kitten from a friend's cat and needed a home, so in a moment of I can't believe what I just did, I said I'd take her. She was a cuddly thing and, as cats go, was pretty ordinary other than her propensity to bite me. Oh I know. Cats do that when they're feeling affectionate. But when Wedee did it, it was more like she was completing a homework assignment. She'd saunter over to me after supper, jump up onto my lap, and start her evening ritual of tiny little bites; sometimes my arms, sometimes my legs or feet, and sometimes even my neck and head. Weird, I know, but by that time of day I'm usually a lump of tiredness, so she got away with it. Sometimes I wondered if she really did think it was her duty and if she would ever think she'd accomplished the homework she had assigned herself each evening. After she was done, she'd snuggle in as though she'd not just sent little cat saliva coursing through my veins. That was six years ago and since then Wedee had pretty much determined my schedule, including, apparently, grocery store runs in dense fog.

I was on my way back when a faint light shone in the distance. I couldn't tell how near or far. It was just there. I slowed my car, thinking to avoid spending money I didn't have at the auto shop. It suddenly burst so brightly on my windshield I cringed and slammed on the brakes, waiting for the crunching sound to come. It didn't.

It was foolish, I know, but I pulled over and walked back to the approximate location of the light, now gone. Nothing. I walked in a zigzagging circle, but neither stumbled upon, heard, nor (of course) saw anything. I slid back into the car, pulled back onto the road as well as I could, and started for home. The fog had lifted slightly, though I passed a car that still crept along as though no one could see an inch in front of them. We could, but the driver must have been one of those extra careful types; the type of person who checks their locks twice and wears Vicks to bed rain or shine. Not that there's anything wrong with that.

I hauled Wedee's dinner into my crackerbox house, scooped out a serving which Wedee sniffed, then devoured like she'd been starved for a week, and I tugged off my jacket. Ugh. Something fell onto my arm. I seemed to have acquired a hitchhiker in the dewy fog. A little lightning bug spread its wings, then began to crawl. I shook it off, and it flew to a corner of the room.

After I'd made myself a huge tuna sandwich, I grabbed the TV remote, switched on the nightly news, and awaited Wedee to saunter over for her evening ritual. The news seemed more ridiculous than usual, and I shut it off and grabbed a book instead. And Wedee jumped up and snuggled. Not one bite. And the lightning bug settled down in the corner with a friendly glow.

It Can Be Found

My story is about a natural love lost, then found; of hesitancy and regret; and of the kindness of time. In that sense, it is a story about us all.

Claire had known Knox since kindergarten. They were best friends then, playing together, choosing each other for coloring partners, and hanging their coats side by side. But as often happens during growing up years, they grew apart. They exchange shy smiles in school hallways, attended sports events and concerts where they sat close enough to glance but not to speak, even attended the same parties where they might begin a conversation which interruption prevented them from finishing. Never a goodbye. Only a studied, unnoticed look or furtive glance. Graduation sealed their separation, a way-parting that left each feeling a little empty, though introspection skirted around the possibility of the childhood affection being the cause of it.

Five years is a long time, but then again, not that long.

"Claire?"

Her heart beat quickened slightly as she turned. "Knox! Is that you? What are you doing back in town? Last I heard . . . not that I . . . I mean . . ."

"I'm back for an interview in Cartersville tomorrow morning."

"Cartersville!'

He nodded and they stood, each trying to think of something to fill up the space between them. In between stutters and false starts, they agreed to meet for supper that evening. But it didn't happen. Claire's father had a heart attack and she was called away.

Twenty-five years is a long time, but then again, not that long. Knox grabbed the nurse's notes as he walked into the hospital room of a new patient, then stopped in his tracks.

Claire shrugged.

Knox cleared his throat and studied the notes in his hand.

"How is your foot feeling?"

Claire grimaced, then began laughing – a good alternative to crying. And he laughed with her until they both had to wipe tears away. Small talk distracted from pressure on bruised skin, and they caught up on unimportant matters.

And every so often they would see each other – through life's stages, marriage, children, gain and loss. And they might speak, but something always interfered and finally ended the conversation.

Forty years is a long time, but then again, not that long. It was at a large party of old friends, they once more found each other: uncoupled by death, living lives as fully as they could muster. Those forty years and their accompanying experiences and lessons did what Claire and Knox could not manage on their own. In a finger snap the familiar hesitancies fell away. The stutters. The shyness. The putting up with interference. They were friends again; the kind whose ideas piqued the other's curiosity, who found the same things amusing, and whose intuition told them what words do not.

And they were right.

❦

Dear friends, lose not the simplicity of first friendships though time's waves push them far. Put away self-consciousness long enough to speak truly and listen thoughtfully. For love, once lost, does not need to be lost forever. It can be found, though space and time shout otherwise. It can be found.

Beauty Is In the Eye of the Beholder – So Is Justice.

Dim sunlight filtered through the haze of a day that held the scent of rain. Quiet waves whispered their barely perceptible sound to the sandy shore while a chipmunk foraged in last fall's matted leaves. It was there – in a large mass, hardened by rain, wind, and cold – that she found it.

The chipmunk dug into the leaves, pulling them apart, and tugged at it – still shiny in its plastic packet – then, finding it too heavy, yet too delightful to abandon, dragged it to a bush under which she disappeared. She traveled slowly, pushing and pulling her treasure through her burrow's path until she reached an impressive stash of nuts and seeds, berries and mushrooms. She placed her new acquisition alongside of the rest. Chipping with satisfaction, she nudged her jellybean-sized pups, still too blind to see what the excitement was about.

It was here. I know it was, he mumbled to himself. He'd stolen it from an employer last fall and hidden it just to be sure he wouldn't be blamed. Now that winter was past and his job was, too, he'd cash it in. No one could outsmart *him*.

And two little eyes peered out at him from underneath a bush.

———❖———

"Beauty is in the eye of the beholder", attributed to Margaret Hungerford in her novel "Molly Bawn," 1878; "Justice, like beauty, is in the eye of the beholder." Zora Neale Hurston

The Day After Mother's Day

A tiny voice at her bedside whispered, "I had a bad dream". Opening her eyes, she held out her arms and helped her little one into bed with her. As he snuggled and fell fast asleep, she ran through a list of things the coming day held.

* * *

After waiting for her little fashionista to choose the day's clothes, then change her mind – twice – she helped the parts of getting dressed that little hands could not quite manage. A glance at her watch told her there would be just enough time for a dawdling breakfast and another change of clothes before preschool.

She pulled her jacket closer as she watched tee-ball practice on a cold May morning. The excitable players threw balls that managed to land halfway to their destination, swing bats at a batting tee, and run as fast a short legs could carry them. She opened her large bag to doublecheck the after-game snacks she had brought. Yes, there would be just enough.

* * *

An irritated voice shouted from the bedroom. Her heart wanted to give way, but she stood her ground. Make-up at this age would pave the path for the next life step to be premature. The morning promised a sullen breakfast and silent car ride to school.

* * *

Tears and despair. She'd heard stories about this particular class. Leaning over, she asked, "Could you do it this way?" NO! came the hopeless answer. Why was math even a thing?

* * *

Car lights shown down the street as she watched them light the late night dark. They passed by the house. It wasn't her. She sat down again. She was glad the Good Lord never slept and that He was up at this time of night as she prayed over her fears. Car lights flashed on the wall and the sound of a car in the driveway diminished her worry. She picked up a book and pretended to be engrossed in it as her child crossed the threshold on the dot of curfew.

* * *

"Remember, stop if you get too tired. It's a long trip." Her son gave her a goodbye hug. She could feel his college road trip excitement and held back her tears until his car disappeared down the street.

* * *

"Mom? I just thought I'd call and wish you a Happy Mother's Day. Sorry I'm late! Did you do anything special?"

Anything special? She pondered the question. No. Nothing special at all.

Nondescript

He couldn't figure it out. He'd been careful. *Beyond* careful. He'd left his apartment at different times each day. He'd taken varying routes. His meetings with his contacts had been quick and discreet, the notes and thumb drives tucked in a slim, black bag identical to the one he exchanged with his contacts. He'd even found a nondescript shop at which to meet each one. The shop was nothing, really. It sold scented candles with names like *Cozy Evening* and *Misty Rain*. Along the wall were two shelves of used books for sale. Garden art items were tagged to sell quickly. And it sold teas made of herbs, flowers, and mushrooms, with curious names like *Meetme*, *Gotcha*, and *Moribund*. There were other names, too. He'd read them often during meetings at which no word was spoken and a hand-off was imperceptible. *Rosalie* and *Mill Stream* were two other names he recalled. The rest scattered from his memory just now; not that it mattered.

The shopkeeper sat the back of the shop with a cup of tea and a book. Always the same teapot, sometimes a different book. Whenever he entered, she'd barely raise her eyes other than to acknowledge him. One time she startled him by asking if she could help him, but he pretended to browse, and shook his head. Foolish woman, he thought — with nothing to do but sit all day hoping to sell a dollar's worth of goods. He wondered how she made enough to live. She fit the shop perfectly.

But the game was up now. He'd been discovered, along with notes he'd copied and quietly shared. It wasn't actually embezzlement, he'd reasoned, because business ideas were fair game. How could they be trade secrets when they were no longer secret? He'd quietly laughed over that joke. It was worth it. They were paying him enough to buy a country house and take an island vacation.

Someone higher up had somehow gotten wind of the scheme, though, and just when he and his associates were patting themselves on the back, they'd been yanked up short. He sat in his office, wondering if his future held anything worth salvaging and waiting for his lawyer to get him out of this mess.

"Mr. Stears sent me to ask if you would like anything," his secretary looked both sorry and scared.

He looked up briefly.

"Here. He left this for me this morning. It's pretty good. Why don't you try it?"

She offered a cup of tea, the bag still steeping.

He took it and she left. He set it down, pulled the tea bag from the cup, and glanced at the saucer. Then he froze.

A familiar voice floated down the hall. "Thank you again, Rosalie. I don't know what we'd do without you. Here's your check. You take that long vacation you've been promising yourself."

His eyes drifted down to the tiny tea tag labeled simply: *Gotcha.*

Warm With a Whisper of Cool

She kicked through the orange leaves, their crunchy response somehow reassuring. How far was it? Five miles? Yes, she thought, five or nearly that from her deserted car to who knew where. A balmy fall evening had wandered seamlessly into the dawn of what promised to be a replica of the day just past — warm with a whisper of cool undertones. How could she sit at home on such a day? So before the sun had barely announced it's presence, she'd hopped in her old Pontiac. She'd tossed her favorite merino wool blanket into the back seat along with a turkey sandwich, an apple, and large bottle of water in an insulated lunch bag.

Just that week she'd been accused of being (gasp) boring. She knew she shouldn't pay attention to an accusation coming from someone she barely knew. Who knew where that co-worker's opinions came from? The worker's own insecurities, no doubt. Still, it had bothered her enough to lead to the day's impromptu outing. And, really, her usually preferred choice of sitting at home on her reclining lawn chair reading a book could stand a little shaking up. The little duplex she called home was a sanctuary to her, though. The other side of it hadn't been rented for years which was just fine with her. In fact, she'd never laid eyes on her landlord. A rental company had shown her the place, and she simply mailed her rent each month to the address provided. The peace and quiet suited her.

The trees seemed almost luminescent as the sun's rays nipped their red and yellow leaves. The miles had flown by on the untraveled country road, and she didn't care. Why should she on such a day? She turned last minute toward what appeared to be some decent hiking trails. And they were. Decent. But a few miles' hike was suddenly enough. She was ready for a quick picnic and drive back to the little duplex she called home. After all, anyone who thought she was boring didn't know squat about her cozy sanctum.

She made quick work of her lunch, and turned her key in the ignition. Her car's whine grew louder with each effort and then stopped altogether. She rubbed the tender spot where she'd bumped her head when she'd lifted the hood of the car and peered at the engine. Who was she kidding? She had no idea what to look for. Everything always looked the same when it came to cars. She squinted at the sun and guessed the time that was left before dusk.

How far had she driven that morning? She wished she had paid closer attention to that little detail; but then she remembered the gloriousness of Fall that she *had* paid attention to and promptly forgave herself. Except. She gazed ahead at the road in front of her, briefly glanced back at the turnoff which had led to the hiking trails, and sighed. It was going to be a long hike home.

A car slowed behind her and stopped. She looked over her shoulder and saw a black Maserati.

"Do you need a lift?"

Should she answer or quicken her pace? The fleeting thought of racing a Maserati both amused and alarmed her.

"I," she turned and found herself staring at a man near her age but clearly not her league.

She cleared her throat. "I was hiking and my car wouldn't start."

Great. Lovely explanation.

"I could try to start it."

As she wondered how safe it would be to backtrack to a hiking trail with a stranger, he added, "Or I could give you a lift home."

It is an inexorable fact of life that one choice always leads to another. She wished that just now her choice wasn't between a proverbial rock and hard place. The sun was setting, and hiking along a deserted highway wasn't remotely appealing even on this warm fall evening. Boring had its own appeal just now.

"I won't hurt you and," he squinted at the setting sun, "I hate the thought of you out here by yourself."

She nodded, slid into the passenger seat, and directed him to the turnoff she'd taken earlier.

"It's a beautiful evening – warm," he remarked.

"With a whisper of cool." She couldn't seem to help herself.

He smiled. "I like that. Yes. A whisper of cool. Complementary features of Fall."

He pulled up next to her car, jumped out, and looked under the Pontiac's hood. Pulling a gadget from his pocket, he hooked it up to her car battery, waited a few minutes, and motioned for her to try the ignition. Her jaw dropped as her car roared to life. He smiled, waved, and pulled out ahead of her.

There really were angels who walked the earth, she thought as she neared her cozy, boring, beautiful duplex. She would make it home before night's dark made fitting her key in the lock more a matter of touch than sight.

What?! Lights filled the other side of the duplex that had stood vacant for so long. Of all the days for her to have been gone. Someone must have moved into the attached unit. She grabbed her things and pulled a note from her screen as she unlocked her door. The note explained her landlord would be staying *for an unspecified amount of time.*

Landlord? Well at least she might put a face to the heretofore featureless recipient of her rent.

Apologies for missing my new neighbor, the note continued. *Arrived later than anticipated.* She studied the handwriting. The block letters suggested it wasn't a little old lady who received her rent. Other than that, she couldn't tell.

After making the first cocoa of the fall season and changing from hiking boots to fuzzy slippers, she peeked out her back window to the duplex garage. She used it only during winter months to save on rent. But she concluded with no car in the driveway, the landlord must've parked in the garage.

It was probably too late to go next door and introduce herself, but her curiosity got the better of her. What did he – or she – drive? A truck – maybe Chevy? Ford – probably. She opened the door a crack, then swung it wide. There it stood. A Maserati – black as the oncoming night and anything but boring.

Great Worship

"It's just easier, you know? I click the link, sip coffee in my pajamas, and even get a little housework done during the boring parts."

"Plus I don't worry about the kids getting antsy. God is there where two or three are gathered, right?"

The people in Berea were more open-minded than those in Thessalonica. They were so glad to hear the message Paul told them. They studied the Scriptures every day to make sure that what they heard was really true.

And continuing daily with one accord in the temple, and breaking bread from house to house, they ate their meat with gladness and singleness of heart.

"What a great sermon!"

"I just can't get enough of him, can you?"

"I don't know how he does it week after week. But he does!"

And upon the first day of the week, when the disciples came together to break bread, Paul preached unto them, ready to depart on the morrow; and continued his speech until midnight.

"And the worship! I felt transported!"

"The worship is the best around, for sure."

Therefore, since we receive a kingdom which cannot be shaken, let us show gratitude, by which we may offer to God an acceptable service with reverence and awe; for our God is a consuming fire.

Speak to one another with psalms, hymns, and spiritual songs. Sing and make music in your hearts to the Lord.

And God watched. He heard their voices and music and words. And He listened to what hearts were saying.

Of All the Times
For This to Happen

Of all the times for this to happen. Passover is my favorite holiday: a week of recalling God's mercy on His enslaved people, envisioning the death angel examining the doorposts for lamb's blood and passing over those who had it as their protection. And, of course, since it was close to that time, we remember about them escaping through a sea that God actually parted. A sea! Split! You might as well expect a boulder to break apart or a dead man to live again. It just doesn't happen. And to top it off, the army chasing them got stuck. Run aground in the sea. It's as hard to envision as — say — an evergreen growing in the desert. It can happen, sure; but it's hardly likely. The Red Sea event can give you goosebumps if you close your eyes and imagine it.

We are painfully acquainted with the Roman method of torture and execution. Sometimes we see crosses planted along the road with criminals in various stages of dying hanging from them. It's a form of torture for us, too, in a way. A reminder of who's in charge and what could happen if you say or do the wrong thing. Pax Romana is peace at the point of a spear. Don't worry. I wouldn't say that in public. But I'm not the only one who thinks it.

Jesus was – well – he was perfect. He was funny and creative and compassionate and strong and smart and a deep-thinker. Perfect. He had a way of teaching us that made us feel like God was right there with us. He said that, you know. That he was God's son. And some of us actually believed such an unbelievable claim. I would've followed that man to the ends of the earth.

And as his following was increasing exponentially, they pounced. Those Pharisees. Those law teachers. They paid one of the guys who were with him all of the time to turn him in. And that scum of the earth did it. For money. For MONEY. Jesus didn't care about money. He cared about a larger than life mission. He wouldn't have done something just for money. For love, maybe, but not money.

And now? He's dead. They took him and gave him a bogus trial and whipped him and hanged him! On a cross! It was brutal. I won't describe it. Some things are better unspoken. But I'll see it for the rest of my days. I'll dream it for the rest of my nights.

Passover: A lesson in obedience despite fear. A tutorial in trust. God's amazing rescue plan. But now? Like I said. Of all the times for this to happen.

Apple Slices Dipped in Caramel

It wasn't that he was the most handsome man she'd ever met nor even the most quick-witted. But he was kind. She'd witnessed it whenever she saw him with other people or animals or birds. And there was something in his eyes that indicated he was thinking beyond what was heard or spoken. She couldn't say what it was that kept her thinking of him even when he was out of sight, why she thought of him as she left the office each day and when she got home, nor the reason she saw him in her dreams.

The problem, of course, was that he had no idea she existed. None! She sat at the same spot every day, reading while she ate her favorite lunch – apple slices dipped in caramel, a favorite because when she was a little girl, her grandfather had made it their very own treat, and memories of love and home rushed in whenever she ate them.

And the man passed the very spot every day, chatting with a friend or looking at his phone or simply whistling. Today was no different. He'd passed without noticing. Enough! She gathered her things and slid them into her bag. She wasn't someone who approached attractive strangers nor any stranger, for that matter. It just wasn't in her. Maybe one day she'd find someone like him; someone kind who had more within him than he let anyone know. Today would be the last day, she decided. No more pining. No more wishing. She'd take lunch at her desk and let go of thoughts of which only she was aware.

And she did. And it was boring. Oh, she made mindless conversation with co-workers who took lunch at their desks, too. She read a book, but it felt flat. She distracted herself with Pinterest. But she missed her little spot near the fountain outside her office building.

Depressed. That's what she felt, though nothing had really been lost other than an intangible hope of something more. She still passed by the fountain after work. At least there was that, but she did not sit. She did not read. And something in her heart broke a little. Until.

Until a week had gone by. And there, as she passed the fountain after work, waiting for her, was the not most handsome man holding something out to her.

Apple slices dipped in caramel.

Winds of Change
and the Witch

Rain blew through the forest as the storm tossed limbs and branches in its torrential fury. On through the night the wind blew, lightning flashed, and thunder rolled and crashed. The crack of a birch, weakened by unseen pests eating it from the inside out, reverberated over the commotion as it slammed to the ground, crushing the brush and bushes around it.

And then – in an instant – it was over. Droplets glistened on both bough and leaf. A nearby river rushed loudly with the memory of the storm just past. A chipmunk's bright eyes peeked out of its hiding place and a couple of deer took tentative steps nearby. And the oldest tree of the forest seemed to shake itself as the sun caressed its shadow.

It was on that night that a little girl was born. She was given all she desired and more than she needed. And she grew, through the seasons and signposts of life, diligently working toward her goals, finding beauty and glory and seeking more. Always more.

And every year she visited the forest that called to her and spent a day at the base of the old tree thinking – no, pondering

– as hope and discouragement, good and evil, light and dark played tag in her soul.

And although myriad paths lay open to her, she considered prestige and power a worthy aim and chose that path which offered most and best. And she got it. For there are in life ways some do not recognize or chose to know; but for those who seek them, their allure calls clearly and relentlessly.

She attended the best schools where she learned to think in the accepted manner; not only learned, but embraced the lessons that scoffed at old wisdom and blessed those that tore its fabric. She acquired beauty at the cost of dignity, fortune at the cost of integrity, and success at the cost of legitimacy.

She followed the clear and relentless path to dark places and shadowy travelers. She made everyone around her a servant and thought of those she did not know, slaves. Others' lives became a means to an end, and she didn't hesitate regardless of hurt or harm her actions might cause; until life became as expendable as used package wrapping.

She gave in to gluttony, but was never satiated. Whatever of the many things she'd dreamed and worked to gain were never enough. She began to think of herself as a god, really. No one was higher or should be. She was greater than anyone! Larger than life, even bigger than creation! She had it all and would control it all, too!

And then a storm came; quietly and slowly at first, as some storms do. It continued, and disturbed her. Putting her hands over her ears, she demanded it stop. But the wind rose higher and the rain pelted harder. On through the night the wind blew, lightning flashed, and thunder rolled and crashed.

It occurred to her that the old tree beneath which she had sat and pondered and planned in her youth, and later neglected until it was forgotten, could be a shelter. Running to the forest, she looked but couldn't find it. At last she was spent. Raging at the storm and any who had the audacity to cross her, she lay on the ground, cursing until the very end. The ground swallowed her weaselly body, and the rain washed away the filth of her life.

And the oldest tree of the forest seemed to shake itself as the sun caressed its shadow.

A Last Look
at the Upper Room

It was clean except for one – no, two things. They were unobtrusive, but caught her eye. On the floor near the wall lay a towel; a muddy towel, now dried. And near it sat a basin of dirty water. Strange things left in such a clean room.

She wandered over to the table. She'd heard the stories. You couldn't live here and not have heard about the man who said things so remarkable they sent shivers down your spine; who healed – healed! – lame people who hadn't felt the earth beneath their feet for years, if ever; and who talked with anyone, not just the important or educated or honored. Oh yes, she'd heard. She, herself, had heard from her neighbor's daughter's friend about a woman caught in a situation that shouldn't be spoken of and, instead of hurling accusations with the rest, he had asked some questions that had sent her accusers running. There was something very gratifying in that, though she couldn't say exactly what.

She'd heard the rumors, too. He had said – reportedly, mind you – that "Anyone who has seen me has seen the Father". The Father. God! He'd actually said that! That comment right there did it for some people. It was a bridge too far. But others? Not so much. They'd stuck with him. They believed it was true.

And herself? Hmmm. She wasn't sure. But those healings — you couldn't deny them. Or the creepy guy in the tombs who was freed from demon-possession. Really. Who does that? Or the huge storm that was stilled in an instant. Seriously.

And now the worst. Because whether you believed him or not, he hadn't done anything deserving a crucifixion. Those were the whispers spreading through the city. The ones who were offended by his defense of unremarkable, diseased people were crowding together. It's the way mobs were. And others joined in, of course, because they did whatever anyone else did. They thought whatever anyone else thought. It was almost like they didn't know they could act or think for themselves.

A loud sound startled her. As it grew louder, she ran to the window and looked out. Oh no! The man! No! NO! Soldiers surrounded him. One of them flicked a whip his way every once in awhile for his own amusement. The man was carrying a cross — those heavy, dirty, terrible, tortuous things. As her breath caught in her throat, he glanced up at her for an instant. And in that instant, her doubt vanished.

Tears started slowly, then ran down her face as her body shuddered with heavy sobs. Why did some people blacken light with dark? Good with bad? What was the point? She wished she could fix it. She wished there was something she could do to chase away the hardened hearts and evil mobs. She wished she could drive them from the whole world, or, at least, from hers. From here. From the street the man with the cross was trudging down.

He was so good. Really good. And kind. And, as she thought about it, one of the purest souls she'd ever known – or at least known about. She harshly brushed her tears away.

Her eyes roamed the room in a last once-over. Ah. Here was a crumb on the table. Unleavened bread. How could she have missed it? Oh. And a drop of wine. She began to clear them with one swipe, hesitated, and placed them on the tip of her tongue instead. Then she picked up the towel and basin and walked out.

A Change of Pace

They walked past the house every day at the same time: the man with green tennis shoes and the Scottie dog. He didn't scroll through his phone like some walkers did, and the Scottie dog was content to match his master's pace without pulling on the leash. And then one day they didn't.

It gave the man who noticed them every day pause. He'd grown used to taking a second sip of decaf and looking up from watching the news at exactly 6:10 every evening. He barely noticed he did it. But this evening was different. This evening he noticed because the man with the green tennis shoes and the Scottie dog didn't walk by. He put down his coffee, rose from his chair, and peered out the window; then, seeing nothing, he hurried down his front steps and looked both ways down his street. No one. Nothing.

The next night, the man took a first sip of decaf and sauntered over to the window. No reason. No man with green tennis shoes. No Scottie dog. It shouldn't bother him. It really shouldn't.

The third night, the man didn't pour a cup of coffee at all. He didn't turn on the news. He sat on his front steps and watched the street. A neighbor slipped quietly into his driveway and tinkered on the new car he'd purchased just a month ago. Another neighbor stared blankly out her picture window, petting the cat in her arms.

The fourth night, the man gave a tentative wave to his neighbor who happened to, once again, be tinkering with his new car. The lady with the cat in her arms mistook his wave, and waved back.

The fifth night, the lady ventured into her yard – minus her cat. She set out a card table with lemonade and lemon cookies. The man tinkering on his car went over and chatted as he ate a cookie.

The sixth night, the three neighbors found themselves once again in the lady's yard eating cookies and drinking lemonade and talking all at once. Did something bad happen to the man with the green tennis shoes? What about his Scottie dog?

More neighbors congregated on the seventh night – so much so, that the lemonade pitcher had to be refilled three times. And then – then a hush fell over the crowd as they watched the man in the green tennis shoes and his dog stroll by. He waved. They all waved back. And that, dear reader, is how a week's vacation can help a neighborhood.

Don't Panic

I was pretty sure it was time to panic. I'd exhausted all other options.

Retracing my steps? Of course, and it had made things worse. I now had no earthly idea where I was.

Praying to the Good Lord Almighty? Obviously. And we can agree He heard me. What He decided to do with the desperate request was a whole other matter. Take Jonah, for instance. I honestly don't know if he had a wife, and I don't suppose he made it home in time to ask her to work on those nasty whale vomit stains before they were a hopeless case (which – of course they were), but suffice it to say, the Good Lord Almighty took a different perspective than Jonah did. Of the sense I *do* have, it is enough to know that my perspective diverges from holy more often than not. Need I say more?

Yelling for help at the top of my lungs? Mmm. Well you have to understand it's usually a bit complicated to take that option. After all, maybe someone kind and helpful would hear me, but then again, maybe someone unhelpful and not at all kind would hear me too. Or maybe only one of them would hear me and how would I be able to tell if the one who came was the kind person or the one who was not at all kind? Or maybe kind and unhelpful? And, in trying to be helpful, they told someone who was of the not at all kind type? You see? Things aren't nearly as easy as one might imagine.

And believe me, I was imagining enough for you and me both. You see, it all started with a birthday present. I had years ago expressed interest in going to Radio City Music Hall (an unattainable extravagance for someone like me) and one of my friends with a long, but not terribly detailed memory made the major effort of fulfilling my dream. That is, she got the radio part right, and I had to give her major credit for that. I unwrapped one part of a two-way radio. Ahem. *One.* And I think it was used. No one ever claimed my friends and I were flush with cash. Every one of us was more of what you call thrifters – or, more honestly, scavengers. But I was curious, and I thought to myself that I might just find the owner of the other part of a set by walking around and speaking into my walkie every so often.

The following day was beautiful, and I was in the mood for a long autumn walk. I ended up at the edge of town and proceeded down a road where I found myself at the edge of Tamarac National Wildlife Refuge: 43,000 acres of fresh air and sunshine; and, I might add, a reasonable place someone might carry a handheld radio. I admit now that sometimes things that seem reasonable at first, don't seem at all reasonable after awhile.

Clouds began to gather so innocently that I didn't notice, but by the time an hour had passed and I was beginning to think it was time to go back, the sky was filling up and the innocent fluffy clouds I hadn't at first noticed were turning a bit gray. After another rambling speech into my walkie that resulted in nothing but silence from wherever the other one was (probably now deceased in a junk yard), I hurried back on the path and made pretty good time. I congratulated myself on recognizing an unusual bush I'd taken note of when I passed it before, but, weirdly enough, spied another one just like it at the bend of my track. I retraced my steps and noticed another unusual bush that apparently wasn't quite as unusual as I had originally believed.

It was then that I felt a few pangs of doubt, then a few drops of rain, then a sudden downpour. Looking left and right, I ran into the torrent and noticed a fuzzy shadow ahead. As I approached it, I was grateful to make out a cave of sorts; not a huge one by any means; rather, a sort of respectable indentation into rock. Breathing heavily, I reached it and slumped onto its floor, my back to the wall. If daylight held, maybe I could find my way back after the rain lifted.

It was beginning to grow a bit chilly and I thought of how the weather in these parts can drop fairly quickly this time of year. Tamarac National Wildlife Refuge seemed to me now to be not the 43,000 acres of fresh air and sunshine I had entered, but 43,000 acres of not so great possibilities. Pheasants, then fox, then bears traipsed through my thoughts. I closed my eyes in an effort to rest and regroup, and when I opened them, there were two strangers standing in front of me. I hadn't heard a thing.

I believe it was at this point I was concluding it was time to panic, not that I had to think it through. Some things in life come as naturally as – well let's just say prayer in a foxhole and leave it at that.

"I told you I heard something!" the woman said, giving the follow beside her a friendly nudge.

He looked at her with delight and disbelief, and they started muttering things I couldn't understand. I caught odd-sounding words and phrases like *torsion field* along with algebraic-sounding back and forth chatter that I didn't care to dissect.

Soon the man looked at me and asked about my half of a two-way radio I was holding. I told him it was a birthday gift and how, with good intentions, my friend had remembered the "radio" part of a comment I'd once made about wanting to go to Radio City Music Hall. The two friends apparently thought it extremely funny and I was relieved enough at their demeanor that I chuckled along with them.

"Would you?" he asked.

"Would I what?"

"Like to go to a concert?"

I shrugged my shoulders. He couldn't be serious. We were in the middle of nowhere and the temperature was dropping. "I guess."

"It is her birthday, after all," the woman remarked.

"Hm. Seems like a fair exchange," the man said.

The woman raised her eyebrows, but he ignored her and held out his hand.

"Mind if I look at it?"

"This?" I held out my walkie.

I can't really tell you how it happened: Just that one minute I was sitting in a cave and the next minute I was taking in an Il Volo concert at Radio City Music Hall. Granted, I was still rather damp and underdressed (to say the least), but it was a concert I'll never forget. The minute it ended, I found myself standing at the edge of the Tamarac National Wildlife Refuge with enough daylight left to walk back to town.

Some people use their money to travel the world. Some travel only in their imagination. Me? All I know is that one autumn evening I seem to have traded my half of a two-way radio for a concert at Radio City Music Hall, and I'm more than satisfied with the trade.

Because I Took a Walk

It happened because I took a walk. I love taking walks. Okay, not all of the time. On days when the pavement is slick with ice and snow and I have to watch my step more than the surrounding scenery, I'd rather stay inside with a cup of cocoa and read. No, not newspapers. I used to like to do that, and did so every day. But, well, no comment other than to say I cancelled my subscription. Too bad. I really did like to read it – except the middle of the business section with all the letters and numbers that I didn't quite follow. Not that. But the rest of it. But not now. Now I can't even make a cup of cocoa. But I'll get to that in a minute.

Today, however . . . today the temperature could be best described as balmy. Balmy! That's not easy to find near the close of October, but it was today. Though many had fallen, some leaves still clung for their beautiful red, orange, and yellow lives to the branches. You had to admire their will to live. And the sky was a faint blue: the color of my grandma's eyes after her cataract surgery.

I waved to my neighbor, Merl, as I started out. He sat on his porch nearly every day and just watched. I don't really know what he watched, but he seemed to find enough to interest him. Maybe he saw more than the average person. Who knows. He waved back as he took a sip of his lemonade.

I needed this. Our town's water system was low, and we were on a strict limit – even to drink. Weather pundits claimed we'd been in a year-long drought. Unlike some fortunate souls who lived out of town, I had no cistern. The whole situation made me not only thirsty, but more than a little grumpy.

I'd passed the local grocery store (there was a line inside, each customer holding a 12 pack of Dasani or one of its poorer cousins), and was approaching the church on the corner, when the largest raven I've ever seen swooped so close I automatically ducked. In fact, I dived so low, my hands slammed on the pavement and I skinned the palm of one hand. As I brushed myself off, and was deciding whether to turn home or continue on, I noticed a small envelope on the ground just where the raven had flown so low.

I retrieved it and opened the flap. Inside was a crude map and one word: **Walk**. My eyebrows shot up and I thought, *Well that decides that.* I followed the trail as far as I could understand from the crudely drawn map. I glanced up at the sky. Still faint blue with no cloud in sight.

I came to the edge of a stream. It was nothing remarkable, burrowing a shallow channel, often more of a muddy trail than legitimate stream depending on the amount of rain. That was probably why hardly anyone ever paid attention to it.

That is where the map ended. I was more than a little puzzled and looked around. What had I been thinking? An envelope dropped by a raven was certainly nothing to waste my day over, was it? But I had. And by now it was no longer balmy. I was getting chilled. To the bone. It no longer felt like the close of October, but instead, the edge of November. I scolded myself as I pulled my thin sweater close and started home.

As I walked, I pondered over the events of my day. My mind wandered over the non-descript scene the map had led me to. With a start I stopped, then turned and hurried back to the stream.

Sometimes it's the things we don't see that are the very thing we need to notice. My mind and memory finally saw what my blind eyes had missed. The stream that was more of a muddy trail held a treasure greater than gold!

How can a stream be muddy in a drought? I dug until my fingernails were caked with mud, and there it was: An underground spring, small and beautiful!

The next day, though it was chilly, I decided to sit on my porch and just watch for awhile. I looked over and raised my cup of cocoa to Merl as he raised his glass to mine.

Just Like That

"*No! I said it should go **there**!*" The overseer slammed him against some rock and pointed.

The workman picked up the heavy stone and moved it two feet to the right. He rubbed the place on his back and shoulder where he'd hit the rock. The overseer was not only inconsistent, but easily angered. *This needs to go here. No, there – are you deaf! We don't have time for a lunch break. Get back to work. A funeral? Really! And who's supposed to pick up your slack when you're not here?!*

Maybe he should find another place to work. But where? His shepherding days were past. He didn't mind manual labor. He was proud to have worked on the Masada, but the space had a weird feel to it for some reason; and although it was a feather in his cap, he was glad to move on. He'd worked on a few small synagogues and now on the temple complex in Jerusalem. It was steady work, and didn't appear to be slowing down soon. But the overseer! He dreaded coming to work each day. A tightness in his chest took hold, and he didn't try to release it. He didn't believe he would ever be able to forgive the man for his harshness. Or want to. No, it would take some kind of miracle to forgive the guy, and he wasn't asking for one. He was the worst he'd ever encountered.

He mulled it over. He *could* use a miracle about now – but not to forgive. No, he could use a miracle to lead him to another job or help him endure the one he had. He'd heard of miracles taking place. Some didn't believe such things. But he did.

He was picking up another block when a cacophony broke out on the other side of the wall. Searching for the overseer and not seeing him, he moved toward the crowd to see what the noise was about. He saw a man carrying a cross. It was nothing new these days. But something stopped him from returning to work. And the man carrying the cross looked at him, caught his eye, and held his gaze for a moment. A chill he couldn't identify ran through him.

He wished he could look at those eyes forever, for it was then he remembered. He recalled a quiet night that had been disrupted by the loudest shout and song he had ever heard. He remembered falling to the ground in fear, and running to a manger in the little town nearby. And he saw once again in his memory a baby in a manger just as he had been told, the steaming breath of nearby animals, and how, when the mother picked up the baby, the tiny one looked at him over her shoulder.

And just like that, nothing else mattered.

. . . Or Was It Two?

He walked through the tall grasses as the soggy ground beneath hugged the edges of his boots. It was a glorious day, the temperature nearly touching 50 and the sky a brilliant splash of deep blue verging on periwinkle, his favorite color.

It had been a year – or was it two? Maybe more. Yes, maybe more. Time was like that, clear at some points, offering Monet-like images in others. What he *did* know was that it didn't seem like a year or two or more ago. It seemed like yesterday. And it seemed like a lifetime ago.

Whenever it was, he'd been walking along the railroad tracks sorting through his financial troubles and wishing them away. His thoughts had turned to the tons of money (lucky sport) that had been made with something beginning with the likes of the Tom Thumb. Most folks thought of the name as belonging in English folklore stories of the 1600's rather than a steam locomotive. Then his mind had wandered to the buildings and towns that had sprung up along the railroad and drifted into curiosity about how the people of those towns had lived and loved and died. He hadn't reached much past the beginning of those thoughts, however, when something along the edge of the tracks caught his eye – a flash of brightness made him stoop to look closer.

The gold coin that had glinted in the sun covered another one or two. Maybe more. He looked around and, seeing no one, dug down, pocketed them and hurried home.

The time that passed offered both good and bad, excitement and boredom, fun and trouble. He learned that, while it made life easier, money did not make it better. What made it better was purpose. He found one, maybe two, and found many ways to accomplish them, some with money and some without.

And then one day he was tired. No, not tired of his purpose, but tired of the wealth and of the things that went with it; tired of false friends, tired of those living in pretense of either importance or victimhood, and (curiously enough) tired of always getting what he wanted. His mind wandered back to the Tom Thumb and the buildings and towns that had sprung up because of it. He thought again of the lives affected by it — lived in glory or ruin or everything in between. And he wondered if in some grand tangle of meaning the Tom Thumb that had brought newness and greatness was somehow inextricably linked to the miniature folklore character who found trouble.

In such ponderings he found himself as he walked through tall grasses on a beautiful day. Ah. Here it was. The spot. He looked around and, seeing no one, dug down and placed one or two — or maybe more — gold coins just visible in the ground. Maybe some lucky or unlucky soul would come upon it as he had done. He wished whoever it was well, but did not wish it again for himself. After all, troubles of the rich aren't necessarily dwarfed by troubles of the poor.

He began his return walk without a backward glance and no regret.

Tumbleweed

He squinted into the blackness; white, directionless flakes blinding any hope of seeing shadowy forms. There was nothing to be done. He'd been warned. Forecasters had talked about it for weeks and the past week it was all he heard about. Well, not all. Actually, he'd been distracted by a flurry of phone calls: his. He had been calling around seeking information about Tumbleweed. Not a plant. His dog. He felt bad for the name. He'd have chosen something like Bear or Duke or Hank. But it was his wife's choice. She'd gotten the little yellow lab just a month before they married. She said having a dog in the country was good sense. She moved into his bachelor house on their wedding night and put her cozy chic stamp on it within the first month. Seven months later, on a clear summer night, she'd run to town for some ingredient her peach pie needed, and on her return had been killed in a head-on collision.

He'd been sitting outside, Tumbleweed rummaging around the yard, when the police pulled up. The dog seemed to know immediately and let out a long, mournful howl. When an officer handed him a plastic bag with newly purchased cinnamon and a small bag of flour, the world went black for a few moments.

The days following were filled with too much of the business of death, but after – After. It had taken his breath away.

He was glad he lived in the country where he didn't need to make conversation with sympathetic people. Tumbleweed provided as much conversation as he needed and, he thought, he gave to the dog as well as he got. They were a good pair. He'd started calling him Weed, and the dog seemed amenable to the change.

It was close to Valentine's Day, and he took Weed into town with him to get a box of chocolates. It seemed fitting maybe. Boy, he missed her. And he'd stopped to chat with a few folks several different times before he made the purchase. But when he got back to the car, Weed was nowhere in sight. He'd looked and called. The townsfolk had spread the word. But night had fallen and the dog was still gone. He'd driven home alone with a lump in his throat.

It had been two days and, despite his sorrow, or perhaps because of it, he unwrapped the box he'd purchased. He might not be adept at pink heart types of things, but chocolate? Chocolate would be his defiance of loss. He realized as he sat at the window that they'd not even celebrated their first wedding anniversary. Not only was his dog gone, but this Valentine's Day – his wedding day one year ago – he was all alone.

He took a small bite of chocolate and forced it down, then opened his front door and whistled and called. The wind blew and snow began edging it's way over the threshold. Though he closed the door, he strained to see in the black winter storm because he'd learned that there is no such thing as lost hope. People may say there is no way out of a hopeless situation; that hope, once lost, cannot be recovered. But no. Hope is never lost, even in the most desperate times or trying day. He knew that from the experience of a lifetime and from a difficult year. Hope is always present: Perhaps misplaced or difficult to see, but it is never gone. It just takes on an appearance different than known or expected. But it is there just the same. He would not yield that point.

He brushed a slight bit of moisture from his eye, then blinked. Something seemed to tumble with the wind. And it grew larger as it came closer. He slammed open the door.

"Weed! Weed! Tumbleweed!!"

And the dog bounded panting out of the night, nearly knocking him down. They hugged and played and wrestled until he was as soaked with snow as Weed was and the floor was a soggy mess: A glorious, grateful, wonderful mess!

The blizzard wind howled louder, and the two took a last look outside before he firmly shut the door. Then they both settled down enough to have a bit of supper and settle into the comfort of the cozy chic she'd left behind, secure in the light and warmth of home.

Spring Sleet

I hopped around on one foot, trying to dislodge the sleet from my boot. How had it gotten there in the first place? Let me go back a few hours.

It was actually a beautiful spring day when I stepped out my front door. I was wearing a new pair of fashion boots that went beautifully with a skirt I had picked up for a song at the same store. I use the term fashion boots loosely here. I guess they were more like booties than boots. Not that I didn't like the knee high things that made you look a step away from a magazine spread, and not that I didn't have a pair. I did. They were in the back of my closet. After wearing them once, and then again to prove to myself my ankles could take the punishment, I silently admitted I would never be a step away from a magazine spread. I would be a block away at least, and that was if I was a distant relative of someone who worked there – which I wasn't. My relatives worked at unglamorous places like recycling centers and school buildings and discount stores. I, myself, was on my way to my job at the local library. And I was pretty thrilled due to my new skirt and the boot(ie)s that matched. Camel brown. I never said I was a flashy dresser.

I'd arrived to the accolades of my fellow librarian – she knew how to flatter, believe me, having access to Roget's College Thesaurus on a regular basis – and settled into another uneventful day behind the desk by the door. Polly (the aforementioned co-worker) had the jitters today. Since it was a quiet day (librarian humor), I sauntered over to the stacks where she was replacing returned books to their proper alphabetical home in between tapping her fingers on the cart, and asked her how it was going. There was no doubt she'd tell me what made her jumpy the minute I took a step into the aisle. She did not disappoint.

"See that guy over there?"

She nodded in the direction of a table near the back.

I raised my eyebrows. No one ever sat in the back. The folks who came to our library were starved for anything that looked remotely like friendship, which included people who walked past their table nodding hello.

"Why do you think he's back *there*?"

"Who is he?" I answered helpfully.

Polly shrugged and returned to tapping her fingers on the library cart.

The man began gathering his things at the table, so I scooted back to the front desk in case he planned to check something out.

"Hi," I smiled as friendly as I could when he approached the desk.

He nodded, and put a couple of books in front of me.

"Would you like to get a library card?"

To my surprise he shoved one in front of me. He'd clearly been here before, though neither Polly nor I had any idea who he was.

I tried to look disinterested as I checked out his books. He grabbed them and hurried out.

Polly rushed over.

"Well?"

"Stuart Demone."

"Never heard of him."

"Me neither. He checked out *How to Build a Compost* and *Autolysis.*"

Polly's sharp intake of breath told me she knew what it meant and it wasn't good.

"Body decomposition! Body decomposition!" she whisper-shouted. "Go! Go!"

"What?"

"Follow him to see where he goes!"

"And what if he sees me?"

"Tell him . . . tell him you want to know if he needs a book about worms," she said pushing me out the door.

I should've known that wouldn't be a good excuse.

As she pushed me out the door, the fleeting question of why Polly was so insistent rang in my thoughts. Granted, her life was nearly as routine as mine. At least I thought it was. We'd both lived in this town long enough to know everyone's histories as well as each other's; okay – admittedly assumed histories. As with people the world over, we knew what we were told.

Stuart Demone was easily a block ahead of me. I was slightly curious about him, but nowhere nearly as curious as Polly was. What would following him get either of us? He arrived at an average house on an average block midway through town. Well that was just perfect. Nothing here promised to jolt me out of my boring librarian existence, but I kept walking as he opened his front door. If I continued on to the block behind it, I would be able to see if he had room for a compost bin. I craned my neck to see in between houses. It appeared his backyard was every bit as average as his house. Yes, there was room for a bin, but that was no surprise. What was a surprise is that there was already one there. It was by the side of his garage.

I gathered my nerve, approached the back of his garage, and peeked through the windows that lined the top of the wide door. A lawn mower, shovels and rakes, a hose, some buckets, and boards enough that they rose probably four feet when stacked along one side of the building. But what was missing from the garage was a car.

Now I suppose it's not out of the question for someone to be without a vehicle, but in this part of the country most people have one. Otherwise, where would you find a battery to jump on cold days or take to the repair shop on others? However, a grown man living alone without a vehicle was curious, at least to me. It lent itself to all sorts of questions.

There wasn't much else to see. I'd followed Stuart Demone and discovered he had boards in his garage and no car. I would report back to Polly and wash my hands of her jitters. If she wanted more information, she could scout it out herself.

As I started back to the library, the air grew chill, then it began to rain, then sleet. My boots! I began to run. It was more of a jog, but it is what it is.

Rather distressed about the weather and its effect on my new boot(ie)s, I dodged into the first building I reached. It was a coffee shop called Ground Zero, and it was there that (as you recall) I pulled off a boot to shake the sleet from it.

It was also there that, just as I was doing so, someone nudged open the door nearly knocking me over. I guess I'd not moved over enough to be avoided; plus hopping on one foot tends to diminish one's balance, so there's that. I looked up from the sleet on the floor and into the eyes of Stuart Demone.

One thing sprang to mind and slipped out of my mouth.

"Autolysis," I whispered, dropping my boot in the process.

A puzzled frown flitted across Stuart Demone's face. "What?"

"What?" I congratulated myself on the dodgy comeback and busied myself with putting my boot back on. When I looked back again, he'd gone to place his order. It seemed perfect timing to make my exit. But one look outside at sleet still falling changed my plan. It was an uncomfortable situation, but I chose boots over comfort. I was determined to save them. Plus, it had grown plenty chill and I was without a warm coat, considering it had been a lovely day when I left for work. Perhaps I could find a table out of his sight until the weather cleared.

I ordered a turtle latte and a cinnamon scone. I might as well have something enjoyable to come to my aide during this awkward situation. Consoling myself with the thought that maybe I wouldn't have to stay out of his sight if Stuart Demone left once he had his coffee, I perused the menu on the back wall. The server was quick, and presented me with my order in a few minutes.

To my dismay, Ground Zero had grown quite popular just now and, as my eyes roamed for a place to sit, they landed on the one empty chair in the entire room. Stuart Demone motioned for me to sit across from him. I stifled a sigh and tried for a friendly smile instead. As I made my way over, I wondered who he had killed, where he had hidden the body, and how long it would take for autolysis. (It appeared Polly was more of an influence on me than I'd realized. After all, maybe he had a dead pet fish he was wondering about rather than flushing it down the toilet.)

To my chagrin, Mr. Demone wasted no time.

"Funny," he said, "I thought you said autolysis when you saw me."

"I . . ." I searched my brain for something that rhymed with it so I could claim he'd misunderstood me and could only come up with 'paralysis'. No help.

"Actually, I *am* doing a little research in the area."

I nearly choked on my scone.

"It's quite interesting, really."

He suddenly sounded like a professor.

"Is it?"

"Why yes!"

His speech quickened, but I have to admit, I didn't miss a thing.

By the time he had taken me on a journey of the Egyptian pyramids clear over to the ones in Alaska (Alaska??), described estivation (it's hibernation for worms – I know, right? Clearly he didn't need a book about worms and my original excuse for following him would've fallen flat.) and delved into some history I'd never read, much less heard of or thought of, I was done with my latte and on my second scone.

Stuart Demone suddenly looked at his watch.

"Why look at the time! I must pick up my car. It needed new tires."

Looking across the table at Mr. Demone, I thought to myself I'd never met a more curious person in my life.

I got back to the library with a only a few hours left of my shift. Polly was distraught and actually hugged me when I walked through the door.

"I thought I'd never see you again! Are you okay? Tell me everything!"

I did, and by the time I finished, the work day was, too. Polly had gradually calmed down and hesitantly agreed her imagination might have run a bit too far. I scolded her. That was what she got for haunting the stacks that held mystery fiction. Perhaps she should stick to non-fiction like the rest of us with both feet planted solidly on the ground.

Polly had evening plans, so I told her I'd lock up. I went to the desk for the key and noticed some returned books stacked to the side. I might as well get a head start on tomorrow's work and put them away.

I replaced a Jan Karon book and a worn Daniel Defoe. I glanced down at the last two books in my hand . . . *How to Build a Compost* and *Autolysis.* My heart skipped a beat. Nobody reads that fast. When had Stuart Demone even returned them? I hurried to the back stacks to put them away. Locking up quickly suddenly seemed like a good idea.

As I scanned the shelves, I felt slightly faint. What was this? *A Complete History of the Alaskan Pyramids* and *Heaven's Water* by none other than Stuart Demone. I pulled them both from the shelf, backed into a chair where I sat and began to read. *A Complete History of the Alaskan Pyramids* discussed some of what Mr. Demone had described at Ground Zero. It was intriguing to say the least. Even Polly would have a hard time believing what I read. Time passed too quickly, so I decided to take both books home with me. I didn't check them out.

Once I'd had a light supper, I settled into my most comfortable chair and picked up *Heaven's Water*. It was amazing! The book spoke of bright water whose color was a sort of azure and turquoise with glints of pink and green. The author said it was impossible to describe in this world. I rubbed both hands over my scrunched face. What? He went on to say that it bubbled and rippled; that one could sink underneath the surface and still breathe; and that its delightful sensations tingled and refreshed, healed and energized.

I read until the moon was high in the sky and continued until the sun peeked over the horizon. It felt like an hour.

I couldn't get enough. Too soon I reached the last page. Inscribed in the author's own hand was a note. To me! I shakily pulled it out and read:

Life is not as average as it appears. Around every corner is something unseen, in every person is a hidden treasure yet to be revealed, and time holds more promise than anyone understands. Yet there is given to those of us who have stepped from this world to the next an opportunity to share what we are learning here: history hidden from most, science yet undiscovered, and beauty indescribable and unattainable to the most gifted artist. So when you see something out of order – for instance, winter's sleet in the spring – it is then that a few of us are instructed to step back over the portal and share some of the work we enjoy in heaven's realms with those still bound to the misunderstandings

of earth. You are not unglamorous! You are treasured.
—S.D.
P.S. Great boots!

I called in sick to work. I needed time to think. I wandered to the window – maybe I would take a walk. The spring day was as beautiful as I'd ever seen. I pulled on my new boots and stepped out the door.

. . . and then it began to sleet.

The Heirloom

Rain pelted the window as the wind shook it. He pulled on some woolen socks, scraped a kitchen chair out from the table, and picked up the pocket watch. It had been handed down for six generations and had landed in his possession when his father died.

He didn't need it. He had a watch. It was a Tissot. No Rolex, granted, but not bad for an accountant. He'd thought of getting cash for the heirloom at a pawnshop, but then had thought better. He examined the pocket watch, turning it over, and thought of family members who had owned it before him. Most of them had kept it hidden away in a drawer, as far as he knew. His family wasn't one for following each other's dreams; only their own. Besides, he chuckled to himself, who would want to be an accountant? But it held interest for him, and interest was good in oh so many ways.

He ran his thumb over the words in pretty script at the bottom of the watch: *World's Fair Chicago 1893*. What the Great Chicago Fire didn't accomplish, the World's Fair was designed to finish. What a morose thought! Still. Was a sullen truth worse than a happy lie? He knew he wasn't alone in thinking that despite the story of Mrs. O'Leary's cow, it wasn't likely that a kicked-over lantern would have burned down over three miles of a city. Poor Mrs. O'Leary: living out her life in relative reclusion what with the notoriety of the story! But, he thought, a fire can destroy as surely without a conclusive origin as with one. And destruction is useful for someone who wants to build back better. Yes, what the Chicago fire didn't do, a World's Fair might. He scolded himself for thinking it. It was a nice-looking watch, after all.

He pulled an old book from his bookshelf and paged through it, not for the first time. His eyes drifted to the part about the Midway Plaisance, but despite it's name, he didn't feel pleased. Those at the very top of the Fair's planning, the ones with the money, said they were celebrating the past, while in reality planning a future the unsuspecting attendees wouldn't have believed. Albert Pike and his green ink would have approved. But he felt no attraction to the glorious accounts of the spectacle. He was not impressed, and he knew why. Over the years he had read more than he wished he had read. It had changed his initial curiosity to distaste. Oh yes. He knew why he felt no attraction. He didn't worship their god.

He rose and went to the window. The rain had stopped and even the little droplets from the storm had found their home at the bottom of the outside sill. The *Fair that changed America.* Give them bread and circuses! People still wanted a progressive utopia with all of its moving parts, and those who had planned it all long ago would have been pleased to hear of it. *He* appreciated one thing – a very big thing: Nikola Tesla's alternating current. History claimed Tesla's lights illuminated the Fair as the first rays of Arcturus began to show themselves. He added Arcturus to the short list. He could appreciate a very old star such as that. Stars, after all, were time keepers, too. And light in the darkness was grand whether through electricity or nature or Spirit. Yes, there was always something to appreciate among the detritus of history.

He felt the weight of the pocket watch in his hand. And time. He could appreciate – even value – time. He stared into space. Light broke darkness with time. He needed time. The whole world needed time. Precious, precious time. He started over to his desk drawer to stow the heirloom as generations before him had done, then paused, and slipped the watch into his pocket instead.

Buyer's Remorse

When I clicked, it was more of out of curiosity than intent. Then I decided I was hungry, and fixed myself a scone with grape preserves. That, of course, needed a cup of coffee to go with it, giving me even more time to ponder the possibilities from the admittedly vague listing on my computer. I don't know if they do that for you, but scones always put me in an agreeable mood. By the time I'd followed possibility after peculiarity after potential, and after I'd polished off both scone and coffee, I'd contacted my bank, signed some papers, and become the proud owner of a house sight unseen.

Oh sure. Like you've never done something on impulse!

Don't mind my defensiveness. The jitters I get when I think of what I've done could send me into the next decade, not that those years look any more promising than the ones everyone is bemoaning this year. Or last year. Or even the year before that. Maybe I should stop counting.

Anyway, that original, innocent click on the listing on my computer led me to a weekend trip outside of my usual paths. In addition to jitters, I was also a bit excited. Me! A homeowner! Visions of cute cottages with herb gardens and hunting lodges surrounded by bendy pines filled my imagination.

I rechecked the directions, and turned onto a long dirt lane. Yes, I have GPS. I'm not 60. I'm 27 and I know a thing or two. But my cell service stopped working about 20 miles back. Fortunately, the guy at the last gas station assured me with a creepy sort of smile that cell service is spotty in these parts, so after I'd gassed up and before starting out again, I'd taken advantage of what I hadn't known would be the last of the reassuring, if not somewhat annoying, voice telling me which way to turn, and had written down directions I'd pulled up from a phone map service. Did I say the lane was long? And dirt? Because I feel like that's something you need to know. At least I think *I* do.

Finally I pulled up to the front of my new house, which was neither cottage nor hunting lodge. And as I sat behind my steering wheel peering at the structure in front of me, I thought to myself that I should've sworn off my love of scones long ago.

Not without a huge sigh (part uncertainty and part regret), I disembarked from my car and just stood, looking. The house was surrounded by trees on both sides, in addition to the long lane I had just trekked. But some wild daisies sprinkled amidst the long grasses lent me comfort. A meadow of what appeared to be weeds of different sorts was visible if I leaned to peer around the side of the building, which I did. Weeds. How apt.

The house, itself, well, not really a house — I don't know what to call it; was more than a shed, less than a respectable cabin — was fronted with a sagging porch with four steps ascending. I took the challenge, and, as I did, heard some scurrying underneath. I had company without even sending housewarming invitations! Lovely.

I fished the key from my pocket and unlocked the front door. It was sturdy! I took the win and stepped inside. Remarkably enough, it was furnished with decent furniture, clearly from past generations.

I blew dust from a side table holding a lamp and the lamp wobbled until I grabbed it. It seemed a nice piece, perhaps even valuable in its day. I would hate to be the owner that broke it. Then I wondered how many owners there had been: if I was the second after an original or near the end of a long line of proprietors. I wandered through the rooms: a living room, kitchen, bedroom, and even a small bathroom (I was pleasantly surprised, though held no certainty that it worked). Beyond the kitchen, to the back of the house, was a sleeping porch, complete with a swinging bed held to the rafters by sturdy chains. My eyes scanned the mattress full of acorns.

Dusk was creeping over the yard by the time I brought in my belongings. There had been more to explore than at first glance. For one thing, there was a root cellar. I know! I saved my examination of it for daylight when I could clear the spiderwebs with greater assurance of seeing whether the spiders were elsewhere.

In my inspection of the bedroom, I had literally stumbled into what sounded like a hollow place in the wall near the head of the bed. I scraped the bed across the floor in order to get a closer look. With a little effort, I broke through the false part and found a compartment which held my interest as well as, it appeared, things from a past owner.

I pulled out my sturdy flashlight and spent my evening reading the papers I had found. By the time my eyes were gritty with sleep, I knew my new house was not the tumbledown shack it appeared to be.

It wasn't the sun's rays that woke me, but the scampering of little feet belonging to who knew what. On the heels of the sound, though, the sun peeked over the horizon, and I watched as red turned to orange and pink, filling the sky with indescribable color and hope.

I sipped day old coffee (bought from the gas station the day before and surprisingly still hot) from my thermos and mulled over my options. I had one more day to explore . . . okay, I know it shouldn't take even a half hour to explore something like my "new house", but the things stored in the wall told me otherwise.

It's interesting, isn't it, what you can learn from letters, journal entries, recipes, newspaper clippings, and the like. And hand-drawn maps. Innuendo isn't only for mainstream media, politicians, and trashy novels, you know. And some of the things that I'd read in that place between wakefulness and sleep made me think that my house was like the lid of a jar. I determined to open it. I spread out some of the things I'd read and read them again to make sure I hadn't been dreaming.

By the time dark enveloped my property, I'd made a plan. Now I'm not saying you should follow my example. In fact, I'm pretty sure you shouldn't. But I concluded that if I was to honestly own this place, I should be more than a curiosity seeker. What I'm saying is that some people are owners in name only. They might have something, for instance, from an inheritance, but rarely visit it and value it only for its eventual monetary worth. Getting back to my conclusion: if I was to honestly own this place, I should take ownership – you know, like people do who actually believe something is theirs and that they are in charge of it. Like that. Which meant (in my mind) I needed to be more than a visitor on convenient weekends.

It had begun raining before I went to bed, and I took advantage of it by setting out some pots and pans to collect the water. Even *I* am amazed at how well I think ahead sometimes. The next morning I cleaned. Okay, I mostly swept and sprayed the all-purpose cleaner with a "light lemon scent" I'd brought with me all over everything. At least I had rinse water!

I put away things I'd planned to take back with me and locked the door. I'd written my letter of resignation to my employer the night before, but hadn't sent it. Sometimes spotty cell (and in this case, internet) service can save you from yourself, not that I planned on being saved. You have your personality, I have mine.

I watched my new house grow smaller in the rearview mirror as I drove down the long lane and back to my normal that would never seem normal again.

I was about halfway down the lane when I began to regret that it wasn't paved. The rain from the night before (the one I had commended myself about thinking ahead and putting out pots and pans to catch the rain – that one) had left not only friendly puddles here and there, but an unfortunate puddle the size of my ex-boyfriend's propensity for lying – excuses with holes in timelines and logic that defied the imagination of any reasonable person . . . but I digress. For those of you uninterested in detours, let me just say it was a very large puddle that covered the breadth of the road, and leave it at that. However, I managed to skirt it by going off-road for the minute it took to go around it.

The next morning I dropped off my car at the auto shop (the off-road minute had compromised the front axle), walked the extra mile to work, and stepped into the office as though I hadn't entered another world in one weekend.

I had decided to be dignified and personally hand in my resignation. Before I could hand it to my boss, he pulled me aside. He had a special assignment requiring some amount of delicacy and would I be willing to work remotely for the next six months or however long it would take to complete it? To wit: was I willing to disappear while on assignment?

Okay. I must take another detour here, and I'm sorry for those of you who get hives from such things, but it must be done. You see, I work in forensics, my boss is a fairly well-known lawyer, and there have been things that have crossed my desk from time to time that have given me pause. And while I can be impulsive, I can also be circumspect in office conversation. And although there are gaping holes in some of my life skills, I've become rather good at my job. So you'll understand that when the word "delicacy" is used, the reputation or worse of someone of note is very possibly at risk.

I scrunched my face as though I needed to think about it, not as though I had to guard against jumping up and down. He hurriedly assured me the firm would pay any related costs. I blinked fast, which made him offer me an increase in salary. I inquired whether paving a lane could be included in the offer and he gave me his hasty affirmation. I began to think that if I stayed any longer I would own the firm, but who wants that headache? We shook hands, I cleaned out my desk, and made arrangements for a satellite internet that would impress Tim Cook.

It's been two months, my lane is as smooth as a baby's bottom, the electricity and utilities work as well as the government, and

I've settled in. I've uncovered pieces of the lives of the people who lived here before me, thoroughly cleaned the root cellar and began to stock it, and found a use for the weeds behind the house (yes, I'm calling it a house in order to reassure myself that my future isn't as bleak as the person whose delicate matter I'm researching). The weeds? I discovered that many of them were herbs or had some kind of usefulness. It's going to take me longer than two months to figure it all out.

The puzzle that keeps me up at night, though, isn't the weeds. It's some of the letters that were hidden in the wall. Oh I fixed it. Who wants a hole in the wall? But I mean to say that those lives – the ones of the people who wrote the letters – they were full of courageous words. And as I look at my surroundings, I can't for the life of me figure out why they would need to be brave and wish I knew. What's the expression? Be careful what you wish for.

I woke with a start at the edge of morning while it was still dark. And it was. Pitch black. My heart was racing, but there was no dream in memory that could have prompted it. I reached for my bedside lamp and turned it on. It's a gift, isn't it, when the electricity works? The utilities in my new home being what they were, I was quickly learning gratefulness for those little things.

There was nothing out of place. I looked at my watch. It was 4:00. Some people go to work at this time of day, I reasoned. I certainly wasn't in the mood to return to pitch black.

I was dressed and at my computer, files spread on the table, and a cup of coffee accompanied by a lemon poppy seed scone next to it by 4:30. I'd stocked up on scone ingredients before I left the city. Don't judge. It's harder to think freely or analyze when feeling emotional, and I needed both in my work. Scones were my way to rise above the fear I had felt upon waking. Emotional eating has its uses. Due to my early start, I finished for the day by early afternoon.

I was by now in the habit of using my afternoons to (try to) fix the broken down mess I'd bought, and was accomplishing at least a little. I had reconstructed my front porch. That was somewhat of an accomplishment, I assured myself. I'd pulled down cupboards, sanded and painted them, and somehow gotten them back in place so my dishes didn't slide toward the cupboard door like they had at first. You have no idea the pleasure it is to open a cupboard door without bracing for destruction. This afternoon, I'd pushed and pulled and carried everything out of the living room whose floors I planned to sand as my evening entertainment.

In the meantime, I brought my box of the things retrieved from the hole in the wall, sat on the porch to await the sunset, and mulled over loose connections floating around in my brain.

I got to bed later than usual. Sanding can be a messy project. One board, in particular, had given me terrible trouble until I realized it had been pulled up and nailed down again. It didn't take much to pull it up, and what I discovered had kept me awake until the wee hours.

Deeds! There had been an actual treasure trove of stuff underneath the floorboard, but deeds — as in plural — were what caught my attention. I wondered, and not for the first time, if the information I was finding in the house had been hidden out of distress or laziness. I couldn't tell. What I *could* tell, however, was that I apparently owned more than I had initially believed and most probably what the seller had known about as well.

I also learned that there was a tunnel starting behind what I had originally thought were just boards to supply a sort of underpinning to the root cellar. One Saturday I took a flashlight and a broom for both spiderwebs and weaponry – okay, I know (But still) and explored it. It traveled underneath the sleeping porch and then another two or so miles and ended at the far end of an old-fashioned covered bridge (I own a covered bridge!). I'm still not sure why someone dug a tunnel, and a long one (at least to me) at that. I found nothing to smuggle from my house and wondered what had been of such value or danger in the past. So many whys.

But I do know a thing or two about deeds and I confirmed my ownership of the additional property I hadn't known about.

I couldn't do things as quickly as I would have liked, because I still had to sort out "the delicate matter" to which I'd been assigned. Looking back, I should've figured things out more quickly. But I didn't. I blame myself for that, but I also forgive myself for it because all of God's children sometimes stumble even with the lights on. It took 7 days straight of waking up at 4 a.m. before it clicked. Somewhere in the back of my mind, I'd heard the term 4 a.m. talking points. It must have tweaked my unconscious until I made a waking connection. Once I did, I could see clearly that the information I was given – the talking points as my subconscious told me – wasn't the whole story. I won't discuss the matter other than to say I found myself having to confront my boss and resign from my job and what lately had been a decent remote work arrangement. Oh I could've stayed and lived with the pretense that I hadn't connected him to the matter needing discretion. I could've kept my mouth shut. I had done so in the past, and that's probably why he gave me the assignment. But having learned about courage from the former inhabitants of this place, I couldn't very well do it now. Finding myself in the line of owners of this crumbling edifice, for some reason I didn't want to let them down. I became an independent contractor and found more than enough remote work to stay at my new old rundown home. I can assert it is no longer new to me, but it is still definitely rundown.

It's been a year! One year ago today I bought a house sight unseen. It was a ridiculous decision, and I clearly understood the term *buyer's remorse* the minute I pulled in front of my ill-considered purchase. Do I still have buyer's remorse? About the house – yes, indeed. It's terrible and will take more time and money than I want to invest to make it comfortable and appealing. But I bought more than I knew.

And this is what I learned: The things in this life that we are given to own may look to us like a tumbledown bit of nothing. They may appear without merit or too far gone to salvage. And yet. And yet what is hidden from us, what is unseen, and what, if we make the effort to uncover, we eventually discover is far greater than what meets the eye.

Now excuse me while I drink a cup of coffee, enjoy my lemon poppy seed scone, and watch the sunset. Oh yes – and admire the sign I placed in front of my house just this afternoon. It is the name I have given my property: ***Hole In The Wall.***

Christmas
Miracle
Stories

Two Blind Men

The snow fell like little diamonds on the two as they walked, deep in conversation. Oblivious to the scenes around them, they reminded the company president of two ants as he glanced down from the window of his top floor office before returning to his work. As the friends made their way past the large window of a corner café, a patron looked out and saw that in the intensity of their conversation, they did not notice the woolen scarf of the one closest to the window had caught on the window ledge, was pulled from where it had carelessly rested on his coat and now lay in the gathering snow beneath. An old woman in a thread-bare coat turned the corner they had just rounded, found the scarf and, crossing herself, bent to retrieve it, wrapping it around her neck to gain its precious warmth. The stars began to come out, winking here and there in the dark velvet sky and casting pinprick lights from their million miles away in the heavens. The two increased their pace, as they trudged up a slight hill in their walk.

The voice of one rose, "I'm telling you, all of us want a miracle,"

"If such things exist," the other interrupted.

"If such things exist," the one acknowledged, "but no one wants to be in the place it would take to get one. Nobody wants to be in the place where a miracle is their only option. Who wants to have everything taken away with nothing to fall back on? Who wants to feel so desperate they think they'll go crazy?"

His companion nodded his head.

"At any rate," the companion replied, "if someone did witness a miracle,"

"If such things exist," the one reminded him.

"If such things exist," the companion agreed," he would have had to wish for it or ask for it for a very long time, I would think."

"Oh, no doubt about it," the one remarked, as they unwittingly passed the life-size crèche in the yard of a local church, "a person would absolutely need to know they needed it before they witnessed a miracle."

The Box

She picked up the box and examined it. It was ivory with the raised shape of a deer in the center and outlines of vines and berries traveling over its surface. How often had she passed by this box without noticing the detail that had gone into its design? How many days had she seen it without really looking at it?

Hers was a lifetime of inattention, she thought. A lifetime of distraction and hurry. Life was, after all, so full of details and important things that could not wait. It had happened so quickly that thinking of it now still made her shake her head as if to clear it. A knock at the door interrupted her thoughts.

"Ms. Stryker?"

She turned and looked at the care attendant.

"Sybil. Just Sybil," she answered.

"Ms. Stryker, the van is here to take you for your doctor's appointment."

A lump began forming in her throat. It would be the same as it had been for over two years now. Always the same. Probing and asking questions over and over again, questions she had by now memorized. The prognosis was set in stone.

"I'll be there in a minute," she answered, dismissing the attendant with a nod.

Upon learning of her paraplegic state, it had not taken long for her husband to leave her and even less time for her to lose her job. Visitors had come and gone. Family members showed up on a rotating basis, except for her grandmother. Her grandmother had come that first horrible night and had taken a taxi every Sunday after church thereafter, sitting and visiting; telling jokes; singing in her warbling, wavering, winsome soprano; and bringing some small thing now and then – a tin of cookies or an article from the newspaper or a little memento from home. And sometime during each of those visits her grandmother would sit in silent prayer, intent and immoveable.

One time Sybil had said out loud what she thought whenever she saw her grandmother's eyes begin to close or to stare off into space into a realm through which most others didn't pass. "Grandma, stop praying for a miracle. It's done. I've accepted it. We need to move on."

Her grandmother had simply glanced up and caught her eye with an intensity she remembered from her childhood. It was a look that said, "Do not presume to know more than your elder".

The next Sunday, her grandmother had brought the box from Sybil's parents' home where she had left it along with the things of childhood so many years ago. It was one that her grandmother had given to her when she was born. She had stored little treasures in it when she was young, then it had sat on her dresser through years of other, more important things. The Sunday she brought it, her grandmother had set it on her dresser and there it had remained without a glance from its owner.

Just this week, she had felt an inexplicable prompting to examine it, but ignored its pull. Why? It wasn't as though she had pressing meetings any longer, nor appointments nor social engagements nor visits from friends. Not many, anyway.

The care attendant came to her door again.

"Ms. Stryker, the driver says he's on a schedule. You really need to come. Here, let me help you," she said as she moved to take the handles of the wheelchair.

"No," Sybil said more firmly than she had in a long time. She softened. "No, tell him I need just another minute."

She lifted the lid, expecting to find some little trinket of a forgotten childhood. None was there. Instead it was filled with slips of paper. She picked up one near the top and read, "Please help her to be a good girl. Bless her life. Keep her safe."

Sybil's eyebrows knit in confusion. She picked up another. "I don't know what's bothering her at school, but would you please help her? Please send a good friend. Please give her success."

"She says she's in love and she doesn't see him clearly, so I'm asking you to help her see. Or change him. Either one."

"Oh thank you, thank you, thank you for this dear girl."

As she pulled slip after slip out of the box, tears burned her eyes as she began to realize what she was reading. Long after the slips should have run out, long after there were more in her lap than could have ever fit in the box, they continued, spilling onto the floor.

"If only that deer had crossed the highway a minute later. If only she had been delayed or left for home sooner. Oh, I know I'm going on like you know I do. Please heal her. Please make her walk again."

"Please, somehow help her to believe that you are bigger than she is or her doctor is or anything is in this world. Help her to believe in miracles."

Sybil reached for a Kleenex and dabbed harshly at her eyes. She pulled her chair closer to the dresser to set the box in its place, but as she picked it up, she lost her grip and it began to fall. It would break, she knew. There would be no putting it back together. She lunged for it, and that's when it happened.

She didn't fall. And as she stood for the first time in two years, the rescued box in her hands, she looked up. There in the doorway was her grandmother.

"I had a feeling you might want to go for a walk today," was all she said as Sybil left the wheelchair and walked to the door.

A Sparrow Falls

A film of ice crystals hung in the air, obscuring the faint light of the gibbous moon and adding their frosty touch to the piercing cold. The woods, quiet in the approaching night, cast long shadows over the sparse ground. A crispy, brown leaf, the refugee of the fall just past, scuttered over the ice-covered snow, caught briefly on a downed tree's twig, then, slightly ragged from its collision, was caught in the wind's updraft and smashed against a tree trunk, its crumbling pieces disappearing into the night.

The cold this year had come suddenly, like death; anticipated in the future but never expected in the present. One morning the frost of the evening before had warmed to the happy coolness of autumn. Hardy plants that had withstood the night's cold showed their oranges and rusts and ambers to a day that warmed the ground again with the promise of more. The sun shone high and bright in a sky of faded blue.

Geese had stopped to rest on the lakes, then rose up again, beckoned by some silent call and formed their V in a goodbye for now salute. Sparrows had danced in the sky in an undulating arch as they made their way to warmer climes.

Then it hit. A cold Arctic wind swept down into the day of promised Autumn warmth and stripped it of its heat. In the bluster of snow and ice that surprised even the birds, one was swept from its migrating course, left behind by the others struggling now to fly fast and high. Carried by the wicked wind, it found some relief in the shelter of a nearby woods; but the wind continued until the day waned, and the exhausted bird huddled under a bare bush as the wind died and the cold remained.

The little bird, its brown feathers covering a downy layer underneath, began to shiver. Its energy was spent, so as day turned to night it lay, as it must, ready for its fate, understanding somehow it had seen its last dawn. It lay under the white light of the moon in the impenetrable cold with nothing to shield it when above the bird the dancing movement of a tiny light caught its attention.

About the size of a quarter, the light sparkled and danced and bobbed and flashed within the space of a square foot or so. Seeing it brought to the bird a sense of happiness; the kind of happiness and freedom it felt in the spring when the plants broke from the earth in a carefree chorus of liberation. Watching it gave the little bird a temporary reprieve from its cold nest of hardened earth and icy snow and reminded it of warm rains and sweet air and dependable sunlight. The light took away its fear. As it watched the light, entertained by its dance in the middle of the cold night, it sensed another presence.

A wolf walked silently through the woods, watching the light, too, as if it was calling him by name. The bird tried to blend into the bush as much as it could. The wolf would be hungry on such a night. But as surely as birds migrate south for winter, as surely as light breaks through darkness, the wolf padded softly right over to where the little bird huddled. It lay down so closely to the bird that its black and gray fur touched the brown feathers. It, too, watched the dancing light, and through the long night the little bird was warmed by the heat of the wolf until it slept and regained its strength. As morning dawned and the sun broke through the sharp cold of the night, the wolf rose from its place of rest and trotted deeper into the woods.

And, after a snack of dried berries from the bush under which it had hidden, the little bird took flight.

Miracle on Hoover Street

It started out like a typical morning. She woke up at 6:00, prayed for various things and people, lacking the energy for the fervent prayer mentioned in the Bible, but with the knowledge that when you don't have the energy to do something right, you do what you can. She got up at 6:30, plodded into the kitchen in her bathrobe and slippers, poured a cup of yesterday's cold coffee with a splash of milk, and settled into her rocking chair to read a chapter in the Bible, something she'd done nearly every day since she was baptized when a 4th grader. It was a habit. It was a good habit. It did for her what she could not do for herself. It grounded her. It supplied wisdom that wasn't hers. It made her believe in miracles.

It was December 23rd, and a few things still needed to be done before Christmas Day. She ran down to the laundry room, started a load of laundry and was grateful that some things did most of the work themselves, like a washing machine. She drove to the mall and picked up a few last minute gifts, then to the grocery store and home again to put everything away. She still needed to run into the city to shovel a walk or two at the home of her parents and their neighbors and fix greenery and berries in their window box — something that had been delayed due to the cold. It didn't appear the cold would abate anytime soon, though, and Christmas was two days away! She would have to haul out the ladder and get it done despite the single digit temperature.

She called her teenage son to help her (the ladder would be too heavy for one person, or at least for her to manage alone), threw a shovel in the backseat, and pulled out of the driveway.

"Slow down, Mom," her son cautioned.

The newly licensed driver was telling his mother what she sometimes said to him when their places were reversed. When did he get to be so responsible? However, five or ten miles per hour over the limit wasn't hurting anyone, and Christmas was two days away!

A train whistle sounded in concert with her son's voice. She looked to her left, and there it was. What?! She had never, in all the years she'd taken this route, seen a train on this rarely used track. She braked, but the car slid on the snowy street into the path of the coming train. She could see every detail on the approaching train and as crazy as it was, considering the situation, thought it was pretty. Things do that. During the emergencies of life, things slow down, details sharpen. Maybe that's the way things really are, and all of the other times, the times when we go about our daily business, are when we see least clearly. She gunned the accelerator and flew over the track as the train passed behind them.

And that was when two facts made their way to the front of all of the other things that needed to be done two days before

Christmas. Christmas would come whether or not there was enough food in the refrigerator or the house was clean or cookies were baked. It would come despite the most beautiful decorations or no decorations at all. It would come because birthdays aren't dependent on what we do in the days and months and years afterward to celebrate the event, but because the event happened at a place in time and cannot be changed whether people want to celebrate it or ignore it or despise it.

The second fact she remembered was that life is a series of doing what you can with God filling in the gaps. She was grateful for that because she would never be great or even adequate, but God would always be more than enough.

<hr>

And that, dear readers, is a miracle that is personal; because the she in this post is me, and Christmas is one day away, and I'm still here.

The Light of a Flickering Candle

The year was at its close, and while the green and red of Christmas had turned to the silver and gold of New Year's Eve decorations, one house stood still ensconced in its Christmas best. It had been ready for Christmas since before Thanksgiving, as though this Christmas held such goodness it could not wait for its allotted time on the calendar. To the passing observer glancing inside the window of the house there appeared to be stripes moving around. The stripes were red and blue, like a candy cane, running up and down a man's pajama pants and ending at the new brown suede slippers he wore on his feet. There was a time when those feet walked up and down and streets of the city delivering mail to its residents. Now, however, bad knees the man had acquired playing college football and the hip replacement he'd had just two months ago gave him more of a shuffle than a gait. He'd taken early retirement in the face of the surgery. For a man once strong and active, it was a hit, but he'd made the decision and was living with it and the surgery's resulting loss of strength.

Determination had helped him put up a tree for Christmas. Oh, it wasn't real. He'd succumbed to practicality when he finally climbed out of the depression that had come with his wife's death three years before, and just last year at his son's suggestion written in a hastily scrawled letter, he had bought one at the local hardware store. It went up a lot more quickly, but it didn't have the *je ne sais quoi* of the real ones sold at the lot six blocks away. Still, the lights he'd strung twinkled in the waning light of evening and ornaments collected over years of Christmases told stories of babies and childhoods and hobbies and beautiful things.

He'd climbed unsteadily on a chair and hung the mistletoe his wife had bought when they were newlyweds. He'd put out some throw pillows embroidered with poinsettias and manger scenes. As his eyes roamed over the room, it really did look like Christmas, he thought. It just needed one thing more. Every Christmas Eve since he was a boy, he'd set a candle in the window. It was for the Christchild, you see; for Mary and Joseph to find their way through the dark night to the safety of a warm place to stay. Though the first Christmas was long ago, maybe there was someone else needing that light and the warmth of home. That candlelight was more than just a light, like the star of Bethlehem. It was hope. It was invitation. It was love. It was peace. His mother had taught him that when he was old enough to light a match, and from then on that was his tradition. He'd passed it on to his son and hoped that one day his son would pass it on as well. He hoped, but he lacked certainty. Time could blur things from a son's memory, he knew. Experiences could change a son's priorities.

The trouble was his hand had grown unsteady from some of the medication his doctor insisted he take, and a creeping arthritis of late had made it weak. This night he'd tried and tried to light that match, but had only managed to achieve the slight odor of sulfur.

A knock at the door startled him and he shuffled to open it. It was the neighbor boy, there to belatedly collect the money he'd promised when he'd bought his wreath.

"Oh, Sammie, come in, come in," he said when he saw him. "I've got it right here."

He fished a twenty and a five out of his billfold lying on the end table and handed it to the boy.

"Say, could I ask a favor? You're a Boy Scout, after all, you do a good deed daily," he chuckled.

The boy looked bored, but nodded his head.

The man led him over the front window, and pulled a matchbook from his pajama pocket.

"Would you mind lighting this for me?" he asked.

"But it's after Christmas, Mr. Simmons. We've already got our Christmas tree down."

The man nodded.

"Yes, yes it's time to put things away, isn't it? But I just want to light this candle tonight and tomorrow I might think about putting things back in their boxes."

The boy struck the match and lit the candle. The man patted him on the back and walked him to the door.

"Thanks, Sammie."

Sammie nodded and jumped off the porch to join the friend who was accompanying him on his rounds.

"What took you so long?" his friend complained as they started down the street.

"Oh, the old man wanted a candle lit."

For some reason the boys found it funny and began to laugh as they went on their way. And the man watched them, lost in thought, as they jostled each other as boys will do.

The man finally made his way to the couch and watched some T.V. Then he did a crossword puzzle until, finally, his head drooped to his chest and he lightly slept while the candle burned. His dreams were filled with images of his boy; the boy he'd taught to ride a bike and catch a football and shoot a gun; the boy he hadn't seen in three years.

The sound of a taxi pulling up at the curb woke him, and he made his way to the window. A young man in uniform sat for a moment looking through the window of the taxi to the candle dancing brightly just inside. He climbed out, pulling his duffle after him. Running up the walk, he smiled broadly as he caught his father's eye through the light of the candle he had often thought of from a distant desert where such a thing had seemed very far away. Its glow reached beyond Christmas Eve, beyond an enlisted soldier's cot, beyond changes like death and retirement and surgeries, and wrapped the father and son in its promise.

Backdraft

She exhaled a puff of white that momentarily hung in the air before vanishing into the darkness. Hugging herself with her arms, she shivered; but she would stay just awhile longer to enjoy what she had come to see. They were pretty: twinkling beauty against the cold, night air. The lights had been strung the weekend before on evergreens encircling the skating rink. The tiny white bulbs that had graced the pines all the years before had been moved to the bushes and deciduous trees outside city hall. Resting in the now bare-boned branches, the lights gave a certain panache to the surroundings of the otherwise unremarkable building by which they stood.

But the red and green, blue and purple lights now lending their sparkle to the rink's evergreen edge were amazing. She thought, as she gazed at them, she hadn't seen anything so stunning in a long time. A very long time.

It had been ten years now since the fire, but in her mind it was yesterday. A neighbor – one she barely knew – who had resented her happy life even as she smiled and waved each time they met had channeled her jealousy into a lighted match thrown onto her morning paper resting on the jute rug in her small, enclosed

249

front porch. Her morning ritual to switch off the outdoor light and get the newspaper had resulted in a backdraft which sent her to the hospital for treatment she wished she could forget and a future she wished she could escape.

A morning jogger had provided testimony of the event, and the neighbor had gotten five years and the satisfaction of destroying the irritating happy life.

Knowing what had happened and why and punishing the perpetrator couldn't change the image she saw every time she looked in the mirror. Her scarred face and neck, once pretty – some said beautiful – were oppressive to see. The scars seemed to thicken with every year and a quiet, gnawing sadness grew with them.

She had avoided anything to do with fire, even light, at first. After its inhabitant had returned from the hospital, the neighbors saw a dark house, its interior as devoid of light as its owner's soul. Light was unavoidable, of course, and gradually she had allowed it in its many forms to filter back into her life. She had left all light switches untouched for a long time; but one day she had turned on a lamp, and the next week she turned on the kitchen light. She was able to flick those switches now, but only one room at a time. There was no point in wasting electricity.

It had been easy to remove reflective surfaces – vases, silver-plate, mirrors. The bathroom mirror had stayed. It was like living with an old friend she no longer appreciated. She didn't need a mirror to remind her of the fire's wrath. She saw it in the pitying faces of friends and the curious, repulsed, stolen glances of strangers. She felt it in the webbing between her thumb and forefinger.

A visitor to her hospital room had told her that maybe one day her skin would be as good as new, but forgiveness was more important than skin. It had to do with the inner pain, the pain that would never go away without it. He, she supposed, was an old chaplain looking for something to do or say; but his words were harsh. Forgiveness of the neighbor? Forgiveness of someone who had caused her such grief and pain seemed ridiculous. She hoped that neighbor would live hand to mouth, that she would have trouble finding work because of her criminal record, that she was disgusted with herself. The nurse attending her just then had completely ignored him. People could give care without caring, she had thought at the time. She had ignored him, too.

She had ignored everyone at first. It was two years after the explosion when she saw the old chaplain in a dream. He just stood, looking at her, waiting. The next time was at the grocery store. Well, actually, she couldn't be sure about that. She had thought she'd caught a glance, but when she looked more closely, he was gone. She thought about the jealous neighbor, and wondered where she was now.

Standing here looking at the lights, she felt a presence and turned her head to see the old chaplain standing next to her.

"Have you forgiven her yet?"

He said it as though their conversation begun with his comment in her hospital room had continued through the years. Here beside the Christmas lights the question seemed as natural as the evergreens in front of them.

"Does it matter? It's been so many years."

She could hardly believe it, but his standing next to her didn't bother her as it had that very first time. It didn't frighten her as it had in her dream, nor surprise her as it had at the grocery store. It seemed, in fact, somehow good – like he was a very old friend.

"Forgiveness always matters."

She stood, breathing white puffs into the night while the tree lights sparkled, the darkness exposing their beauty and color.

She thought about the neighbor, the woman whose jealousy of her happy life had inflamed the hostile act. That day's destruction was not limited to dwelling, but extended to thought and emotion, trust and memory. She breathed another vapor of white into the air. She was tired of it all. She knew now that she really did want to let it go; let all of it go. She wanted to release the debt. She nodded her head. Yes. She forgave the neighbor. She knew she could, and she really did.

Gazing anew at the Christmas lights, she breathed in their beauty and goodness. It seemed suddenly that their friendly, sparkling light shot into her soul baptizing it with warmth and brightness. She looked into the old chaplain's compassionate eyes and saw in them her reflection.

She blinked and peered more closely. Slowly she brought her hand up to her face, the skin between her thumb and forefinger no longer webbed. As she ran her fingers over her now smooth skin, she closed her eyes against the tears pooling there. Was it true? Had the stranger's comment long ago in the agony of her hospital room really taken place? Surely not. But she had forgiven – she knew that much – and when she had determined to let the transgression go, she really had felt a very strange pulse run through her body.

"What happened?" she asked as she opened her eyes.

But the old chaplain wasn't there, and the Christmas lights glowed brighter into the cold, dark night.

253

One Forgotten Thing

"Tonight, folks, you see the miracle of Christmas all around you. It is in the help given to a neighbor, the music resounding through stores and churches, in resplendent parades and pageants. It is in the tinsel and color and sparkle shining through each window. It is in the light of the eyes of a child. It is in our hearts."

Dan shrugged into his jacket and plucked the key from his pocket to lock the door. He had hit all the right notes tonight. The audience had chuckled and nodded at just the right places. It had become second nature by now. Just as his grandmother had hoped, he had become a very good speaker. Very good. He knew how to move a crowd, how to fill them with questions or anger or, like tonight, fill their hearts with the blessed joy of the holiday.

He stepped quickly down the cement steps, breathing in the cold night air. He stopped and looked around him at muted lights of a city gone dark and quiet on a night when most turned to home for nurture and entertainment. Christmas Eve.

As he turned the lock of his home, a striking building on an upscale city block, his foot nudged something on the top step.

Picking it up, he turned it over in his hands. A small piece from a crèche. Whose it was or how it had landed on his step he had no idea, but someone would be missing this tonight. Surely they would want it to complete the Christmas scene.

He bent down and dropped the infant Jesus back in its place as he stepped over it and shut his door. He would turn on one of those wonderful Christmas movies tonight and appreciate the stories with happy endings. He would drink cocoa and eat some fudge someone had given him. He would play games on the new computer he had indulged in as a Christmas present to himself.

And the baby Jesus lay in the quiet night outside in the cold.

Curtain Call

The weather forecasters all agreed. It was going to be a doozy. The balmy warmth that had washed November with its counterfeit promises was about to be blasted to smithereens by a winter storm of snow and ice and the kind of cold that froze not only toes, but bones. Newscasters, mayors, hospitals, and the police force throughout the Midwest pleaded with anyone who watched or heard: Stay indoors.

Thea had pleaded, herself. Stay put. Don't come. But it was the first Christmas since her husband had died, the first Christmas their only child had been without her strong, dependable papa who always made everything better. He had owned a small theater company that barely scraped by. His grand plans to expand and change lives had never materialized. But it didn't matter to Clara. To Clara, he surpassed all the directors in New York and London combined. His words echoed in her memory: "Follow your spark, sweetheart. Follow your light."

She had finally turned off her phone to ignore her mother's messages. She didn't want to hear them because they told her something that didn't accommodate her desires. She didn't want to listen because she was nineteen.

She wasn't a child anymore. She could take care of herself. If the roads became impassable, she'd simply take the nearest exit and find a café to wait it out.

Miles multiplied, and as millions of tiny snowflakes pelted her window, obscuring dark from light, Clara began peering down every passing exit, each town's darkened signs a testimony to businesses closed to the impending storm.

Thea jumped at the teapot's whistle, then scuffed to the kitchen. With a shaking hand, she poured the steaming water into the cup of peppermint tea, then held the cup close to her face the better to feel the warmth of it. She glanced at the clock. Clara would have been on the road ten hours now if she had left as planned. Then, in a sudden act of faith, Thea poured a second cup.

She placed it on the fireplace mantel, then stood in the spot she had haunted for hours this day as she had watched the sky turn from winter white to darker gray until light receded into wind-whipped, snow-covered darkness.

What was that? She squinted, then blinked. Her breath fogged the window and she felt its cold pane on her cheek. The infinitesimal light grew larger. A light, but not headlights. A spotlight shone down on the car as it inched its way down the street following a string of footlights that lit its path.

"And then," Clara concluded her story of sliding on the icy road and desperate prayers for help, "the lights came on. It felt like I was back at Dad's theater."

They held hands as through the window they watched the curious lights dim, then go out in the whiteout of the night's blizzard.

The Star

The house was a wonderland of tiny snowflakes and bells, of gingerbread men and spritz cookies and fudge, and of wreaths of every size in every room. Scents of cinnamon and orange peel lightly infused the air. Candy canes bunched together in a cut-glass jar. On the dining room table stood a gingerbread house, carefully baked and designed with loving hands. And on a bookcase shelf near the mantel, not too obvious, but fitting in just so, the crèche.

Her eyes roamed over each scene as she walked casually from room to room. She'd always loved Christmas and her habit of decorating for The Day was one of the few things that had outlasted her troubles. The only thing that was missing was the star. She had one at one time and not too long ago, either. A few Christmases ago, it had fallen from the top of the tree and broken beyond repair. That was the year she had retired. It was the year she had been diagnosed with something that sucked the life from her until modern medicine and sheer determination had killed it. And it was the year she had sat alone in silence just as the last minutes of the day had ticked away, and city dwellers were welcoming in the new year with little horns and midnight kisses.

Oh, she didn't mind the silence. Before – before she'd battled death – she'd loved joining in life with those around her. But she'd changed. Since her illness, she'd become a bit of a loner and quietness soothed her more often than not. Still, at this time of year when families were traveling long distances just to spend the day together and friends gathered for dinners and teas and parties, her quiet life tweaked her. She thought maybe she should read again the Christmas cards sent to her and send her own in return. Perhaps she should join the coffee party announced for the next day by old friends, the annual event she had ignored during her silent years. Maybe she should go to church. An inaudible, dismissive laugh escaped her lips. No, of the many things she could think of only the loveliness around her merited her attention.

She looked at the beautiful tree placed in front of her window. She'd done at least that; a gesture to those passing by that someone in her house believed in the light of life. But it still bothered her that the topmost branch of the Christmas tree from where the little star had pronounced its benediction for over forty years was now bare. It troubled her that the tree's top missed the star which most assuredly belonged there.

She turned off each light, sat for a time in the dark, then stretched out on the couch thinking of better days and happier times. She must have drifted off, for it was two in the morning when she woke. She rubbed her eyes, then rubbed them again. There above the crèche was a little light. It wasn't the shape of anything, but it made her happier than she recalled ever being. And she watched it as, in the stillness of the night, it glowed with a warmth she had forgotten. As she watched it in its tiny place above the Christ child, peace flooded her spirit. It was as though goodness, itself, was in the room with her, filling her up with hope and love.

She glanced at the clock. Who cared for sleep? If she hurried, she could address those unsent Christmas cards and still make it in time for the coffee party.

The Gift

She couldn't recall the last time she'd had a present. It may have been the necklace she'd received from her grandmother when she was twelve, or maybe it was some other little thing she'd received from one of the foster families in the years after that and before she'd run away. But it was all so very long ago now.

She'd never blamed anyone. She'd never known her parents, them both being the kind that disappeared when troubles arose – troubles such as a baby. Her grandmother had cared for her until she, herself, needed care. It had just seemed best to start out on her own. She'd done pretty well, too, if she did say so, herself. Never married. No, not that. Too much – trouble.

But she'd made a decent living and a few friends here and there, and had retired before they'd let her go, though no one would have said anything about age.

When December came, she had carefully lifted out cardboard boxes holding the treasures of her favorite time of year and had pulled each piece out to put in its proper place. She wasn't certain why she felt compelled every year to do such a thing. There wasn't anyone to make happy by little Christmassy touches, and she didn't actually believe in the baby in the manger. Jesus was a word that slipped out when she was frustrated, though why she should use the name of the one she didn't actually believe in mystified her if she thought about it, so she mostly didn't.

Christmas Eve descended into a clear, dark sky sprinkled with stars. As she sipped some cocoa, she sat back and took in the sight of her house decorated for a day celebrating the birth of someone who she deemed unworthy of celebrating and wished this year would be different. She wasn't one of those who believed something you bought for yourself could be called a gift, but she wished, this once, she might receive a gift.

The doorbell rang, and she jumped up. No one ever came to visit. Who would come now? She opened the door to nothing but cold air on a dark night. She leaned out and peered down the street. No one. Yet there, on the top step was a box with her name on it. She pulled it into the warmth of her home and slit the tape.

And there . . . nestled in straw . . . was the best gift of all.

God Watched

Don't read this Christmas miracle story. You won't like it, and you won't like me for writing it. Save yourself the stress, skip this story, and come back next week for something to give you the sense of warmth and Christmas joy we all love; unless, of course, you don't mind the fact that sometimes truth is stranger than fiction.

* * *

Semi-surrounded as it was by three oceans, the dear little country seemed to be encircled with the shelter of angel's wings. Its founders had, in fact, asked for wisdom from heaven, itself, in its structure, and for many years it seemed to be blessed because of it. Sure, it had its ups and downs. Every country swings between the forces of good and evil with the pendulum of history. It praised its heroes. It mourned its defeats. It witnessed its share of error as well as of greatness in the comings and goings of all that happens through the course of time's river.

But of late the country had been badly beaten and bruised. Its recent rulers had done what damage they could by pitting its citizens against each other (skin, sex, culture, religion, language, you name it), by reducing its protections — both of individuals and as a whole, by abusing its sense of morality and common sense, by denigrating the church and even the country, itself, and by putting a stranglehold on those who attempted to use their nerve and smarts to make a go of it. The rulers held out the apple of benevolence injected with the poison of increased governmental control, and the people ate it.

How did it happen? It wasn't as though its citizens desired their own country's demise. They were, for the most part, very good people: People who loved what was right, or thought they did; who cared about their fellow-man; who honestly wanted good to prevail. But schools of thought differed about how to best help people and preserve a nation. Passions inflamed. Those who would use those passions to create destruction rather than discourse were loud and persistent. The gem of youth was accessed. Slowly and surely young children grew to believe things they were taught about history, economy, and morality regardless of the lessons' veracity. They were young. They didn't know differently, their teachers were both sincere and skillful, and their parents were oblivious of the intensity of indoctrination. The very definition of words was changed to influence thinking about right and wrong, good and evil. It became difficult to tell what was true and what was false, and voices from many sources created a cacophony of confusion.

For belief, as we all know, is a stubborn thing. It is strong and rarely yields. Why should it? The question, of course, is which belief is right? Which belief is true?

And now the country's demise was nearly complete. In only a short time, its transformation from freedom to communism would take place. The powers and their followers were nearly ecstatic with the thought. And the people? Half of them were alarmed at the thought and half of them were at peace with it.

In just one election, it would be entirely possible to wrest what control a free citizenry maintained and implement their own philosophy: Marxism leading to socialism leading to communism. It was, according to everyone who knew anything, a sure thing.

But prayer can't be outlawed, even when thought seemingly is controlled and speech surely is – if not by law, then by name-calling. Small utterances in quiet homes and loud pleas in large gatherings were offered to the God who had watched, as He watches all countries, with care and concern, and suddenly the little country found reason to hope.

That hope came, as hope often does, in an unexpected way. A blustery man of no political background challenged the plans so carefully laid. His language wasn't skilled nor did it hold the smooth enticement of a politician, but he was brave and he was tenacious, whatever else people thought of him. Some said he thought one thing, some said he thought another. And said. And did. And his character was this. Or that. His election caused some to fear. They worried about the opinions others claimed he held and were concerned for the future. Some people rejoiced at the thought of the country being snatched from the precipice of Marxist policy and of the possibility of it returning to its origins; not the origins taught by the sincere and skillful teachers, but its true Constitutional origins that people needed to learn about; some, for the first time. And some people felt uncertain about who they should believe, sighing while they continued in their daily tasks.

And the country watched and waited to see what the blustery man of no political background would do. And as they waited, God watched them.

After

It had been howling for, oh, two hours straight. The wind that had begun as a hesitant breeze had grown swiftly to unrelenting gusts. Hard pellets of icy snow filled the air, swirling and crashing on streets and cars and homes. No one in their right mind would be out in this weather. And no one in their right mind was.

"Jiffy!" His words were snatched by the wind and tossed into a sea of soundless air. Still, he persisted.

"Jiffy! Jiff, please! I'm here. Follow my voice!"

How had it even come to this? He'd been a slug for days on end after. That's how he'd begun to think of it. After. After he'd lost his job due to cuts because of one more regulation the small company just couldn't afford. After he'd discovered his girlfriend had been seeing another man on the side. Well, that was that. As they say, once trust is gone, what else is there? After he'd had to move from his apartment to a much smaller, less expensive place in another part of town.

The 'after' part of his life hadn't been long – just the weeks between Thanksgiving and Christmas – but it had been brutal. The road ahead was dark and hopeless, the girl he'd once considered his best friend — wasn't, and despite knowing it would just make things worse, he'd begun to allow himself to sink into the despair that knocked incessantly at his door.

The one thing that had kept him from crawling under the covers and checking out completely was his dog, Jiffy. He'd rescued Jiffy from the pound at a bargain price the day before he was scheduled to be put down. They were as close as it was possible for man and dog to be. When he went anywhere, Jiffy was right beside him. They ran together every morning and every evening. Before. Yet even when he'd begun his long slide, Jiffy hadn't deserted him. He'd nudged him out of bed, snuggled next to him with camaraderie's warmth, and made him keep going somehow.

And now, on a lonely Christmas Eve night, his one loyal friend was lost during a walk around a block of the new part of town; an impulse that, like everything else in his life of late, had gone horribly wrong.

Wasn't Christmas, if not a time of joy and gladness or lights and presents, at least a time of hope?

He sank to his knees and the snow seeped through his jeans with its numbing cold.

"Jiiiiffyyy! Ji . . ."

He covered his face with his hands. There was no light for him. No joy. No warmth.

Something made him look up: A sound; small, but real, and getting louder. It was a sound he knew by heart. By heart.

And his dog jumped up on him and licked him over and over, and he wrapped his arms around his wriggling, wet, cold, snowy, wonderful friend and kissed him back.

After. After they'd gotten back to his apartment, after he'd rubbed Jiffy down with a thirsty towel, after he'd changed into warm, dry clothes, after he'd grilled a steak to split between the two of them, and after he'd turned on some Christmas music, he and Jiffy sat close together and watched the busy snow against a dark sky. He didn't have a tree this year. There were no lights. Yet something he'd missed began rising up inside him.

And he and Jiffy celebrated like there was no tomorrow. But there was.

The Midnight Promise

Snow fell outside as winter's cold touch frosted the pane of glass next to her. She wrapped her hands more tightly around her coffee cup as she sipped and peered into the velvety dark of an empty street. Other than the cook and a waitress, she was alone in the all-night diner. She wished she wasn't, but she was. Her mind drifted back to another night just like this one. Just like this one it had been close to midnight on Christmas Eve.

She'd been on top of the world then. After three years of hard work and loneliness, she'd been offered a promotion in an exciting city away from this bland town and she'd accepted it. Her things had been moved and she had just finished up final details on a day when everyone else was home or at church celebrating. She'd passed the little diner and decided to stop for a hot cup of coffee to warm her fingers, for though future's promise held some light, the night was bitterly cold.

Her fingers had just begun to thaw when he walked in and cheerfulness suddenly filled the room, touching everyone including her. He hailed the cook and the cook waved back with his spatula. He got the waitress talking, and marveled at her two children's accomplishments. He told a joke and the two workmen at the counter joked back, laughing.

As he was served his bacon and eggs, their eyes met; and he'd motioned her to join him. And in two hours that felt both like a lifetime and no time at all, she learned he was leaving — as she was — in the morning. Yet it wasn't for an exciting city, but a dusty country where he would fight for someone else's freedom and, perhaps, for a freedom she daily took for granted. And they had agreed that night, that, barring other relationships or death, they would meet here again in five years to the minute.

Those five years had been good. She'd met with success. She'd made some friends, friendly acquaintances really. But a life filled with trivial things holds little satisfaction, and she'd learned that, like everyone else, she was not without a yearning to go below surface amusements.

Oh, she'd made an effort to find him. She'd tracked his name down every possible avenue, but had come up empty. Maybe she'd been had. His easy manner invited trust, but perhaps it was a ruse. She'd chided herself, but she couldn't forget that night five years ago nor their easy conversation nor the depth of his gray-green eyes nor the way his left eye squinted when he smiled. Nor their promise.

And here she was. Little had changed in this old town, but somehow it pulled her back. She'd even come a few days early and curiously perused real estate listings.

The dark night whispered doubt and tragedy. Minus the occasional clatter of dishes, it was too quiet. She had been foolish to think about it at all. She should have left it, as he most certainly had, in the booth as she walked out the door.

She should have left the memory. She should have forgotten the promise.

She squinted again into the darkness, then down into her steaming coffee. She closed her eyes and held the cup to her cheek. Please. Life had to hold more than what she'd experienced. Please, on this night when all the world somehow knew hope was real and love wasn't just for the fortunate, let him remember. Let him care. Let him come.

The bell on the door jingled. She opened her eyes and they met his: gray and green and deep as the sea.

One Gift

She'd turned it over in her mind for months. She was allowed to give one gift. Cost was no object, but it was the only gift she would be allowed to give ever again. Just one gift.

She'd gotten the message in her mailbox on a sweltering August day. The envelope was sealed with gold leaf and the writing was in excellent calligraphy. Choose a gift for the letter writer's choice of recipient. She might never know who, might never meet the person, but would know he received the gift. At first, she'd dismissed it as someone's effort to amuse himself. Maybe it was some sort of game show, and she was the only one not in on the joke. Why her? Why had she been singled out? She wasn't anyone special. But as the days cooled and no other message arrived, she began to consider the project. If this was a real offer – responsibility, really – she shouldn't pass on it. One gift. Any amount of money could be spent and would be made available as required.

Money no object? She could dismiss the usual gifts of clothing or nearly anything else found in the mall. Technology? Now there was an idea. A person could do things with the newest gadget. But technology was always changing. Who would want something that would be obsolete within a year or two? Ditto for vehicles of all kinds.

She didn't dismiss books as readily as someone else might. A book – the right book – could elevate thinking. Why, it could change a life if a person took the author's premise to heart. Maybe she could give a first edition. Hmm.

Real estate was a great alternative. You can't go wrong with real estate despite market trends, because that was just it. If the price fell, it could as easily rise after enough time. A house? Maybe an estate. What was she thinking?! She could buy an entire island. Who wouldn't want their own private island? No one she could think of.

She could arrange for tuition and room and board at a university. Of course, not knowing the recipient, she couldn't be certain such a thing would be appreciated nor even useful.

Or a vacation somewhere! Really. Didn't everyone need, or, at least, want a vacation? France, Greece, Paris in the spring . . .

She supposed she could buy stock. Didn't rich people do that type of thing? Stock could make someone a millionaire. Or not.

Days and weeks passed. She researched. She wandered around the neighborhood wondering about the letter-writer and then thinking about the gift recipient. Leaves changed color and fell. Icy weather settled in. She sipped cocoa and looked out the window, thinking. Wondering. Turning it over in her mind. One gift. Only one and then, never again.

And it was Christmas Eve, the date given to reveal her choice. Despite the crunchy snow underfoot, she walked to the mailbox and deposited her choice within. It was a small manila envelope with two 2-inch symbols and a letter inside. It read:

Dear Gift Recipient:

I've spent a lot of time — make that an enormous amount of time — wondering what to give you. I finally concluded that, of all the things available the world over, my choice is the best one. It's small and great at the same time.

I hope you like it. I hope you will accept it.

Cost: Me — nothing. Him — everything. You — pending.

Seven

She liked little things: the shape of bark on a tree, the tickity sound of that one machine she didn't know the name of, Christmas, of course, and the smell of dirt just before anything sprouted in the spring. And she *loved* math. It was logical and dependable. It was actually beautiful in the way the same conclusion could be reached in a variety of ways. And the answers were never fuzzy, never tentative. They were solid.

One January day she felt a little dizzy. Maybe it was the flu. Then she fell during recess. And in one day a brain cancer diagnosis stole the little things, her favorite sights and sounds and scents. She was six.

She lost her hair overnight, and wondered if anyone's hair could grow back overnight, too. When she lost her bowel control, her dad reminded her of all the things she could still control, and gave her some equations to work just for fun. Her appetite left her, and she didn't wonder or think anything. She just felt weak. And then one day she sensed her math skills slowing; and it was on that day that hope became transparent. That day her world was no longer solid. That day was the worst day.

One night voices filled her dreams. She could hear bits and pieces here and there of what they were saying, of what they were praying. Sometimes she heard her name. She saw a man standing in front of her and liked him instantly. He told her the number seven was one of his favorite numbers and asked her how old she would be on her next birthday. She laughed when he threw up his hands in surprise. He told her his birthday would be celebrated soon, and they talked about the sound of stars and the warm breath of sheep. He told her that miracles are as dependable as math if you know who to ask. The man seemed so real and his words so solid. She felt happy and, for the first time in a year, a weight lifted. But when she woke up, she was in her same bed with accustomed pain and saw the familiar troubled look in her mother's eyes.

In one year things had grown so hard. Spring and summer had passed without tree bark or the smell of fresh dirt because tests and worry had taken their place. Her world had grown smaller and quieter in the hospital. Math ceased to bring the satisfaction it had one time brought. It hardly seemed possible her days could ever become better.

Christmas wasn't far away now, but she would lose that favorite thing, too. How would she celebrate it with such a tired body?

And then it was Christmas Eve. Before she went to sleep, she thought again about the nice guy she'd seen in her dream. She could almost hear him telling her about how miracles really do exist, and she prayed for the miracle she wanted most of all. A small smile crossed her face as she thought about the sound of stars, the warm breath of sheep, and how he liked the number 7.

Christmas morning dawned cold and sharp, but bright and clear. She stretched and felt a tug. What in the world? She jumped out of bed and ran to the mirror. There – just touching her shoulders – was the hair she'd missed for too long. Her eyes grew wide. She breathed deeply.

"Mom! Dad! I feel good! I feel great! Nothing hurts! I! Have! Hair!"

She ran into the living room and jumped on the couch. Up and down, up and down. She couldn't stop! She ran back into her room and grabbed a math worksheet. Ha! How could anyone not like math?! And the answer was seven! Seven! Seven! Seven! She ran back into the living room, plugged in the tree lights, and felt the glow of Christmas, itself: promise and hope. Today she would celebrate her friend's birthday with all her might. It felt so right. So real. Solid. She was home. She was whole. And miracles? Miracles are as dependable as math if you know who to ask.

White and Red Christmas Eve

Wind whipped the branches and slammed snow pellets against the brick until red became white. City dwellers had heeded the forecasters' warnings and had stocked up on necessities including rock salt, sand, and kitty litter. Shovels were sold out. Streets had emptied. Here and there a window blinked a hint of brave light otherwise muted by the blizzard.

She'd heard the warnings just as everyone else had, but how often were forecasters right, really? When she'd started out, it had been simply cold and windy. But the forecasters had been right, and she had gotten it very wrong.

She wanted to make it home for Christmas – surprise everyone for once in her life. Oh, they'd planned on her coming, but with this weather, had urged her to stay put. They'd get together another time. Still, it had been too long.

Last Christmas she'd been invited to Aspen and you'd have to be crazy to turn down an invitation like that. The Christmas before that she'd worked because, well because she needed the money, and at the time money seemed more important than going home. It wasn't the same. Working made the day seem like just another day. She'd gone back to a quiet apartment and ate leftover quiche that had lost some of its texture and toast that tasted like sawdust. Aspen had been exciting and beautiful, but . . .

As December 25th approached, she'd begun to think of the pine scent of the Christmas tree she knew stood in front of the window and the cookies her mom always made, the ginger ones with sugared orange rinds on top. Every time she heard a Christmas song on the radio or in a store, she thought of the little church down the block from their house that held Christmas Eve services no matter the weather.

Now her Christmas surprise had made an awful turn. God was in heaven, and Jesus wasn't just a baby in a pretty story. She knew that. But she never prayed. Wasn't sure she knew what to say even if she tried. How, after all, did one ask for Rudolph the red-nosed reindeer?

She pulled over as she approached the edge of town. Ten more miles on a blowing highway and she'd be home. Ten more miles might as well be ten hundred. She couldn't even see where the road ended and the ditch began.

Squinting into the whiteout, suddenly she caught sight of a light up ahead! Not white light, but red and red enough to break through the blinding flakes. She pulled out and crept onto the highway, following it. A lone trucker needing to make it a few more miles would've laughed to think he was an answer to prayer. No matter. The driver of the car behind him was humming Rudolph.

Lights Out

"The important thing is that we focus on the diversity this campus is known for."

"Right." He paused. "Everything gets equal attention."

"A..a..a"

"Well of course I don't mean Christmas. It's had too much preference for far too long in this country. Besides, it's passe."

"Right. Twinkly lights are fine as long as they don't mean anything. And Christmas carols . . ."

"Ach! Don't even mention them. I can't stand them."

"I hated to see the Santa display go, but it was for the best."

"Haha! I'd forgotten about that one!"

"What in the world? Did you see that?"

"I think it's the Fine Arts Building. I'd think they'll be on it before too long. Painting in the dark would be a challenge, eh?"

"Of course, red and green were fine for awhile, but—I don't know—do you think it's associated too closely with Christmas?"

"Let's just go with white and gold. No reason to ruffle any feathers."

The two men stopped and peered down the street for a moment.

"The English department will howl, for sure."

"Oop! And Languages. Ah! And a few of the street lights! I wonder if it's something with the electrical system?"

"Ooo, watch out there. Are you okay?"

"Just a minor stumble. It's a bit hard to see without those lights."

"Did you see the creche in front of the gas station down on 7th?"

"I can let the student group know. They love a good protest."

A loud buzz echoed through the evening air.

"Look! The History department! They've probably all fallen asleep anyway."

The two men chuckled.

"Science and technology will feel that."

"I wonder how it will affect research?"

"But to the main point. This time of year shouldn't be any different than any other time. I think we've done a fine job of cleaning up the campus. I don't see evidence of the C word anywhere, do you?"

"How much better our campus is without Christmas!"

The other man nodded. "Nothing to take offense at here."

And the campus went dark.

Something New

The house had been cleaned from top to bottom. Candy canes hung in ribbon above the windows and the tree was resplendent with ornaments of sentimental value. The scent of gingerbread filled the kitchen as she began rolling out sugar cookies while she thought about it all. If only everything could be washed clean and made new. If only . . .

For, you see, something new crossed her path every day. Normally that would be a good thing. Something new meant something fresh and exciting! But now the something new was stomach-churning. Every day. And the season which had before brought beauty and sweetness, sparkle and peace had been tarnished with unrelenting tales of deception, perversion, and anger. It was as though a spider of darkness was determinedly spreading its sticky web over the season of light.

But people's hearts seemed impossibly hard and the enormous amount of disgusting behavior seemed darker than a black hole. How could such contempt for what was right be turned around? How could those who allowed themselves to wallow in a gutter mindlessly covered by glamour and status or blame and suspicion be redeemed? How could both accused and accuser find peace? It was hopeless! What was needed was a miracle. An unconscious sigh escaped her lips.

And she gave birth to her firstborn son, and wrapped him in swaddling clothes, and laid him in a manger; because there was no room for them in the inn.

And there were shepherds living out in the fields nearby, keeping watch over their flocks at night. An angel of the Lord appeared to them, and the glory of the Lord shone around them, and they were terrified. But the angel said to them, "Do not be afraid. I bring you good news of great joy that will be for all the people. Today in the town of David a Savior has been born to you; he is Christ the Lord. This will be a sign to you: You will find a baby wrapped in swaddling clothes and lying in a manger."

Suddenly a great company of the heavenly host appeared with the angel, praising God and saying, "Gory to God in the highest, and on earth peace to men on whom his favor rests."

In evil times to desperate people comes One who makes everything new and redeems those willing to be saved. It is an astounding miracle that crosses time and space to every culture and generation. It is offered to a multitude and available for a single soul. And *that* is the best miracle of all.

Luke 2:7-14

Shadow and Light

Three days. That's how long it had been since the power went out. At first it had been kind of fun, and after she and her cat watched white snowflakes in their persistent descent against a storm-gray sky, she'd gone to bed under cozy covers and dreamed she was at the North Pole.

Morning had brought the chill of winter indoors and realization flashlight games with Simba would hold little amusement in a room cold enough to see her breath. She'd slipped long johns on under her clothes, and pulled on two pair of socks, a hat, and gloves. Simba slipped under the comforter.

She called the power company again and got the same recorded message she'd heard the day before. It would be at least a week before everyone's service was restored. Her small house on a little-traveled road was at the bottom of the priority list, which meant power to her house would come in seven more days at the earliest! Tonight was Christmas Eve and Christmas would essentially be blacked out. Typical. Okay. Okay. She preferred soft shadows to glaring light anyway, didn't she?

She'd bought it – the house – with money from her grandfather's inheritance, for solitude she'd wished for during ten years of living in the concrete jungle where she'd found comfort only in the shadows. At the time of purchase, she hadn't thought of emergencies; only of getting away from too many people, too much light, too much everything.

Getting away from it all was good, right? The shadows of tall pines secreted her from the world. She admitted, though, that as the years passed, she'd begun to wonder if, by leaving behind some things she'd pegged as needless, she had shut out something else. Something important, perhaps.

She wrapped a blanket around herself more snugly and stared at the Christmas tree she'd set up in the corner. It seemed somehow ridiculous with all light stripped from its branches. Little ornaments hung listlessly. Suddenly, a glass ballerina she'd had since childhood broke from the cold. Was it a sign? She shook her head to clear it. The cold must be doing things to her mind. She began to wonder if the shadows that had weaved in and out of her life were of her own making. Did no one love her or had she simply shut love out? Humph. Nonsense. She laughed mirthlessly as she swept up the pieces.

And as a nearly invisible weak winter sun sank below the horizon, the shadows began to change from cozy to ominous. Warmth and light suddenly seemed unattainable. Her life wasn't one to which good things came, something she'd repeated for years like a mantra. And miracles (for that's what it would take)? That was just a charming word, more fiction than fact. Two days had passed and she was already quite miserable. It hung over her like an unlit candle: that sense of dread that night would stretch on forever and light would disappear.

She stretched out on the couch, Simba next to her, and wished for the week to be over, the week the power company claimed it would take to turn the power back on. Wind from the storm rattled the windows and drafted through minute crevices.

She closed her eyes and allowed herself something she'd always strictly forbidden: She thought of Christmases past; of people from long ago; of out-of-key church choirs and imperfect cookies and snow-trampled sidewalks. And she began to remember stories told by long-silenced voices she had dismissed as out-of-touch. A baby born in a shadowy cave and placed in a manger. Of a God so loving He sent His own Son and called Him Light. If only it were true. If only light filtered into sad, sightless, cold shadow and brought warmth. Please. Please send light. Please, she thought. Or was it a prayer? She drifted in and out through the night, the unforgiving cold disallowing sleep. Then sometime near the dawn of the third day it happened. She saw it first, then felt it. Light! Warmth! And Christmas Day – the day God sent Light into the shadows of the world – broke through. After all, light casts no shadow.

The true light that gives light to everyone was coming into the world.
John 1:9

The Church Bell

The bell had last rung in 1945 on Christmas Day, its peal joyful and jubilant. The bell was twenty years old then, and the one who rang it was strong and sinewy. He could still remember the sweater he'd worn that day. It was of heavy knitted wool, handmade by his girl, Betty. He planned to ask her to marry him the next evening and knew she'd say yes.

He knew, because that's the way life was for him. It was almost as if he could make what he wanted appear before his eyes. If he wanted a job, he got it. If he wanted a girl, she loved him. When he wanted a house, he'd be moving in the next month.

They'd had a small wedding in the church where he was bell-ringer, but the bell didn't ring on his wedding day. It didn't ring on any Sunday or holy day afterward, either. He'd checked to see what the problem was. The clapper seemed fine. There were no noticeable cracks and the bolts were tight. He'd climbed up to examine the mechanism of ropes and pulleys. Nothing. So there it remained, in its ordained place high above the church, looking for all the world like a working bell, but in reality doing only that and nothing more.

He and Betty had raised a family. Five strong boys and a daughter whose life had been cut short by a high fever and misdiagnosis. Betty, his Betty, couldn't stand the loss and she had died within a year. Neighbors were puzzled. She'd seemed in good health. But he knew it wasn't her health. It was her heart.

He'd soldiered on, looking up at what he called "his bell" each time he crossed the church threshold. He hadn't been able to fix the bell just as he hadn't been able to fix Betty's grief. It bothered him, not being able to make things right. But the bell was the first to teach him that life can clobber even the luckiest man.

It was Christmas Eve, and the years had marked time as they do in everyone's life. He was tired and the church was, too. And he thought, as he listened to sweet carols sung by weary voices, that what he needed was what the church needed. And what the church needed was what the world needed.

He slipped out of his pew before the last song and climbed the tower stairs to stare once again at the bell. And he did something he hadn't done when trying to fix it nor in all the trials in his life that he'd found to be unfixable.

The good Lord had more important things to do than listen to an old man make a needless request. But this time, well this time, he'd approach the throne. After all, even Kings give presents to their servants.

"Father," he whispered, his breath making puffs in front of him. "I'm so tired, and this here church is world-weary. And who are we, anyway? We aren't any of us impressive or even good. I've tried, Lord, how I've tried to get this bell to ring. It was my job, and I failed. I couldn't figure it out. I couldn't fix it. And it won't matter, I guess, if you don't do this. But it'd mean a lot if this old bell could ring again; If it would do what it's meant to do, and on Christmas Eve, no less. Let it ring, Father. Let it fill the night with the voice of the angels."

And the old man, full of years, grabbed the rope and pulled with all his might. And clarion rings called from the church tower, echoing through the town and fields. Its peals were taken up by bells across the town: big, booming bells; choir-like bells that rang in harmony; even tiny bells hanging from Christmas trees in homes of the townsfolk. The church people rose from their pews and ran outside to look up in wonder. And the old man pulled and pulled with tears streaming down his face, while voices of the angels sang.

Eight Quarters

Eight quarters. That's what did it. It was two dollars sucked into a laundromat dryer with nothing to show for them that cracked her final effort to put on her game face. And now, as she sat on a cold bench, holding a large bag of wet laundry and waiting for the bus, a few tears burned her eyes. She blinked quickly to chase them away.

It had been six months since she moved from her small town back in Oklahoma. Her parents had worn worry on their faces like freckles; but they had bravely waved goodbye, whispering prayers – prayers for her to remember where she came from, prayers for a sense of home in a strange city – they thought she hadn't heard. Her dad had flipped a quarter in the air and she'd caught it.

"Remember," he'd said. "Remember even a quarter says to trust God."

"And if a quarter knows as much," her mom had added, "then you do, too. And whenever things get troublesome, just take a quarter's advice."

Only she had used her last quarter in the laundromat dryer – the dryer that didn't work. She didn't even have a quarter to look at. Oh, she went through the motions of bedtime prayers and thanks for food, but . . . The baby in the manger seemed very far away.

Now it was Christmas Eve. She would be missing the special stew her mother always made and cocoa and cookies as they decorated the tree. But if she thought about it too much, it would just depress her. She would ignore the day. She had rejected her parents' offer of transportation money. Too proud, she admitted. She would take their phone call and pretend she had gone somewhere exciting. A trickle of water seeped from the laundry bag in front of her and ran down the slanted pavement.

"I haven't seen you here before."

She glanced over at size 13 shoes. At *least* 13, she thought. Her eyes moved to a wooden cane topped with an engraved solid brass cane head in the shape of a tree branch, and upward to a wrinkled, leathery face.

"Looks like you were in a hurry," he chuckled.

"I . . ."

"Dryer on the fritz?" he tossed her the question that felt like a lifebouy.

"Yes, that's it." She wouldn't admit the quarters she'd lost in it were some of the last until her next paycheck. At least she had a bus ticket.

Fumes from the bus clouded the air as they climbed the steps. It occurred to her that steps might be hard to manage with a cane, but when she turned to look, the old man seemed strong and spry.

As she stepped off the last stair at her stop, she heard a familiar voice.

"Imagine living so close," the tall stranger marvelled. "Say – I have a washer/dryer in my unit you can use."

She considered. Was it safe? Her wet load made her decision, and she nodded.

His apartment building *was* so close – only a couple of buildings from her own. But she supposed it wasn't unusual to not have met him before.

She couldn't have said what she'd expected, but she stepped into a surprisingly cozy home. For that's what it was. The very air was a welcoming hug. He plugged in lights on a Christmas tree in the corner, then showed her to the dryer.

While waiting for her clothes to dry, he brought her a heavy blue bowl of beef stew along with buttered french bread, perfectly toasted. The simple meal warmed her through. It reminded her of home.

"I was going to finish decorating the tree this evening. Care to help?" he asked.

He held out an ornament with an iridescent glow. She took it and carefully hung it on a branch. It was one of a kind. Truly stunning.

As she lay in bed the next morning, the events from the previous evening played in her memory. She could almost taste the gingerbread cookies and hot cocoa the old man had brought out while they finished decorating his tree, a tree that rivaled any she'd ever seen.

The phone rang: a Christmas morning call from her parents. Was she doing okay? Had she made any friends? They still prayed every day for her to encounter some sort of family-like support when she needed it. They missed her, and had hung her special ornaments on the tree. She told them of the tall old man she'd spent Christmas Eve with, leaving her wet laundry and missing quarters out of the story.

She slipped into her newly laundered jeans and sweater. She couldn't remember laundry smelling so fresh! Energized, she decided to hand-deliver a thank you note to her new friend. The winter sun muted the light as she stepped onto the sidewalk on her way to the old man's apartment two buildings down. She passed the first building and – wait. She turned around. No, this was where his apartment building had been. Had been! She stared at an empty lot. Yet not completely empty. For there, a few steps in, was a pile quarters. Eight, to be exact. And snowflakes gently fell as she read, IN GOD WE TRUST.

A Tree in the Forest

There is an ancient pine tree deep in the Forest of Dirgel that stands taller and stronger than any other variety, of its own and others. No one knows when it sprouted nor how long it grew. Perhaps the mysterious forest originated with the tree, or maybe lucky placement gave it enough room and light to stretch to the beckoning sky. But whether it was the first in the forest around it or was the result of a pinecone dropped by tree or animal, it became the reigning presence that lent itself to the old story.

The legend is nearly as old as the forest, itself, handed down from generation to generation; though two pilots recounted seeing the very tree on Christmas Eve, and a rugged ranger, long gone, witnessed it, himself.

On the day before Christmas, goes the story, as the light dims, fading from winter white to periwinkle to black, the moon dips slightly lower in the sky, lighting the forest with its winter beams – a spotlight on the ancient tree. The air, sharp with cold, begins to shimmer with golden flecks of light, turning the night into a velvety backdrop. Then the branches of the tree reach lower, and lower still until they brush the ground. And in the glittering, gleaming night something amazing begins to happen!

Tiny red, blue, and green berries sprout along the soft green needles. Gradually little bits of corn and pumpkin spring up in concert from the branches; and fruit of all kinds drop from the already laden boughs.

Then one by one forest animals begin to gather around the old tree. Some internal knowledge tells them there is a miraculous feast awaiting them as the glittering light breaks through the darkness. First, little chipmunks, fresh from their winter hibernation, peek up from the snow. Then squirrels: gray, red, and brown chatter to each other as they scamper near. Deer and wolves, friends for the evening, sniff the air and begin to munch on the feast. Birds drop down onto the higher branches and lend music to the night when they break from dining on the abundance of the old tree. The quiet of the forest erupts with happy sounds of animals, some very hungry from too many snowy days, as they enjoy the profusion of good food.

And in the still and sparkling Christmas Eve the stars glimmer and shine as they watch the gathering. They know how the legend began, for they saw the One who calls them each by name and hears their songs in the night reach low and create the hidden gift in celebration of another most spectacular gift one silent night long ago.

What the Soldier Saw

It had been a rough day. Gunfire's repetitive staccato had rattled his bones and jarred his nerves. But it had ended for now, and he was assigned Fire Guard while others slept. Though he was deployed in a part of the world he had always associated with heat, he could see his breath in the night air. It was downright cold!

He'd quieted himself to the point that he was better at discerning the difference between a rogue footfall and the crack of cold, but though a soldier might appear quiet or still, guard duty was never a time of rest.

Something caught his eye, and he zeroed in on it. Oh. A star. Only a star. But its brightness pulled his gaze back to the sky, and he thought of the old story – the one about wise men following a brilliant star and shepherds in the night.

Shepherds in the night. Now there was something he could understand. Men of varied ages spending time in the field. Without decent food. Smudged and dark from dirt and sun. Always slightly on edge, a result of their responsibility to protect. To fight when necessary. To be invisible, unremembered, and essential. They guarded sheep. He guarded freedom.

On a night not unlike this one and in a place relatively near to the station he guarded, those shepherds watched; watched the sheep and the undiscernible darkness. Their eyes, like his, might have blurred from tiredness. Some of their comrades might have been collegial – others, not so much. But, unlike him, their night had exploded in light and sound and magnificence with the announcement of the ages. Glory! To God! In the highest! A baby was born who would first save the world for all history, then rule for all eternity. History! Eternity!

The One who was announced did battle with the forces of evil. Yes, he knew something about that. And He loved. Yes, he knew love. Wished he knew it better. And He finished what He started. Yes, it was part of the Soldier's Creed.

The soldier felt suddenly small in the grand scheme of things. He stretched and gazed as far as his eyesight would allow. He wouldn't see magnificence tonight. He would only see the stars over the hills. His view was magnificent, was it not? It would have to be enough on this Christmas night. While those he loved and those who hated him and those who didn't give him a thought celebrated with feasts and presents and songs and candlelight, the stars would have to be enough.

"Merry Christmas", he whispered.

And then, then he saw . . . something. Were his eyes playing tricks? No, no, he was as sure as anything he'd seen it; if only for an instant. Angels! Not a multitude. And not glowing and beautiful like the pictures he'd seen in books when he was a child. But fierce. Profoundly scary and somehow comforting. No one would believe this. Not his buddies. Not his friends and family back home. But when you witness the unseen, you never forget it. He knew what he saw.

And his heart beat fast with awe as he blinked back grateful tears on the quiet Christmas night.

The Cabin on Buck Creek

It had been, oh, how long? More years than he cared to think about. Life had taken him away from familiar places and people into a world they and he knew nothing of. It was a world of tall buildings and bridges, masses of people and multi-course meals.

He had faced a steep learning curve; one that had kept him stimulated and focused during most of his waking hours and dreaming of fenestration, tartan grids, and plans during his sleep. It was only a few years ago that his engagement had slowed, then slowed some more until what were once challenges were now no more than mundane tasks. His schedule was so dependable, he could set a Times Square clock by it. Coffee at 6:00. Stepping over the threshold of his office by 7:00. A working lunch at his desk or a quick walk to clear the cobwebs at noon. Home by 7:00 and repeat ad infinitum. His restlessness increased.

One day he looked up from his work, past the steel and glass outside his windows, and acknowledged to himself that something had taken the place of the former puzzles floating through his consciousness and had instead filled his dreams with increased yearning. He couldn't quite believe it, but it had grown until its undeniability filled the room.

So it was that he found himself back in a familiar place, now slightly changed. There was no decent road in. It was a place only off-road vehicles could manage, and even then, the trees blocked most paths. He scuffed through dried leaves on the track to the shaded snowpack near his Grandpa's old place. Little animals scurried to hide. The cold walk filled his lungs with crisp, fresh air. He dug his hands into his coat pockets, and the vapor from his breath increased with the distance. He used to pretend it was pipe smoke when he was 5. He wanted to be like his Grandpa. And God. For somewhere in his little boy imagination his Grandpa was pretty near as close to God as anyone. He wouldn't have been surprised if God smoked a pipe.

He'd spent every summer of his boyhood in the sturdy three room log cabin filling his days chasing frogs, swimming in the creek, and climbing trees. And every other winter, he'd been allowed to spend his Christmas vacation from school with his Grandpa. The crunch, crunch, crunch underfoot stopped as he pulled the key from his coat pocket and unlocked old, forgotten memories.

For a few hours he swept and scrubbed dirt from neglected surfaces. He started a fire in the fieldstone fireplace, then sank down in the chair his Grandpa had favored. His mind wandered back to evenings by the firelight and wisdom the world he had come from couldn't touch. He closed his eyes and wished – oh how he wished . . .

A sigh escaped his lips. So many years. Had he chosen the right path or was the simpler one his Grandfather had taken the better one? Was money, hobnobbing, and status the best reward? After all, they had their merits. Were those years he could have had – of rewards from physical labor and homey leisure – now lost? Probably.

He recalled the last Christmas he had joined his Grandpa at the cabin. His parents had died within a year of each other, and he hadn't wanted to bear the season alone. But his Grandpa was stubborn about one thing. That cabin. He never left it. Something about his lost dog returning, though it never did. He claimed he always wanted it to know where to find him. And they had spent a wonderful week together. That was before his choices. Before the city. Before.

He hadn't come here to sulk. He grabbed an axe – the one that was always in the corner by the door – and walked out to find a tree. It was just the right size, and when he had decorated it with pinecones and berries, it was perfect.

He sat in the dark, firelight and shadow playing over the walls and floor, and he prayed. He prayed for forgiveness of false equivalencies and shallow goals. And he prayed for a miracle. Right here. On Christmas Eve. He didn't want a fancy dinner nor a Tesla nor even a house in the Hamptons. No, tonight he made a different choice. He wished for one more talk with his Grandpa who so reminded him of the Good Lord, Himself.

And the sweet scent of pipe smoke filled the room.

Christmas From Another View

"Wow! Oh wow oh wow oh wow!"

"I know. It's magnificent, isn't it?"

"Not in my wildest dreams could I have ever imagined . . ."

"No, nor in your waking hours either. Christmas celebrations on this side of the veil are amazing!"

They momentarily glanced below, then she knelt and peered into a particular room with great interest.

"During the tribulation, after the rapture, that is; my auntie has been doing the best she can. Look at her," Cecile pointed.

The woman below rocked herself back and forth as she sat on the floor. She had found a place to live – she wasn't allowed to own anything now – but she was glad for shelter and a little food.

"She used to love the Christmas movies on TV – you know the love stories," Cecile commented affectionately.

Her companion nodded.

"She loved the sparkle and glam of Christmas. But," Cecile continued thoughtfully, "she didn't have much time for the main thing. The *real* thing. I once asked her why. Oh, I know. It was rather smart-mouthed of me. She was offended, of course. She scolded me and told me I should go to the concert at her church. Maybe I'd learn a thing or two. The music was . . . I think she described it as 'heavenly'."

The companions smiled in amusement.

"Funny. She scoffed at the simple account when we were together, but now . . . now it looks like there might be a chance. I saw her get this on the black market."

An open Bible rested before the woman as she read and re-read some passages. She closed her eyes, but a pained expression remained.

"It's so hard to let go of old paths. Come on, Auntie. You can do it."

"You can do it," the two companions shouted together.

The woman frowned and looked over her shoulder as though she'd heard something. A thoughtful expression flitted across her face and she turned back to the book in front of her.

Her niece returned alone later to see her aunt asleep on the floor. Her austere surroundings were so different than years past. Maybe, thought Cecile, they were closer to the first Christmas. Just maybe her dear auntie would see a little more clearly the baby in the manger.

An instantaneous flash of light shone from the old book's pages, but only for a moment. The woman's sleeping expression grew softer, and Cecile repeated an oft' prayed request. Perhaps tonight.

Footprints

The church was dark except for a battery-powered candle someone had accidentally left on. It was Christmas Eve, a night when church congregants left their various entertainments and present-opening and buffet tables and came as one to celebrate the holy birth every year. But not this year. This one was online with more music, more varied backdrops, and the comfort of a laptop and a couch. And less, she thought. Less intensity, tenderness, and prayer.

It was nearing midnight when, on impulse, she'd driven the empty streets alone to the dark church for a service of one. Her footfalls resonated a barely audible sound on the carpeted aisle, and the air – the air had that familiar indefinable scent and sense that is part of churches everywhere who welcome Jesus. She often thought you could sense if the Holy Spirit was welcome in a church the minute you crossed the threshold.

Sitting at the piano, she allowed her fingers to play up and down the keyboard. Pretty notes evolved into a few hymns, then Christmas carols, and one last song. Silent Night. They had sung it together every year as candles held by hands young and old lit the room one by one. She missed it. She swallowed hard, and began to play in the darkness.

Wait. What was that? She stopped mid-song and listened hard. A slight sound. She frowned, then rose from the bench and squinted, peering down the darkened aisle. Footprints? Not possible. The sound was barely a whisper, but she could hear them! She closed her eyes and listened as they lined the sanctuary. Such a thing should bring fear, but all she felt was inexplicable warmth.

Opening her eyes, she heard her own intake of breath as bright starlight quietly began to flood through the church doors and windows, lighting the room more brightly than any candlelight service ever had. She shook her head in disbelief. And yet. And yet this was a night for faith. And miracles.

And she slowly settled onto the bench once again to play the carol as heaven's stars and silent voices of congregants from years past joined together in a poignant Silent Night.

Clompy and Perfect

She blew on her chai, causing a pause in the wafting steam. It had snowed last night, and she missed again the steady scrape scrape of her husband's early morning shoveling. The coat closet door stood ajar, beckoning her to the outdoor task, and her eyes darted to the place where his boots had always stood. Always. Rain or shine, heat or cold. She shook her head, but not with disgust like she had done in the past.

In the past the boots had displeased her. Their appearance and the sound they made matched: clomp, clomp, clompy, clomp. She had bought brand new beautiful boots for him that eventually were given to charity. She had bought a different brand. And another. They both rested in a dark corner of the closet until she finally gave up and gave them away as well.

But now? Now she would have given anything to hear clomp clomp clomp and see snow puddles in a line to the closet. She'd asked the dear Lord in heaven to heal him. Asked and asked. But he was gone now and with him so much of what made her treasure her life. And the boots? She'd kept them. It didn't make sense to her, but grief and love are seldom logical.

She brought her empty chai cup to the kitchen, slightly comforted by the greenery atop the cupboards and the poinsettia by the window. Next year she might have more desire to decorate.

Maybe, maybe after she shoveled, she'd hike out to that place they'd loved. The fresh air would do her good, and she could carry the goodness to the family Christmas gatherings where love and sympathy would bring her to tears in an awkward sort of way.

As she drove to the starting point of her hike, her mind wandered to grief in general. How many people were having their first Christmas without someone this year? How were they handling it? For that matter, what did the baby in the manger, grown to a boy, do when Joseph died? And later – did Jesus' friends feel that lump in the throat, eyes-burning burden in the days after the cross? Did they wish, hope, pray for a sign? The Christmas story held plenty: a star, a battalion of angels, shepherds . . .

But for her, well, there were no signs. Eternal life seemed far away and seeing him again did, too.

The newly fallen snow had left everything pure and sparkling. The long hike was absolutely what she needed. Slightly out of breath, she squinted at the sundogs and prayed again, though she couldn't quite find the words to ask for who knew what. A word of thanks for a life, too short, well-lived. Yes. That would do. And she felt better. She really did, even without the reassurances she wished for.

She started back to her car, then stopped. She gazed down intently, squatted and brushed her hand over what she saw. There it was in the untrodden snow. A bootprint. Larger than her own. Clompy and perfect.

The Scent

The door creaked slightly and the scent greeted him. He called it the Holy Spirit scent. Many churches had it. Others didn't. Tonight he was glad for it. Ever since the troubles, churches had found themselves in a different place, a place requiring a larger faith than they had ever experienced. It was good, but it was hard, too. The sifting had left them smaller than ever. It was clear that depth of faith mattered more than numbers through the door, but you'd have to be crazy to not miss the large fellowship. He prayed again one request: just an extra soul at the manger tonight. One single soul won out of the many lost. The longing ended in a sigh, then a tired smile. At least the Holy Spirit scent had stayed. If only he could witness it's miraculous work!

It was Christmas Eve. The worship team had arrived early and someone had put on the coffee. He placed the plate of cookies his wife had sent ahead with him next to the disposable coffee cups, unlocked his office door, shrugged out of his coat, and picked up tonight's message. It would be short. To the point. A timeless story of the event that changed the world and the world's chances of heaven. It was what was needed now. No jokes, though they could all use some laughter; no cultural tripe, though some might love to hear it; but hope. And truth.

Someone walked past his door. He recognized the black jacket, a four inch tear on the left seam. The man had stood outside the church off and on for a month. One time the minister had called out the door for the stranger to come in from the cold for a hot cup of coffee, but the man had pulled up his collar and quickly walked away. He shot up a quick prayer for him, but he had a nagging feeling. It wasn't good. It wasn't good at all.

Cold air rushed in as the entrance door opened and attendees filtered in. Families, friends, and singles dotted the sanctuary as Christmas music softly echoed over the pews.

As he walked to the pulpit, the man in the black jacket shrugged uncomfortably as though he meant to take it off, then thought better of it. And again. The minister began his short homily, attendees' eyes shone with anticipation, and the stranger fidgeted. And the scent – the Holy Spirit scent – grew stronger. Strange. That hadn't happened before.

". . . The event we celebrate so gloriously this time of year was as expansive as the cosmos and as intentional as a train whistle. It started in simple surroundings so that each of us could approach it in a way we could understand. Some come to the manger with the eyes of a child. Some, with jaded sight, like perhaps, some of the shepherds or the innkeeper, himself. And some with humble beauty, like the wise men did later on. So you see, at this very moment in history – what scripture calls 'in the fullness of time' . . ."

The man in the black coat stood and, as though driven by an unknown force, the minister stepped into the aisle, away from his notes, and continued, "It's hard for us to grasp, isn't it? The fullness of time. Because we are used to not having to wait. We grow impatient." What was he saying? Nothing he'd planned.

"Our questions remain unanswered. We become angry. Maybe even defiant. It doesn't occur to us that it could be because we're not yet ready to hear the answer. But God, Who is patient with us beyond reason . . ."

The man stepped into the aisle. The minister continued walking slowly toward him. The Holy Spirit scent increased.

"He watches us. And waits so very patiently. We might even sense it, but choose to ignore it. Even run from it. And if we run, He waits at the place where we run to."

The minister stopped in front of the stranger. "He's waiting for you, you know."

The man fled, and it was only then that the minister saw the butt of a gun peeking out of his coat pocket. The minister wiped a trickle of sweat from his brow. What had just happened?

He led the congregation in a prayer for wandering souls on dark streets. They finished with *Silent Night* sung in quavering voices and left without eating his wife's cookies.

One more night his prayer was unanswered, thought the minister as he pulled out of the parking lot. What had he been thinking? He had chased the stranger away!

And beyond the candlelight of the darkened church, the Holy Spirit scent reached a lost soul just outside the door, obscured by the night.

Partial to Lambs

Dust moats swirled lazily in the air as dim rays of the setting sun filtered through cracks in the wooden slats. A lamb, one day old and too sick to live, bleated. The boy pulled it close to him.

"Are you sure, honey? There's not a thing any of us can do."

"Pleease," his eyes met those of his parents', speaking what he could not.

His father looked down at the boy's leg, still and swollen.

"You cover up good. The cold seeps in faster than you know."

"But you always say the animals keep the barn warm," countered the boy, before his mother could object.

"That's a fact."

"I'll keep the bottles right next to me. He can eat whenever he wants. See?"

His mother sighed audibly. "Keep the phone close now. If anything happens, you call the house."

The boy nodded quickly. He'd done it!

"Hey little guy," he whispered in the lamb's ear as his parents walked out. "We're going to be roommates tonight. I know you're hurtin'. I know."

He rubbed his bum leg and rocked back and forth, then began to sing quietly – Christmas carols mostly. It seemed right for Christmas Eve.

Finally, as the lamb snuggled close and his own eyes drooped, he uttered the prayer he'd prayed through the day.

"God, heal this little lamb. He's a good one – I can tell. Give him a chance. Please, God, please. I know what they all think. But let this one be different. Don't let him die."

Hours passed. Boy and lamb slumbered together as rays of starlight swept over them. The boy didn't know what hour of the night it was, but light as bright as high noon abruptly filled the stall.

"You love football?" the man standing there asked.

"How'd you know?" The boy rubbed his eyes as he took in the tall form. He was wearing a cowboy hat and jeans with a warm jacket. The boy glanced through the slats into the darkness, then at the man's bare feet.

The man smiled. They talked about the boy's dreams, how it felt to be left out sometimes, of this and that as the man knelt and patted the little lamb. And then he was gone. The boy blinked, turned, looked around. . . the stranger had disappeared as suddenly as he had arrived.

Just before daybreak his dad stepped into the barn to dispose of the lamb's dead body.

"What're you doin' awake so early?"

"I've been awake since . . ."

The little lamb stood shakily, then walked over to him.

"How in the world?" His father uttered under his breath.

And the story the boy had to tell was told over and over again; passed from family members to cousins, townsfolk to passersby, until the barn became something of a tourist destination every Christmastime. They say the boy, now a famous football player and rumored to have the fastest running speed on record, returns, too, each year. He sleeps in the barn every December 24th.

For one year a man appeared to him on Christmas Eve: a man whose feet and hands were scarred, who healed a boy given no hope of healing, as well as the lamb with him because, the man had said, he was partial to lambs.

Waiting for the Dawn

Tucked in between two mountains sits a quiet little village where generations of people live and love, struggle and survive. Smoke rises from the chimney of the northernmost house and with it the prayers of each inhabitant within. For their very existence is threatened tonight by those without care for the cost their hostile plans elicit. And across the village, each house sends the same prayer. Come Lord Jesus. Help us.

Snow swirls in the wind, rushes across the plain, and hits the town community center, shaking it with gusts topping fifty miles an hour. But the townspeople within ignore it. They join in little circles of twos and threes and fives as they pray for help against a force far greater than the wind outside. Come Lord Jesus. Heal us.

Lights blink on and off in the city where light and dark coexist. But in little apartments, fancy penthouses, small neighborhoods and boroughs throughout the meandering streets come whispering voices. For down those streets walk those whose intentions are for usurpation. Come Lord Jesus. Rescue us.

And through the expectant air of a Christmas Eve comes their answer. If hopelessness expects nothing, it usually receives it. But if hope calls for a miracle? Oh that blessed, beautiful miracle will come as surely as the One from whom all hope of heaven and earth descended and brought forth glorious LIGHT!

This miracle story depends upon the reader. It waits to hear the prayer, to learn the heart, and to examine the faith. Pray, my dear readers, pray as though your life depends on it. And we of stout heart and unquenchable faith will wait together through the night as we watch for the miraculous dawn.

Tea with Honey

She'd switched out her morning cup of coffee for tea – tea with raw honey – otherwise it was too bitter, and bitterness was something she was trying to avoid. That and, of course, fear. Who hadn't felt at least a tinge of fear these days?

She tucked her long legs under her as she settled into her favorite chair, a soft yellow armchair with a crisscross pattern in forest green. It didn't feel like a chair, but like a pillow with just the right amount of firmness.

She stared into space and thought of current events. For one thing, the vaccine that had everyone disagreeing with everyone else worried her. She'd done all the right things. But now she wondered if she and half the population had been led out of the frying pan and into the fire, and also wondered if there was a way to jump out of the fire and back into the frying pan.

She sipped her tea. Another? Was her DNA really being damaged by toxins from food and water, medicine, and even clouds (of all things) in the sky? Had her body been biologically altered without her knowledge somehow? And what was that article she'd read while waiting at her auto mechanic for an oil change? Could that cutesy test she'd taken three years ago to find out her exact lineage actually allow some bad actor to create a genome-specific pathogen leading to ethnic cleansing? ***Hers?***

The flicker of candlelight in the window caught her eye. The flame was battery-powered, but it was easier and *almost* the same.

What about those poor people she'd read about: the ones who were being trafficked? Enslaved, more like. Or worse. It turned her stomach, and she'd rather not think about it. Was it really possible there were so many? Was she supposed to do something about it and, if so, what?

Border trouble went without saying, and the people who struggled with drug use were more vulnerable than ever. She glanced across the street at her neighbor's house.

Politics and fraudulent elections tracked through her thoughts. Scrunching her eyes shut, she opened them again.

Weather events seemed to be happening so often now. Had it always been this way and she'd just not known of it until fast-access media?

And China. And Russia. And the Middle East.

A soft sigh escaped her lips. In the past few years, fear had become more of a millstone than a warning. It wasn't supposed to be this way. Fear was a tool, not a tyrant.

And it was Christmastime. Three days before Christmas, to be exact. It was the time of carols and cards, cookies and twinkly lights and poinsettias. She wanted it all and had none. She'd need a miracle to find her Christmas spirit this year!

Determinedly, she opened her Bible and read. She might as well start at the beginning. Hmm. Things weren't exactly red bows and wrapping paper that first Christmas. Why were the three kings included in the story everybody knew and not the bad one: the one who arranged for little boys 2 years old and under to be killed? She wished genocide didn't sound so familiar. And as she read, everything else she witnessed each day was somehow in the pages of scripture. Border trouble? Nehemiah. Weather events? God used signs in the sky all the time! Revelation didn't talk of a Christmas star, but promised oh so many other signs. So did Matthew. So did Joel. Even her concerns about DNA were there on the thin pages. The very first thing written was that she was made in God's image. The God above all gods was imprinted in her. In *her*! How kind of Him.

She drained her cup. The most honey was at the bottom, she thought with a wry smile. As she continued to read, two words jumped from the page. She should have known. If not today, tomorrow; and if not tomorrow, eventually. Eventually everything would be okay. Better than okay! It would be more merry and bright than she'd ever imagined! Satan didn't have the last word. Jesus did! She got up and poured another cup of tea. With Honey.

Special Delivery

His clear baritone cut through the icy air. *Jingle bells! Jingle bells!* He pulled up to the curb, pulled two packages from his truck, made the delivery, and was back in his seat and on key within three minutes. *Jingle all the way! Oh what fun it is to ride in a one horse open sleigh! Hey!*

He turned the corner, checked his delivery list, and glanced at the clock. Just maybe he'd be home at a decent hour tonight. He couldn't bet on anything, but it looked like maybe. He mentally crossed his fingers. T'was the season.

He'd be blasted if it silenced *his* music! *Jingle bells! Jingle bells! Jingle all the way!* He pulled up. There it was. His second to last delivery. He was out and back in two. He looked down to ascertain the final address. Rats. It was *that* one: the one that was *always* the dickens to find! He'd think he'd located it, then the house was two blocks down. Or down an alley and behind a tall hedge. It was almost as if it moved, and the trick was on him.

To be honest, one time the delay caused by the troublesome address had kept him from an accident on the way home. He'd 've been on 94 at the very spot for sure had he not spent the extra twenty minutes driving around like a lunatic looking for the house. That night he had sat in backed-up traffic for more than an hour; but when he'd witnessed the scene he thanked his lucky stars time spent looking for the stupid house and waiting in the line of traffic was the worst he'd experienced. Oh! And there was another time he'd happened on a stray dog due to hunting for the house. The dog looked pretty rough – like he'd been in the elements for awhile. He'd gained weight with good food and eventually had a jaunty trot. The delivery man named him Bowser. He was no doubt snoozing on the chair he wasn't supposed to sit on this very minute.

He hummed as he turned on his GPS. He usually didn't have much time for it. It took him indirectly to where he needed to go and the woman's voice was as irritating as heck. But maybe he could find the mysterious address with less trouble this one night. *Oh what fun it is to ride in a . . .*

SCREECH! The old woman appeared out of nowhere. He slammed on the breaks, just barely avoiding hitting her. It mattered little. She'd been startled and fell to the ground anyway. Probably slipped on the ice. He pulled his delivery truck to the side of the road and hurried to help her up. Her moaning wasn't a good sign.

"My back. Ohhh my back." She looked up at him as he squatted beside her.

"Is anything else hurt, Ma'am?" How he wished he'd been a minute later or a minute sooner!

She struggled to raise herself.

"I'm so sorry. Let me call for help."

"It's not your fault. Just give me a minute. I hate to think of an ambulance bill."

He stayed with her then. And they talked of Christmases past and present, how her back had bothered her for years, and how she knew better than to venture out so late. He placed his rough hand gently on her back and nodded sympathetically. Her face grew curious and his hand grew exceedingly warm.

"Leave it there. It feels like, like, I don't know."

His hand tingled and he felt heat radiating from it. What a strange encounter! Then, suddenly, his hand returned to its normal temperature. Her face aglow, she jumped up with no trouble at all.

"My back! My back feels like I'm 20 again! Are you an angel?"

He shook his head quickly. "No, Ma'am. I'm a . . . I'm a . . ." He searched his brain for something. "I'm a Christian."

He didn't know what to make of it.

"A healer then?"

"No, Ma'am. I don't do anything special. I just deliver packages."

"Well you delivered a stunner tonight! Let me pay you!"

He backed away. "No, Ma'am. I'm just glad you're alright."

"Alright? I've lived with back pain for fifteen years! Fifteen! Let me do something for you. Anything."

He looked at his watch, then his truck. All hope of getting home at a decent hour had fled. His route would take another thirty minutes for sure. "Could you tell me how to get to this address?" With little hope he held it out to her.

She glanced at it and laughed – a sweet, tinkling laugh. She turned, then reveling in the motion, twirled around, and pointed. "It's straight ahead."

He couldn't believe his eyes.

She started down the street with a hop and, of all things, a skip. And the delivery man turned the key as his truck roared to life. *One. Horse. O-pen. Sleigh!!!*

Prayer for the Night

Jesus, keep me through the night
safe until the morning light
shines into our window pane
and brings a bright, new day again.
Amen.

The mother tucked in her little boy, running her fingers lightly through his wispy hair. Whispering an extra prayer, she tiptoed from the room. He was already sound asleep.

The clock had just struck three in the morning when the little boy woke. He climbed out of his crib landing with a quiet thump, plodded into his parents' room on little footie pajama feet, and, unable to wake them, wandered into the living room. The Christmas tree's glowing lights twinkled softly bringing a delighted smile to his face.

He stood on tiptoe, looking out the picture window to the neighbor's house across the street. The front door creaked as the little boy pushed it open and slid through the space between doorjamb and door and onto the front step. Oops! He slipped and landed in the snow. But he was up in no time. Snowflakes drifted gently down, crowning his little towhead with white and just touching his eyelashes.

There it was: the blow-up reindeer and an elf beside it! Finally! He'd be able to look at it up close! Snow soaked through his pajamas to his tiny feet, and he hurried to touch the forbidden decoration. It was bigger than he remembered! Reaching out his hand, red with cold, he touched it and – what was that? Did it actually blink?!

The wind picked up and snow skittered across the snowy yards and street. The little boy's ears burned! Why would they burn when it was cold? He covered his ears with his hands. It didn't help. It just made his fingers tingle.

A quiet voice whispered, "Back you go, dear one." The elf? He thought he should go home, but his little feet felt frozen – glued to the ground. He stood there uncertainly as his body shivered. The quiet of the dark night held little to comfort him, and tears began to slide down his cheeks. What could he do? *Jesus, keep me through the night*, he whispered. He couldn't recall the next line of the prayer. *Jesus, keep me through the night*, he repeated. The reindeer and elf stood immovable. He looked over at the pretty tree lights shining through his own home's window. How he wished he was there now! But his feet! They were so cold!

Suddenly he was back in his living room and the front door firmly locked. He took a few steps and lay down on the floor by the beautiful tree.

He grew inexplicably warm, and it was there his mother found him the next morning; soaked to the skin, but covered and tucked in with two cozy blankets.

And his angel sighed with a tired smile. *Safe until the morning light . . .*

⌐———◆———⌐

Original prayer by Mabel J. Cachiaras

www.ingramcontent.com/pod-product-compliance
Lightning Source LLC
Chambersburg PA
CBHW030758210726
48290CB00002B/326